Praise for
Anne Perry's Christmas Mysteries

A Christmas Secret
"Anne Perry has crafted a finely written Christmas
puzzle that has a redemptive seasonal message
woven within its solution."
—*The Wall Street Journal*

A Christmas Beginning
"Intriguing . . . Perry's use of period detail is, as
always, strong and evocative."
—*The Seattle Times*

A Christmas Grace
"Perry effortlessly evokes the region's insularity and
isolation while imbuing religious themes into
a whodunit without being preachy."
—*Publishers Weekly*

A Christmas Promise
"Read Anne Perry's latest and your spirits will
be lifted. That's a promise."
—*The Wall Street Journal*

A Christmas Odyssey
"Perry again delivers a seasonal tale affectingly
celebrating the miraculous transformation
of despair into hope."
—*The Richmond Times Dispatch*

BY ANNE PERRY

PUBLISHED BY THE RANDOM HOUSE PUBLISHING GROUP

The Sheen on the Silk

FEATURING WILLIAM MONK

The Face of a Stranger	*The Twisted Root*
A Dangerous Mourning	*Slaves of Obsession*
Defend and Betray	*Funeral in Blue*
A Sudden, Fearful Death	*Death of a Stranger*
The Sins of the Wolf	*The Shifting Tide*
Cain His Brother	*Dark Assassin*
Weighed in the Balance	*Execution Dock*
The Silent Cry	*Acceptable Loss*
A Breach of Promise	

FEATURING CHARLOTTE AND THOMAS PITT

The Cater Street Hangman	*The Hyde Park Headsman*
Callander Square	*Traitors Gate*
Paragon Walk	*Pentecost Alley*
Resurrection Row	*Ashworth Hall*
Bluegate Fields	*Brunswick Gardens*
Rutland Place	*Bedford Square*
Death in the Devil's Acre	*Half Moon Street*
Cardington Crescent	*The Whitechapel Conspiracy*
Silence in Hanover Close	*Southampton Row*
Bethlehem Road	*Seven Dials*
Highgate Rise	*Long Spoon Lane*
Belgrave Square	*Buckingham Palace Gardens*
Farriers' Lane	*Treason at Lisson Grove*

THE WORLD WAR I NOVELS

No Graves As Yet
Shoulder the Sky
Angels in the Gloom
At Some Disputed Barricade
We Shall Not Sleep

THE CHRISTMAS NOVELS

A Christmas Journey
A Christmas Visitor
A Christmas Guest
A Christmas Secret
A Christmas Beginning
A Christmas Grace
A Christmas Promise
A Christmas Odyssey
A Christmas Homecoming

Anne Perry's Christmas Vigil

Anne Perry's Christmas Vigil

Two Victorian Holiday Mysteries

A CHRISTMAS PROMISE

A CHRISTMAS ODYSSEY

Anne Perry

BALLANTINE BOOKS TRADE PAPERBACKS
NEW YORK

2011 Ballantine Trade Paperback

A Christmas Promise copyright © 2009 by Anne Perry
A Christmas Odyssey copyright © 2010 by Anne Perry

Published in the United States by Ballantine Books, an imprint of The Random House Publishing Group, a division of Random House, Inc., New York.

BALLANTINE and colophon are registered trademarks of Random House, Inc.

Originally published in hardcover as two separate works entitled *A Christmas Promise* and *A Christmas Odyssey* by Ballantine Books in 2009 and 2010.

ISBN: 978-0-345-52491-1
eBook ISBN: 978-0-345-53132-2

Printed in the United States of America

www.ballantinebooks.com

2 4 6 8 9 7 5 3 1

Text design by Julie Schroeder

A Christmas Promise

*T*HE WEEK BEFORE CHRISTMAS, THE SMELL
and taste of it were in the air, a kind of excitement, an urgency about everything. Geese and
rabbits hung outside butchers' shops, and there
were little pieces of holly on some people's doors.
Postmen were extra busy. The streets were still
gray, the wind still hard and cold, the rain turning
to sleet, but it wouldn't have seemed right if it had
been different.

Gracie Phipps was on an errand for her gran to
get a tuppence worth of potatoes to go with the
leftovers of cabbage and onion, so Gran could
make bubble and squeak for supper. Spike and
Finn would pretty well eat anything they could fit
into their mouths, but they liked this especially.
Better with a slice of sausage, of course, but there

was no money for that now. Everything was being saved for Christmas.

Gracie walked a little faster into the wind, pulling her shawl tighter around her. She had the potatoes in a string bag, along with half a cabbage. She saw the girl standing by the candle makers, on the corner of Heneage Street and Brick Lane, her reddish fair hair blowing about and her arms hugged around her as if she were freezing. She looked to be about eight, five years younger than Gracie, and as skinny as an eel. She had to be lost. She didn't belong there, or on Chicksand Street—one over. Gracie had lived on these streets ever since she had come to London from the country, when her mother had died six years before, in 1877. She knew everyone.

"Are yer lorst?" she asked as she reached the child. "This is 'Eneage Street. Where d'yer come from?"

The girl looked at her with wide gray eyes, blinking fiercely in an attempt to stop the tears from brimming over onto her cheeks. "Thrawl Street," she answered. That was two streets over to the west and on the other side of Brick Lane, out of the neighborhood altogether.

"It's that way." Gracie pointed.

"I know where it is," the girl replied, not making any effort to move. "Me uncle Alf's bin killed, an' Charlie's gorn. I gotta find 'im, cos 'e'll be cold an' 'ungry, an' mebbe scared." Her eyes brimmed over, and she wiped her sleeve across her face and sniffed. "'Ave yer seen a donkey as yer don't know? 'E's gray, wi' brown eyes, an' a sort o' pale bit round the end of 'is nose." She looked at Gracie with sudden, intense hope. "'E's about this 'igh." She indicated, reaching upward with a small, dirty hand.

Gracie would have liked to help, but she had seen no animals at all, except for the coal man's horse at the end of the street, and a couple of stray dogs. Even hansom cabs didn't often come to this part of the East End. Commercial Street, or

Whitechapel Road, maybe, on their way to somewhere else. She looked at the child's eager face and felt her heart sink. "Wot's yer name?" she asked.

"Minnie Maude Mudway," the child replied. "But I in't lorst. I'm lookin' fer Charlie. 'E's the one wot's lorst, an' summink might 'ave 'appened to 'im. I told yer, me uncle Alf's bin killed. Yesterday it were, an' Charlie's gorn. 'E'd 'ave come 'ome if 'e could. 'E must be cold an' 'ungry, an' 'e dunno where 'e is."

Gracie was exasperated. The whole story made no sense. Why would Minnie Maude be worrying about a donkey that had wandered off, if her uncle had really been killed? And yet she couldn't just leave the girl there standing on the corner in the wind. It would be dark very soon. It was after three already, and going to rain. "Yer got a ma?" Gracie asked.

"No," Minnie Maude answered. "I got an aunt Bertha, but she says as Charlie don't matter. Donkeys is donkeys."

"Well, if yer uncle got killed, maybe she don't care that much about donkeys right now." Gracie tried to sound reasonable. "Wot's gonna 'appen to 'er, wif 'im gone? Yer gotta think as she might be scared an' all."

Minnie Maude blinked. "Uncle Alf di'n't matter to 'er like that," she explained. " 'E were me pa's bruvver." She sniffed harder. "Uncle Alf told good stories. 'E'd bin ter places, an' 'e saw things better than most folk. Saw them fer real, wot they meant inside, not just wot's plain. 'E used ter make me laugh."

Gracie felt a sudden, sharp sense of the girl's loss. Maybe it was Uncle Alf she was really looking for, and Charlie was just an excuse, a kind of sideways way of seeing it, until she could bear to look at it straight. There was something very special about people who made you laugh. "I'm sorry," she said gently. It had been a little while before she had really said to herself that her mother wasn't ever coming back.

"'E were killed," Minnie Maude repeated. "Yest'day."

"Then yer'd best go 'ome," Gracie pointed out. "Yer aunt'll be wond'rin' wot 'appened to yer. Mebbe Charlie's already got 'ome 'isself."

Minnie Maude looked miserable and defiant, shivering in the wind and almost at the end of her strength. "No 'e won't. If 'e knew 'ow ter come 'ome 'e'd a bin there last night. 'E's cold an' scared, an' all by 'isself. An' no one but 'im an' me knows as Uncle Alf were done in. Aunt Bertha says as 'e fell off an' 'it 'is 'ead, broke 'is neck most like. An' Stan says it don't matter anyway, cos dead is dead jus' the same, an' we gotta bury 'im decent, an' get on wi' things. Ain't no time ter sit around. Stan drives an 'ansom, 'e goes all over the place, but 'e don't know as much as Uncle Alf did. 'E could fall over summink wifout seein' it proper. 'E sees wot it is, like Uncle Alf said, but 'e don't never see wot it could be! 'E di'n't see as donkeys can be as good as a proper 'orse."

Not for a hansom cab, Gracie thought. Who ever saw a hansom with a donkey in the shafts? But she didn't say so.

"An' Aunt Bertha di'n't 'old wif animals," Minnie Maude finished. " 'Ceptin' cats, cos they get the mice." She gulped and wiped her nose on her sleeve again. "So will yer 'elp me look for Charlie, please?"

Gracie felt useless. Why couldn't she have come a little earlier, when her gran had first told her to? Then she wouldn't even have been here for this child to ask her for something completely impossible. She felt sad and guilty, but there was no possible way she could go off around the wet winter streets in the dark, looking for donkeys. She had to get home with the potatoes so her gran could make supper for them, and the two hungry little boys Gran's son had left when he'd died. They were nearly old enough to get out and earn their own way, but right now they were still a considerable responsibility, especially with Gracie's

9

gran earning only what she could doing laundry every hour she was awake, and a few when she hardly was. Gracie helped with errands. She always seemed to be running around fetching or carrying something, cleaning, sweeping, scrubbing. But very soon she would have to go to the factory like other girls, as soon as Spike and Finn didn't need watching.

"I can't," she said quietly. "I gotta go 'ome with the taters, or them kids'll start eatin' the chairs. Then I gotta 'elp me gran." She wanted to apologize, but what was the point? The answer was still no.

Minnie Maude nodded, her mouth tightening a little. She breathed in and out deeply, steadying herself. " 'S all right. I'll look fer Charlie meself." She sniffed and turned away to walk home. The sky was darkening and the first spots of rain were heavy in the wind, hard and cold.

When Gracie pushed the back door open to their lodgings in Heneage Street, her grandmother was standing with a basin of water ready to wash and peel the potatoes. She looked worn-out from spending all day up to her elbows in hot water, caustic, and lye, heaving other people's wet linen from one sink to another, shoulders aching, back so sore she could hardly touch it. Then she would have to lift the linen all again to wind it through the mangles that would squeeze the water out, and there would be some chance of getting it dry so it could be returned, and paid for. There was always need for money: rent, food, boots, a few sticks and a little coal to put on the fire, and of course Christmas.

Gracie hardly grew out of anything. It seemed as if she had stopped at four feet eleven, and worn-out pieces could always be patched. But Spike and Finn were bigger every time you looked at them, and considering how much they ate, perhaps no one should have been surprised.

The food was good, and every scrap disappeared, even though they were being careful and saving any treats for Christmas. Spike and Finn bickered a bit, as usual, then went off to bed obediently enough at about seven. There wasn't a clock, but if you thought about it, and you were used to the sounds of the street outside, footsteps coming and going, the voices of those you knew, then you had a good idea of time.

They had two rooms, which wasn't bad, considering. There was the kitchen, with a tin bowl for washing; the stove, to cook and keep warm; and the table and three chairs and a stool. And there was the bench for chopping, ironing, and baking now and then. There was a drain outside the back door, a well at the end of the street, and a privy at the bottom of the yard. In the other small room, Gracie and her gran had beds on one side, and on the other they had built a sort of bed for the boys. They lay in it, one at each end.

But Gracie did not sleep well, in spite of being very nearly warm enough. She could not forget Minnie Maude Mudway, standing on the street corner in the dusk, grieving for loneliness, death, a donkey who might or might not be lost. All night it troubled her, and she woke to the bleak, icy morning still miserable.

She got up quickly, without disturbing her gran, who needed every moment of sleep she could find. Gracie pulled on her clothes immediately. The air was as cold as stone on her skin. There was ice on the inside of the windows as well as on the outside.

She tiptoed out into the kitchen, put on her boots, and buttoned them up. Then she started to rake out the dead ashes from the kitchen stove and relight it so she could heat a pan of water and make porridge for breakfast. That was a luxury not everyone had, and she tasted it with pleasure every time.

Spike and Finn came in before daylight, although there was a paling of the sky above the rooftops. They were full of good spirits, planning mischief, and glad enough to eat anything they were given: porridge, a heel of bread, and a smear of dripping. By half past eight they were off on errands for the woman at the corner shop, and Gran, fortified by a cup of tea, insisting it was enough, went on her way back to the laundry.

Gracie busied herself with housework, washing dishes, sweeping, and dusting, putting out slops and fetching more water from the well at the end of the street. It was cold outside, with a rime of ice on the cobbles and a hard east wind promising sleet.

By nine o'clock she could not bear her conscience anymore. She put on her heaviest shawl, gray-brown cloth and very thick, and went outside into the street again and down to the corner to look for Minnie Maude.

London was an enormous cluster of villages all running into one another, some rich, some poor, none worse than Flower and Dean Walk, which was filled with rotting tenements, sometimes

eight or ten people to a room. It was full of prostitutes, thieves, magsmen, cracksmen, star-glazers,
snotter-haulers, fogle-hunters, and pickpockets of
every kind.

Oddly enough, the boundaries remained. Each
village had its own identity and loyalties, its hier-
archies of importance and rules of behavior, its
racial and religious mixtures. Just the other side of
Commercial Street it was Jewish, mostly Russians
and Poles. In the other direction was Whitechapel.
Thrawl Street, where Minnie Maude said she
lived, was beyond Gracie's area. Only something as
ignorant as a donkey would wander from one village to another as if there were no barriers, just because you could not see them. Charlie could hardly
be blamed, poor creature, but Minnie Maude knew,
and of course Gracie did even more so.

At the corner the wind was harder. It sliced
down the open street, whining in the eaves of the
taller buildings, their brick defaced with age,

weathering, and neglect. Water stains from broken guttering streaked black, and she knew they would smell of mold inside, like dirty socks.

The soles of her boots slipped on the ice, and her feet were so cold she could not feel her toes anymore.

The next street over was busy with people, men going to work at the lumberyard or the coal merchant, girls going to the match factory a little farther up. One passed her, and Gracie saw for a moment the lopsided disfigurement of her face, known as "phossie-jaw," caused by the phosphorus in the match heads. An old woman was bent over, carrying a bundle of laundry. Two others shared a joke, laughing loudly. There was a peddler on the opposite corner with a tray of sandwiches, and a man in a voluminous coat slouched by.

A brewer's dray passed, horses lifting their great feet proudly and clattering them on the stones, harnesses gleaming even in the washed-out winter light. Nothing more beautiful than a horse, strong and gentle, its huge feet with hair like silk skirts around them.

A hawker came a few yards behind, pushing a barrow full of vegetables, pearly buttons on his coat. He was whistling a tune, and Gracie recognized it as a Christmas carol. The words were something about merry gentlemen.

She walked quickly to get out of the wind; it would be more sheltered once she was around the corner. She knew what street she was looking for. She could remember the name, but she could not read the signs. She was going to have to ask someone, and she hated that. It took away all her independence and made her feel foolish. At least someone would know Minnie Maude, especially since there had just been a death in the family.

She was regarded with some suspicion, but five minutes later she stood on the narrow pavement outside a grimy brick-fronted house whose colorless wooden door was shut fast against the ice-laden wind.

Until this moment Gracie had not thought of what she was going to say to explain her presence. She could hardly tell them that she had come to help Minnie Maude find Charlie, because if she were really a good person, she would have offered to do that yesterday. Going home to tea sounded like an excuse. And anyway, Aunt Bertha had already said that, as far as she was concerned, it didn't matter, and whatever Minnie Maude thought of it, Aunt Bertha seemed reasonable enough. The poor woman was bereaved, and probably beside herself with worry as to how they were going to manage without a money-earning member of the family. There was a funeral to pay for, never mind looking for daft donkeys that had wandered off. Except that he might be worth a few shillings if they sold him?

Probably they already had, and just didn't want to tell Minnie Maude. She was too young to understand some of the realities of life. That was probably it. Better to tell her, though. Then she would stop worrying that he was lost and scared and out in the rain by himself.

Gracie was still standing uselessly on the cobbles, shifting from one foot to the other and shaking with cold, when the door opened and a large man with a barrel chest and bowlegs came out, banging his hands together as if they were already numb.

"Eh, mister!" Gracie stepped forward into his path. "Is this where Minnie Maude lives?"

He looked startled. "I in't seen you 'ere before! 'Oo are yer?" he demanded.

"I in't bin 'ere before," she said reasonably. "That's 'ow I dunno if this is where she lives."

He looked her up and down, all four feet eleven inches of her, from the top of her shawl to her pale, clever little face, down to her bony body and her worn-out boots with buttons missing. "Wot d'yer want wif our Minnie Maude, then?" he asked suspiciously.

Gracie said the first thing that came into her

19

mind. "Got an errand for 'er. Worf tuppence, if she does it right. Can't do it all meself," she added, in case it sounded too good to be true.

"I'll get 'er for yer," he said instantly, turning on his heel and going back into the house. A moment later he returned with Minnie Maude behind him. "There y'are," he said, and pushed her forward. "Make yerself useful, then," he prompted, as if she might be reluctant.

Minnie Maude's wide eyes regarded Gracie with wonder and gratitude entirely inappropriate to the offer of a twopenny job, which might even last all day. Still, perhaps when you were eight, tuppence was a lot. Gracie was thirteen, and it was more than she actually had, but she had needed to make the offer good in order to be certain that it would be carried inside, and that Minnie Maude would be allowed to accept. She would deal with finding the tuppence later.

"Well, c'mon, then!" Gracie said aloud, grasping Minnie Maude's arm and half-pulling her away from the bowlegged man and striding along the street as fast as she dared on the ice.

"Yer gonna 'elp me find Charlie?" Minnie Maude asked breathlessly, slipping and struggling to keep up with her.

It was a little too late to justify her answer now. "Yeah," Gracie conceded. "I 'spec it won't take long. Someb'dy'll 'ave seen 'im. Mebbe 'e got a fright an' ran off. 'E'll get 'isself 'ome by an' by. Wot 'appened ter yer uncle Alf, anyway?" She slowed down a little bit now that they were round the corner and back in Brick Lane again.

"Dunno," Minnie Maude said unhappily. "They found 'im in Richard Street, in Mile End, lyin' in the road wi' the back of 'is 'ead stove in, an' cuts an' bangs all over 'im. They said as 'e must 'ave fell off 'is cart. But Charlie'd never 'ave gorn an' left 'im like that. Couldn't've, even if 'e'd wanted to, bein' as 'e were tied inter the shafts."

"W'ere's the cart, then?" Gracie asked practically.

"That's it!" Minnie Maude exclaimed, stopping abruptly. "It's not there! That's 'ow else I know 'e were done in. It's gorn."

Gracie shook her head, stopping beside her. " 'Oo'd a done 'im in? Wot's in the cart, then? Milk? Coal? Taters?" She was beginning to feel more and more as if Minnie Maude were in her own world of loss and grief more than in the real one. " 'Oo's gonna do in someone fer a cartload o' taters? 'E must a died natural, an' fell off, poor thing. Then some rotten bastard stole 'is cart, taters an' all, an' Charlie wif 'em. But 'owever rotten they are," she added hastily, "they'll look after Charlie, because 'e's worf summink. Donkeys are useful."

"It weren't milk," Minnie Maude said, easing her pace to keep in step. " 'E were a rag an' bone man, an' sometimes 'e 'ad real beautiful things, treasures. It could a bin anyfink." She left the possibilities dangling in the air.

Gracie looked sideways at her. She was about

three inches shorter than Gracie, and just as thin. Her small face had a dusting of freckles across the nose, and at the moment it was pinched with worry. Gracie felt a strong stab of pity for her.

" 'E'll mebbe come back by 'isself," she said as encouragingly as she could. "Unless 'e's in a nice stable somewhere, an' can't get out. I 'spec someone nicked the cart, cos there were some good stuff in it. But donkeys in't daft." She had never actually known a donkey, but she knew the coal man's horse, and it was intelligent enough. It could always find a carrot top, whatever pocket you put it in.

Minnie Maude forced a smile. "Course," she said bravely. "We just gotta ask, afore 'e gets so lorst an' can't find 'is way back. Actual, I dunno 'ow far 'e's ever bin. More 'n I 'ave, prob'ly."

"Well, we'd best get started, then." Gracie surrendered her common sense to a moment's weakness of sympathy. Minnie Maude was a stubborn little article, and daft as a brush with it. Who

23

knew what would happen to her if she was left on her own? Gracie would give it an hour or two. She could spare that much. Maybe Charlie would come back himself by then.

"Fank yer," Minnie Maude acknowledged. "Where we gonna start?" She looked at Gracie hopefully.

Gracie's mind raced for an answer. " 'Oo found yer uncle Alf, then?"

"Jimmy Quick," Minnie Maude replied immediately. " 'E's a lyin' git an' all, but that's prob'ly true, cos 'e 'ad ter get 'elp."

"Then we'll go an' find Jimmy Quick an' ask 'im," Gracie said firmly. "If 'e tells us exact, mebbe takes us there, we can ask folks, an' p'raps someone saw Charlie. Where'd we look fer 'im?"

"In the street." Minnie Maude squinted up at the leaden winter sky, apparently judging the time. "Mebbe Church Lane, be now. Or mebbe 'e in't started yet, an' 'e's still at 'ome in Angel Alley."

"Started wot?"

" 'Is way round. 'E's a rag an' bone man, too. That's 'ow come 'e found Uncle Alf."

"Rag an' bone men don't do the same round as each other," Gracie pointed out. "It don't make no sense. There'd be nuffink left." She was as patient as she could be. Minnie Maude was only eight, but she should have been able to work that out.

"I tol' yer 'e were a lyin' git," Minnie Maude replied, unperturbed.

"Well, we better find 'im anyway." Gracie had no better idea. "Which way d'we go?"

"That way." Minnie Maude pointed after a minute's hesitation, in which she swiveled around slowly, facing each direction in turn. She set off confidently, marching across the cobbles, her feet clattering on the ice and her heart in her mouth. Gracie caught up with her, hoping to heaven that they would not both get as lost as Charlie.

They crossed Wentworth Street away from the places she knew, and had left them behind in a few hundred yards. Now all the streets looked frighteningly the same, narrow and uneven. Here and there cobbles were broken or missing, gutters swollen with the previous night's rain and the refuse from unknown numbers of houses. Alleys threaded off to either side, some little more than the width of a man's outstretched arms, the house eaves almost meeting overhead. The strip of sky above was no more than a jagged crack. Gutters dripped, and most hung with ice. Some of the blackened chimneys belched smoke.

Everyone was busy on errands of one sort or another, pushing carts of vegetables, bales of cloth, kegs of ale—rickety wheels catching the curbs. Children shouted, peddlers called their wares, and patterers rehearsed the latest news and gossip in singsong voices, making up colloquial rhymes. Women quarreled; several dogs ran around barking.

At the end of the next road was the Whitechapel High Street, a wide thoroughfare with hansom cabs bowling along at a brisk clip, cabbies riding high on the boxes. There was even a gentleman's carriage with a matched pair of bay horses with brass on their harness and a beautiful pattern on the carriage door.

"We gone too far," Minnie Maude said. "Angel Alley's back that way." She started along the High Street, then suddenly turned into one of the alleys again, and after a further hundred yards or so, she turned into a ramshackle yard with a sign at the entrance.

"I fink this is it," she said, peering at the letters. But looking at her face all screwed up in uncertainty, Gracie knew perfectly well that she was only guessing.

Minnie Maude took a deep breath and walked in. Gracie followed. She couldn't let her go in alone.

A lean man with straight black hair came out of one of the sheds.

"There's nothing 'ere fer kids," he said with a slight lisp. He waved his hands. "Orff wif yer!"

"Ye're Jimmy Quick?" Minnie Maude pulled herself up very straight.

" 'Oo are you, then?" he said, puzzled.

"Minnie Maude Mudway," she replied. "It were me uncle Alf as yer found in the street." She hesitated. "An' this is me friend," she added.

"Gracie Phipps," Gracie said.

"We're lookin' fer Charlie," Minnie Maude went on.

Jimmy Quick frowned at them. "I dunno no Charlie."

" 'E's a donkey," Gracie explained. Someone needed to talk a little sense. " 'E got lost, along wif Uncle Alf's cart, an' everyfink wot was in it." She glanced around the yard and saw three old bicycles whose wheels had missing spokes, several odd boots and shoes, kettles, pieces of china and pottery, some of it so beautiful she stared at it in amazement. There were old fire irons, a poker with a brass handle, ornaments, pots and pans, pieces of carpet, a cabin trunk with no hinges, unwanted books and pictures, all the things a rag and bone man collects, in with the actual rags or bones for glue.

Minnie Maude stood still, ignoring the scattered takings around her, just staring solemnly at Jimmy Quick. " 'Ow'd yer find 'im, then?"

Jimmy seemed to consider evading the question, then changed his mind. " 'E were jus' lyin' there in the road," he said sadly. "Like 'e fell off, 'cept o' course 'e'd never 'ave done that, if 'e'd bin alive. I've seen Alf as tight as a newt, an' 'e didn't miss a step, never mind fell. 'E knew 'ow ter wedge 'isself, like, so 'e wouldn't—not even if 'e were asleep." He shook his head. "Reckon as 'ow 'e must 'ave just died all of a sudden. Bin took, as it were. Visitation o' God."

"No 'e weren't," Minnie Maude contradicted him. "If 'e 'ad bin, Charlie'd 'ave brought 'im 'ome. An' wot were 'e doin' way out 'ere anyway? This in't 'is patch." She sniffed fiercely as if on the edge of tears. "Someone's done 'im in."

"Yer talkin' daft," Jimmy said dismissively, but his face was very pink. " 'Oo'd wanter 'urt Alf?" He looked uncomfortable, not quite meeting Minnie Maude's eyes. Gracie wondered if it was embarrassment because he did not know how to comfort her, or something uglier that he was trying not to say.

Gracie interrupted at last. "It in't daft," she told him. "Wot 'appened ter Charlie, an' the cart? 'E di'n't go 'ome."

Now Jimmy Quick was deeply unhappy. "I dunno. Yer sure the cart's not at yer aunt Bertha's?" he asked Minnie Maude.

She looked at him witheringly. "Course it in't. Charlie might get lorst, cos this in't where 'e usually comes. So why was 'e 'ere? Even if Uncle Alf died an' fell off, which 'e wouldn't 'ave, why'd nobody see 'im 'ceptin' you? An' 'oo took Charlie an' the cart?"

Put like that, Gracie had to agree that it didn't

sound right at all. She joined Minnie Maude in staring accusingly at Jimmy Quick.

Jimmy looked down at the ground with even greater unhappiness, and what now most certainly appeared to be guilt. "It were my fault," he admitted. "I 'ad ter go up ter Artillery Lane an' see someone, or I'd a bin in real trouble, so I asked Alf ter trade routes wi' me. 'E'd do mine, an' I'd do 'is. That way I could be where I 'ad ter, wi'out missin' an 'ole day. That's why 'e were 'ere. 'E were a good mate ter me, an' 'e died doin' me a favor."

" 'E were on yer round!" Gracie said in sudden realization of all that meant. "So if someone done 'im in, p'raps they meant it ter be you!"

"Nobody's gonna do me in!" Jimmy said with alarm, but looking at his face, paler now and a little gray around his lips, Gracie knew that the thought was sharp in his mind, and growing sharper with every minute.

She made her own expression as grim as she

could, drawing her eyebrows down and tightening her mouth, just as Gran did when she found an immovable stain in someone's best linen. "But yer jus' said as 'e were alone cos 'e were doin' yer a favor," she pointed out. "If nobody else knew that, they'd a thought as it were you sittin' in the cart!"

"I dunno," Jimmy said unhappily.

Gracie did not believe him. Her mind raced over how it could matter, picking up people's odd pieces of throwaway, or the things they might buy or sell, if they knew where. What did rag and bone men pick up, anyway? If you could pawn it for a few pence, or maybe more, you took it to the shop. She glanced at Minnie Maude, who was standing hunched up, shaking with cold, and now looking defeated.

Gracie lost her temper. "Course yer know!" she shouted at Jimmy. " 'E got done in doin' yer job, cos yer asked 'im ter. An' now the cart's gorn and Charlie's gorn, an' we're standin' 'ere freezin', an' yer sayin' as yer can't tell us wot 'e died fer!"

"Cos I dunno!" Jimmy said helplessly. He swung his arms in the air. "Come on inside an' Dora'll make yer a cup o' tea." He led the way across the yard, weaving between bicycles, cart wheels, milk churns without lids, until he came to the back door of his house. He pushed the door wide, invitingly, and they crowded in after him.

Inside the kitchen was a splendid collection of every kind of odd piece of machinery and equipment a scrap yard could acquire. Nothing matched anything else, hardly two pieces of china were from the same set, yet it was all excellent, the most delicate Gracie had ever seen, hand-painted and rimmed in gold. No two saucepans were the same either, or had lids that fitted, but all were handsome enough, even if there was little to put in them besides potatoes, onions, and cabbage, and perhaps a few bones for flavor.

In the far corner stood a magnificent mangle, with odd rollers, one white, one gray; a collection of flatirons, most of them broken; and several lanterns missing either sides or handles. Perhaps the bits and pieces might make two usable ones between them?

Mrs. Quick was standing expectantly by the stove, on which a copper kettle was gleaming in the gaslight, steam whistling out of the spout. She was an ample woman wearing a blue dress patched in a dozen places without thought for matching anything, and she wore a marvelous old velvet cape around her shoulders. It was vivid red, and apart from a burn on one side, appeared as good as new.

"Ah! So you're Bert Mudway's girl," she said to Minnie Maude with satisfaction, then turned to Gracie. "An' 'oo are you, then? In't seen yer before."

"Gracie Phipps, ma'am," Gracie replied.

"Never 'eard of yer. Still an' all, I 'spec yer'd like a cup o' tea. That daft Jimmy kept yer standin' out there in the cold. Goin' ter snow, like as not, before the day's out."

"They come about Alf," Jimmy explained.

"Course they 'ave." She took the kettle off the hob, warmed an enormous white and wine-colored teapot with half a handle, then made the tea, spooning the leaves from a caddy with an Indian woman painted on the front. "Got no milk," she apologized. "Yer'll 'ave ter 'ave it straight. Give yer 'alf a spoon of 'oney?"

"Thank you," Gracie accepted, and took the same for Minnie Maude.

When they were sitting on a random collection of chairs, Mrs. Quick expressed her approval of Uncle Alf, and her sympathy for Minnie Maude, and then for Bertha. "Too bad for 'er," she said, shaking her head. "That bruvver of 'ers is more trouble than 'e's worth. Pity it weren't 'im as got done in."

"Wouldn't 'ave 'appened to 'im," Jimmy said miserably.

"I reckon as it were that golden tin, or wotever it were," she said, giving Jimmy a sharp look, and

35

shaking her head again. "'E said as 'e thought they never meant ter put it out."

Minnie Maude sat up sharply, nearly spilling her tea. "Wot were that, then?" she asked eagerly.

Jimmy glanced at his wife. "Don't go puttin' ideas inter 'er 'ead. We never saw no gold tin. It were jus' Tommy Cob ramblin' on." He turned to Minnie Maude. "It ain't nothin'. Folk put out all kinds o' things. Never know why, an' it don't do ter ask."

"A golden box?" Minnie Maude said in amazement. "'Oo'd put out summink like that?"

"Nobody," Jimmy agreed. "It were jus' Tommy talkin' like a fool. Prob'ly an old piece o' brass, like as not, or even painted wood, or summink."

"Mebbe that's why they killed Uncle Alf an' took the cart?" Minnie Maude was sitting clutching her porcelain teacup, her eyes wide with fear. "An' Charlie."

"Don' be daft!" Jimmy said wearily. "If they put out summink by mistake, then they'd jus' go an' ask fer it back. Mebbe give 'im a couple o' bob fer it, not go off killin' people."

"But they did kill 'im," Minnie Maude pointed out, sniffing and letting out her breath in a long sigh. " 'E's dead."

"I know," Jimmy admitted. "An' I'm real sorry about that. 'Ave some more 'ot water in yer tea?"

That was all they would learn from him, and ten minutes later they were outside in the street again, and a fine rain was falling with a drift of sleet now and then.

"I've still gotta find Charlie," Minnie Maude said, staring ahead of her, avoiding Gracie's eyes. "Uncle Alf doin' Jimmy's round jus' makes it worse. Charlie's really lorst now!"

"I know that," Gracie agreed.

Minnie Maude stopped abruptly on the cobbles. "Yer think as there's summink real bad 'appened, don't yer!" It was a challenge, not a question.

Gracie took a deep breath. "I dunno wot I think," she admitted. She was about to add that she thought Jimmy Quick was not telling all the truth, then she decided not to. It would only upset Minnie Maude, and it was just a feeling, nothing as clear as an idea.

"I told yer 'e were a lyin' sod," Minnie Maude said very quietly. "It's written clear as day on 'is face."

"Mebbe 'e's jus' sad cos 'e liked yer uncle Alf," Gracie suggested. "An' if Alf'd bin on 'is own round, mebbe somebody'd 'ave 'elped 'im. But 'e could a still bin dead."

"Yer mean not left lyin' in the roadway." Minnie Maude sniffed hard, but it did not stop the tears from running down her face. "Yer'd 'ave liked Uncle Alf," she said almost accusingly. "'E'd a made yer laugh."

Gracie would have liked to have an uncle who made her laugh. Come to think of it, she'd have liked a donkey who was a friend. They'd known lots of animals in the country, before her mother had died and she'd come to London: sheep, horses, pigs, cows. Not that there was a lot of time for friends now that she was thirteen. Minnie Maude had a lot to learn about reality, which was a shame.

"Yeah," Gracie agreed. "I 'spec I would."

They walked in silence for a while, back toward Brick Lane, and then Thrawl Street. It got colder with every moment.

"Wot are we gonna do?" Minnie Maude asked when they came to the curb and stopped, traffic rattling past them.

Gracie had been thinking. "Go back 'ome an' see if Charlie's come back on 'is own," she replied. " 'E could 'ave."

"D'yer think?" Minnie Maude's voice lifted with hope, and Gracie was touched by a pang of guilt. She had suggested it only because she could think of nothing better.

Gracie did not answer, and they walked the rest of the way past the end of the notorious Flower and Dean Walk in silence, passing figures moving in the shadows. Others stood still, watching and waiting. The ice made the cobbles slippery. The sleet came down a little harder, stinging their faces and rattling against the stone walls to either side of them in the narrow alleys. The gutters were filling up, water flecked with white that disappeared almost instantly, not yet cold enough to freeze solid. Their breath made white trails of vapor in the air.

Minnie Maude led the way into the back gate of a house exactly like its neighbors on either side. The only thing that distinguished it was the shed at the back, which, from Minnie Maude's sniff and her eager expression, was clearly Charlie's stable. Now she went straight to the door and pushed it open, drawing in her breath to speak, then stood frozen, her shoulders slumping with despair.

Gracie's heart sank, too, although she should have understood better than to imagine the donkey would have come home. She already knew that something was wrong. Probably it was only some minor dishonesty, someone taking advantage of a man who had died suddenly and unexpectedly; a theft, not anything as far-fetched as a murder. But either way, Minnie Maude would hurt just as badly. She would miss the uncle who had made her laugh and had loved her, and the donkey who'd been her friend.

"We'll find 'im," Gracie said impulsively, swallowing hard, and knowing she was making a promise she would not be able to keep.

Minnie Maude forced herself not to cry. She took an enormous breath and turned to face Gracie, her cheeks tear-streaked, wet hair sticking to her forehead. "Yeah. Course we will," she agreed. She led the way along the rest of the short path, barely glancing up as a couple of pigeons flapped above her and disappeared into the loft over the stable. She pushed the back door of the house open, and Gracie followed her inside.

A thin woman with a plain face stood over a chopping board slicing carrots and turnips, her

large-knuckled hands red from the cold. She had
the most beautiful hair Gracie had ever seen. In
the lantern light it was burnished like autumn
leaves, a warm color, as if remembering the sun.
She looked up as Minnie Maude came in, then her
pale eyes widened a little as she saw Gracie, and
her hands stopped working.

"W'ere yer bin, Minnie Maude?"

"Lookin' for Charlie," Minnie Maude replied.
"This is Gracie, from 'Eneage Street. She's 'elpin'
me."

Aunt Bertha shook her head. "In't no point,"
she said quietly. " 'E'll come 'ome by 'isself . . . or 'e
won't. In't nothing yer can do, child. An' don't go
wastin' other folks' time." She regarded Gracie
with only the tiniest fraction of curiosity. There
were dozens of children up and down every street,
and there was nothing remarkable about her.
"Good o' yer, but in't nothin' yer can do. 'E must a
got a scare when poor Alf died." She started chopping the turnip again.

" 'E wouldn't be able ter find 'isself," Minnie Maude agreed. " 'E weren't on 'is own route. 'E were on Jimmy Quick's."

"Don't talk nonsense, Minnie," Bertha said briskly. "Course 'e weren't. Why'd 'e be down there?" She chopped harder, drawing the knife through the tough vegetables with renewed force. "Yer got chores ter get on with." She looked at Gracie. "Yer got 'em too, I 'spec."

It was on the edge of Gracie's tongue to say to Bertha that she'd sold Charlie, and why couldn't she just be honest enough to tell Minnie Maude so. Then at least she wouldn't be worrying about him being lost and hungry, wandering around in the sleet, wet and maybe frightened.

The outside door opened again, and Stan appeared. He looked at Minnie Maude, then at Gracie. "Wot yer doin' back 'ere again?" he said sharply.

"She's 'elpin' me look fer Charlie," Minnie Maude told him.

"She's jus' goin'," Bertha interrupted sooth-
ingly. Her face was pinched, her eyes steady on
Stan. "She were only 'elpin'."

"Well, yer shouldn't bother folks," Stan told
Minnie Maude. "Yer looked. 'E ain't around. Now
do like yer told."

" 'E's lorst," Minnie Maude persisted.

"Donkeys don't get lorst," Stan said, and shook
his head. " 'E's bin doin' these streets fer years.
'E'll come 'ome, or mebbe somebody took 'im.
Which is stealin', an' if I find the bastard, I'll make
'im pay. But that's my business. It in't yers. Now
go and do yer chores, girl." He looked at Gracie.
"An' you do yers, an' all. Yer must 'ave summink
ter do better 'n wanderin' round the streets lookin'
fer some damn donkey!"

"But 'e's lorst!" Minnie Maude protested again,
standing her ground even though she must have
been able to see as well as Gracie could that Stan
was angry. " 'E weren't wi' Uncle Alf's—"

"Don't talk nonsense!" Bertha snapped at her,

putting the knife down and raising her hand as if she would slap Minnie Maude around the ears if she did not keep quiet. But it was not anger Gracie could see in her eyes. Gracie was suddenly, in that instant, quite sure that it was fear. She lifted her foot and gave Minnie Maude a sharp kick on the ankle.

Minnie Maude gasped and turned sharply.

"I'm lost an' all," Gracie said. "An' yer aunt Bertha's right, I got chores, too. Can yer show me which way I gotta go? If yer please?"

Shoulders slumped again, wiping her face with her sleeve to hide the tears, Minnie Maude led the way out the back door, past Charlie's empty stable, and into the street.

"Yer right," Gracie said when they were beyond where Bertha or Stan could hear them. "There's summink wrong, but yer uncle Stan don't like yer pokin' inter it, an' I think yer aunt Bertha's scared o' summink."

"She's scared of 'im," Minnie Maude said with

a shrug. "'E's got a nasty temper, an' Alf in't 'ere no more ter keep 'im in 'and, like. Wot are we gonna do?"

"Yer gonna do yer chores, like I am," Gracie replied firmly.

Minnie Maude's mouth pulled tight to stop her lips from trembling. She searched Gracie's face, hope fading in her. She took a shaky breath.

"I gotta think!" Gracie said desperately. "I . . . I in't givin' up." She felt hot and cold at once with the rashness of what she had just said. Instantly she wished to take it back, and it was too late. "In't no sense till we think," she said again.

"Yeah," Minnie Maude agreed. She forced a rather wobbly smile. "I'll go do me chores." And she turned and walked away, heading into the rain.

Gracie went to help Mr. Wiggins, as she did every other day, running errands and cleaning out the one room in which he lived, scrubbing, doing laundry, and making sure he had groceries. He paid her sixpence at the end of each week, which was today. Sometimes he even made it ninepence, if he was feeling really generous.

"Wot's the matter wif yer, then?" he asked as she came into the room from outside, closing the rickety door behind her. She went straight to the corner where the broom and the scrubbing brush and pail were kept. "Got a face on yer like a burst boot, girl," he went on. "In't like you."

"Sorry, Mr. Wiggins. I got a friend in trouble." She glanced at him briefly with something like a smile, then picked up the broom and started to sweep. Her hands were so cold she could hardly hold the wooden shaft firmly enough.

" 'Ave a cup o' tea," he suggested.

"I in't got time. I gotta clean this up."

"Yer 'ere ter please me or yerself, girl?"

She stared at him. "I'm 'ere ter clean the floor an' fetch yer tea an' bread an' taters."

"Ye're 'ere ter do as I tell yer," he contradicted.

"Yer want the floor cleaned or not?"

47

"I wan' a cup o' tea. Can you tell me why yer look like yer lost sixpence an' found nothin'? Put the kettle on like I said."

She hesitated.

" 'Nother threepence?" he offered.

She couldn't help smiling at him. He was old and crotchety sometimes, but she knew that most of that came from being lonely, and not wanting anyone to know that it hurt him.

"I don' need threepence," she lied. "I'll get a cup o' tea. I'm fair froze any'ow." Obediently she went to the small fire he kept going in a black potbellied stove, and pulled the kettle over. "Yer got any milk, then?" she asked.

"Course I 'ave," he said indignantly. "Usual place. Wot's the matter wif yer, Gracie?"

She made the tea, wondering whether it would be worse to use up what she knew was the last of his milk, and leave him without any, or not to use it, and insult his hospitality. She knew with her gran the humiliation would have stung more, so she used it.

" 'S good," she said, sitting opposite him and sipping it gingerly.

"So wot's goin' on, then?" he asked.

She told him about Alf dying and falling off the cart, and Charlie getting lost, and how she didn't know what to do to help Minnie Maude.

He thought in silence for several minutes while they both finished their tea. "I dunno neither," he said at last.

"Well, fanks fer the tea," she said, conquering a very foolish sense of disappointment. What had she expected, anyway? She stood up ready to go back to the sweeping and scrubbing.

"But yer could go and ask Mr. Balthasar." He put his mug down on the scarred tabletop. " 'E's about the cleverest feller I ever 'eard of." He tapped his head with one arthritic finger. "Wise, 'e is. Knows all kinds o' things. Mebbe 'e di'n't know if Alf fell off the cart afore 'e were dead, or after, but if anyone can find a donkey wot's lost—or stole—it'd be 'im."

"Would 'e?" Gracie said with sudden hope.

Mr. Wiggins nodded, smiling.

She had a moment's deep doubt. Mr. Wiggins was old and a bit daft. Maybe he just wanted to help, which didn't mean he could. Still, she had no better idea herself. "I'll go an' see 'im," she promised. "Where is 'e?"

*S*he found the shop of Mr. Balthasar on Whitechapel Road just about where Mr. Wiggins had said it would be, which surprised her. He had seemed to be too vague for her to trust his judgment. But the moment she stepped inside the dark, narrow doorway, she thought it was much less good an idea than Mr. Wiggins had implied. There was no one to be seen in the extraordinary

interior, but objects of one sort or another seemed
to fill every shelf from floor to ceiling, and be sus-
pended by ropes, threads, and chains from above
so that she was afraid to move in case she dis-
lodged something and brought it all crashing
down on herself.

There seemed to be an inordinate number of
shoes, or perhaps they would more properly be
called slippers. She couldn't imagine anyone
going outside in the wet street in such things.
They were made of cloth, of soft leather, even of
velvet, and they were stitched with all sorts of
patterns like nothing she had ever seen before.
Some had silly curling toes that would make
anybody fall over in two steps. But they were
beautiful!

There were brass dishes with curly writing all
over them, no pictures at all, but the writing was
so fancy it would do just as well. And everywhere
she looked there were boxes of every kind and
shape, painted, decorated with stones, shiny and

dull, written on and plain. Some were so small they would have had trouble holding a thimble, others big enough to take your whole hand. And there was an enormous machine that looked like a cross between a boiler and a pipe to smoke, like gentlemen used. Though what use such a contraption might be, she had no idea.

She was still staring when a voice spoke from behind her.

"And what may I do for you, young lady?"

She was so startled she was sure her feet actually came off the floor. She jerked around and looked at the man not three feet away. He had come in silently, and she had heard nothing. He must have been wearing those velvet slippers.

"I . . . ," she began. "I . . ."

He waited. He was tall and lean and his hair was very black, with just a few streaks of white in it at the sides. His skin was coppery dark, his nose high-bridged and aquiline.

She drew in a deep breath. "I need 'elp," she

admitted. This was not a man you lied to. "An' Mr. Wiggins says as ye're the wisest man around 'ere, so I come ter ask."

"Does he indeed?" Mr. Balthasar smiled with a definite trace of amusement. "You have the advantage of me."

"Wot?" She blinked.

"You seem to know something of me," he explained. "I know nothing of you."

"Oh. I'm Gracie Phipps. I live in 'Eneage Street. But I come cos o' Minnie Maude. 'Er uncle Alf got killed, an' Charlie's lost an' could be all on 'is own, an' in trouble."

"I think you had better tell me from the beginning," Mr. Balthasar said gently. "This sounds as if it might be quite a complicated matter, Gracie Phipps."

Gracie drew in her breath and began.

Mr. Balthasar listened without interrupting, nodding now and then.

" . . . so I think as Jimmy Quick in't tellin' the

truth," she said finally. "Cos it don't make no sense. But I still gotta find Charlie, or that daft little article in't gonna give up till summink real bad 'appens."

"No," Mr. Balthasar agreed, and his face was very grim. "I can see that she isn't. But I fear that you are right. Several people may not be telling the truth. And perhaps Minnie Maude is not quite as daft as you imagine."

Gracie gulped. The room with its crowded shelves and endless assortment of treasures seemed smaller than before, closer to her, the walls crowding in. It was oddly silent, as if the street outside were miles away.

"Course she's daft," Gracie said firmly. " 'Oo's gonna kill a rag an' bone man? On purpose, like? 'E jus' died an' fell off, an' as 'e were on Jimmy Quick's patch, 'stead of 'is own, no one knew 'im, so 'e jus' laid there till someone found 'im."

"And what happened to Charlie?" Mr. Balthasar asked very gently.

"Charlie couldn't pick 'im up," Gracie replied. "An' 'e couldn't get 'elp, so 'e jus' stayed there with 'im . . . sort o' . . . waitin'."

"And why was he not there when poor Alf was found?"

Gracie realized her mistake. "I dunno. Someone must a stole 'im."

"And the cart? They stole that also?"

"Must 'ave."

"Yes," Mr. Balthasar said very sincerely. "That, I fear, may be far more serious than you realize." He searched her face, as if trying to judge how much she understood, and how much more he should tell her.

Suddenly she was brushed with genuine fear, a cold grip inside her that held hard. She fought against it. Now it was not just helping Minnie Maude because she was sorry for her, and felt a certain kind of responsibility. She was caught in it herself. She looked back at the strange features, the dark, burning eyes of Mr. Balthasar.

"Why'd anyone steal it?" she said in little more than a whisper.

"Ah." He let out his breath slowly. "There I think you have it, Gracie. What was in it that someone believed to be worth a human life in order to steal?"

Gracie shivered. "I dunno." The words barely escaped her lips. "D'yer think 'e really were killed?" It still seemed ridiculous, something Minnie Maude would make up, because she was only eight, and daft as a brush. Gracie swallowed hard. It was no longer a bit of a nuisance. She was scared. "She jus' wants 'er friend Charlie back, an' safe."

Mr. Balthasar did not answer her.

"D'yer think they done 'im in, too?" Her voice wobbled a bit, and she could not help it.

"I doubt it," he replied, but there was not even the ghost of a smile on his copper-colored face. "But be very careful, Gracie. It sounds to me as if it is possible that Minnie Maude's uncle saw something he was not supposed to, or picked up something that was intended for someone else. You are quite sure you have the details correct?"

She nodded, her eyes not leaving his steady gaze. "'E done Jimmy Quick's round fer 'im, an' about 'alfway, or more, 'e died, an' Charlie an' the cart, an' everythin' in it, were gone."

"And which streets were Jimmy Quick's round?"

"I dunno."

"But you said you and Minnie Maude went there, at least some of the way."

Gracie looked down at her boots. "We did. I know where I went left, an' where I went right, but I can't read the names."

"I see. Of course." There was apology in his voice, as if he should have known she couldn't read.

"I could find 'em again . . . I think," she offered, her cheeks hot with shame.

"No doubt." He smiled now, very briefly, then

the gravity returned. "But I think it would be wiser if you didn't. Donkeys are patient and useful beasts. Only a fool would hurt them. Charlie will be miserable for a little while, but he will be all right."

He was lying to her, and she knew it. She had seen donkeys starved, beaten, shaking with cold and fear.

He saw it in her face, and now it was his turn to be ashamed. "I'm sorry," he said humbly. "You are right to fear. I will see if I can learn anything. But in the meantime, you should say nothing, and ask no further questions. Do you understand?"

"Yeah."

He did not look satisfied. "Are you sure?"

She nodded.

"What do you know about Uncle Alf?" he persisted.

" 'E were funny an' kind, an' 'e made Minnie Maude laugh, and she said 'e knew about all sorts o' places, and things. 'E saw things in like . . .

brighter colors than wot most people do." She took a deep breath, overcome with her own sense of the loss of something she had only imagined—a companion who'd had dreams and ideas, whose mind had been far away from disappointment and tired streets. She wondered what Uncle Alf had looked like. She saw him with white hair, a bit wild, as if he had been out in a great wind. He would have blue eyes that saw either very close or very far indeed, all the way to the horizon.

Then a flash of memory came to her of what Dora Quick had said, and Jimmy had been angry about.

Balthasar must have seen it in her face. "What is it, Gracie?"

"Mrs. Quick said as Alf picked up a gold-colored box that were special, real beautiful."

"How did she know that?" he said quickly.

"It were someone called Cob wot told 'er. But Mr. Quick said 'e were talkin' daft, an' ter take no notice. An' she never said any more."

"I see. I think that is extremely good advice, Gracie. Say nothing more either. Above all, do not mention the casket."

"Wot's a casket?" she asked.

"A special kind of box to keep precious things in. Now go home and do your chores. I shall look into the matter."

She blinked, staring back at him. "'Ow'll I know if yer do?"

"Because I shall send a message to you in Heneage Street."

"Oh. Thank you . . . Mr. . . . Balthasar."

*G*racie completed her work as soon as possible, knowing she was skimping, and telling herself she would make a better job of it tomorrow. As soon as the cleaning looked finished, at the quickest glance, no rubbing fingers over things to make sure, she wrapped herself up in her heavy brown wool shawl. Tying it tight under her chin so it was thick and lumpy to keep the rain out, she raced into the street holding her head down against the wind and the sleet. She knew the way to Minnie Maude's house even without having to look, never mind ask, and she was there inside ten minutes.

She stopped well short of the house itself. She was a little bit in awe of Aunt Bertha, and she definitely did not want to encounter Stan again. Although since he was a hansom cabbie and it was a bitter day just short of Christmas, there should have been any amount of trade for him in the streets a little farther west, so he was unlikely to be home.

Still she waited, shivering in a doorway opposite, holding her shawl tighter and tighter around her, in spite of the fact that it was wet most of the way through. Eventually she saw Minnie Maude opening the door. She stepped out, her pale, little face bleak, looking one way and then another as if perhaps Charlie might come down the cobbles, in spite of all reason.

"Stupid little article!" Gracie said savagely to herself. " 'E in't comin' 'ome!" She found her own voice choking, and was angry. It wasn't her donkey! She'd never even seen him.

She moved out of the doorway and marched across the uneven road, her boots sloshing in the puddles where stones were missing and the water had collected.

Minnie Maude saw her immediately, and her face brightened into a wide smile.

Gracie's heart sank. She could do nothing to justify it. She waited while Minnie Maude went back inside and then barely a moment later opened the door again and came clattering across the road.

"Yer find out summink?" she said eagerly, her eyes bright.

Gracie hated it. "Nuffink for certain sure," she

replied. "But I told a wise man about it, an' 'e thinks as there could be summink bad. 'E said ter leave it alone."

Minnie Maude's eyes never left Gracie's. "But we in't goin' ter . . ."

Gracie shivered. The wind was cutting down the street like a knife.

"Come up inter the stable," Minnie Maude said quickly. "It's warm in there, up where the pigeons are. Anyway, I gotta feed them, since Uncle Alf in't 'ere anymore." There was only a slight quiver in her voice, and she turned away from Gracie to hide the look on her face. Because she concealed it, it was even more telling.

Gracie followed her back across the street, tugging at her shawl to keep it around her shoulders. They went around and in through the back gate, then across the cobbles to the stable door. This was where Charlie had lived, and Gracie stared at the rough brick walls and the straw piled on the floor. She noticed that Minnie Maude walked through so quickly that she could hardly have seen anything but a blur of familiar shapes.

In the next tiny room, half-filled with hay, a rough ladder was propped up against the edge of the loft, and Minnie Maude hitched up her skirts and scrambled up it. "C'mon," she invited encouragingly. "I'll 'old the top fer yer." And as soon as she reached the ledge of the upper floor, she rolled over sideways and then knelt, gripping the two uprights of the ladder and hanging on to them. She peered down at Gracie, waiting for her.

Wondering where her wits had gone to, Gracie grasped her skirts halfway up her legs and climbed up, hanging on desperately with her other hand. She reached the top white-knuckled and cursing under her breath. Some days she doubted she still had the sense she was born with.

"Careful!" Minnie Maude warned a trifle sharply as Gracie swayed. "Yer don' wanna tip it off. We'd 'ave ter jump, and there in't nuffink ter land on."

Gracie clung on desperately, feeling her head whirl and her stomach knot. She said nothing, concentrating fiercely on what she was doing. She couldn't let Minnie Maude see how scared she was. Minnie Maude would lose all trust in her. She took a deep breath and drew herself up onto the ledge, teetering for a moment, her legs in the air, then scrambled forward and fell flat on her face. She sat up, trying to look as if nothing at all had happened.

" 'Is name was Mr. Balthasar," she said solemnly.

There was a kind of whir of wings and a clatter as a pigeon burst through the narrow entrance in the roof and landed on the wood. Minnie Maude ignored it. Gracie felt her heart nearly burst out of her chest.

"Did 'e say as summink 'ad 'appened ter Uncle Alf?" Minnie Maude asked.

" 'E di'n't rightly know," Gracie said honestly. "But 'e reckoned as it were bad, cos o' them takin' the cart, an' all." She lowered her voice. "Minnie

Maude, 'e said as 'e thought the golden box were a casket, an' could be summink really important, an' mebbe that's why Uncle Alf were killed. 'E said as we shouldn't go on lookin' fer it, in case we get 'urt as well."

"But wot about Charlie?" Minnie Maude asked.

"'E said as donkeys are useful, so they'll prob'ly look after 'im, feed 'im, an' give 'im somewhere ter stay." She remembered Mr. Balthasar's face as he had said it, the dark, sad look in his eyes. She had seen that look before. He did not mean it. He had said it to comfort her. Now she was saying it again, to comfort Minnie Maude.

Minnie Maude stared in front of her. "'S all right," she said quietly. "Yer don't 'ave ter look fer Charlie. I un'erstand."

"I di'n't say I weren't gonna look fer 'im!" Gracie retorted with indignation. "I'm jus' tellin' yer wot 'e said!"

Minnie Maude raised her eyes very slowly, bright with hope.

Gracie could have kicked herself, but there was no escape. "We gotta think fast," she warned.

"It's cold," Minnie Maude replied, as if it were the natural thing to say. "Let's go over inter the 'ay." And without waiting for agreement, she tucked her skirt up again and crawled back into the dark, rich-smelling crowded space in the corner. She went into it headfirst, then swiveled around, and a moment later her face appeared and she smiled encouragingly, a long wisp of hay behind her ear.

Gracie had no dignified choice but to follow her. She tucked her skirts up also and crawled across the space to the bales, then pushed her way in, twisted around, and sat down. It was prickly, but it smelled nice, and it brought back dim memories of the past, of being in the country, long ago. She imagined in time it would be quite warm where they were, compared with the stone floor below.

"Summink really important," Minnie Maude said thoughtfully. "S'pose it would 'ave ter be, ter put it in a casket, an' all." She sat motionless, her eyes very wide. "D'yer think it's magic?"

"What?"

"Magic," Minnie Maude repeated, her voice hushed with awe.

"Wotever put that inter yer 'ead, yer daft little article?" Gracie demanded. "In't no such thing." Then the minute she had said it, she wished she hadn't. Minnie Maude was only eight. Gracie should have let her have a year or two more of dreams.

"There's Christmas," Minnie Maude whispered, her eyes brimming with tears.

Gracie struggled desperately to retrieve the loss. "That in't magic," she answered. "That's . . . that's God. It's diff'rent."

Minnie Maude blushed. "Is it?"

"Course it is." Gracie's mind was whirling like the wind.

Minnie Maude waited, staring at her.

"Magic don't 'ave rules," Gracie explained. "An'

bad people can do it as well as good. It in't always nice. Wot God does is always nice, even if it don't look much like it at the time."

" 'Ow d'yer know?" Minnie Maude asked reasonably.

Gracie was not going to be careful this time. "I dunno," she admitted. "I jus' know."

"Is it an 'oly casket?" Minnie Maude asked her.

"Wot would an 'oly casket be doin' out in the street fer a rag an' bone man ter pick up?" Gracie tried to put the conversation back into some kind of reality.

"Jesus were born in a stable," Minnie Maude pointed out. "Like wot we're in."

"This is a dovecote," Gracie replied.

"It's a stable downstairs, cos Charlie lived in it." Minnie Maude sniffed.

Gracie felt an overwhelming helplessness. She longed to be able to comfort Minnie Maude, but did not know how to. "Yer right," she agreed, avoiding Minnie Maude's eyes. "I forgot that."

"Mebbe it's a present?" Minnie Maude went on. "Mr. Balthasar's a wise man. Yer said so. It could a got stole, an' that's why 'e knows about it. 'E said it were bad, I mean real bad. Ter steal from God, in't that about as bad as yer can be?"

Her logic was faultless. Gracie felt a chill run through her, as if some inner part of her had been touched by ice. She hugged her arms closer around her, and the pigeons cooing seemed louder, as though the birds too were afraid.

"We gotta get it back," Minnie Maude said, moving a little closer to Gracie. "Mebbe Christmas won't 'appen if we don't—"

"Course it'll 'appen!" Gracie said instantly, her voice sharp, too positive.

"Will it?" Minnie Maude whispered. "Yer sure? Even if it were stole by someone wicked? I mean not just bad, but terrible . . . like . . . the devil?"

Gracie had no opinion on that. It was something she had not even thought of. It was a child's imagination, and she was old enough to face the real problems in the world, like cold and hunger, illness, and how to pay for things. She had grown out of fairies and goblins a long time ago, about the time when she'd left the country and had come to live in London. But Minnie Maude was years younger, a child still. Her neck was so pale and slender it was surprising it could hold her head up, and not all her teeth were fully grown in. She believed in magic, good and bad, and in miracles. It would be like breaking a dream to tell her differently.

"Yeah," Gracie answered, her fingers crossed under the hay, where Minnie Maude couldn't see them. "But if 'ooever took it is real bad, then we gotta be careful. We gotta think 'ard before we do anyfink daft."

"If they're real bad, they might 'urt Charlie," Minnie Maude said with a wobble in her voice.

"Wot for? A sick donkey in't no use. Bad in't the same as stupid." Gracie said it with far more conviction than she felt. She had to add something else quickly, before Minnie Maude had time to argue. "If Uncle Alf took the box wot's a casket, Mr. Balthasar said, then wot did 'e do with it?"

"Nuffink," Minnie Maude answered straightaway. "They come after 'im an' took it."

"Then why'd they kill 'im?" Gracie said reasonably. "An' why take Charlie and the cart? That's stupid. Then they got a dead body, an' a donkey an' a cart wot's stole. Fer what?" She shook her head with increasing conviction. "They di'n't find the gold box, or they'd a left the cart. They took Charlie cos they 'ad ter take the cart an' they couldn't pull it without 'im."

"Why'd they kill Uncle Alf? 'E should a jus' give it back ter 'em."

"I dunno. Mebbe they di'n't mean ter," Gracie suggested. "Mebbe 'e argued wif 'em, cos 'e wanted ter keep it."

Minnie Maude shook her head. " 'E weren't like that. Less, o' course, 'e knew as they were wicked?" Minnie Maude blinked. "D'yer reckon as 'e knew? 'E were wise. 'E knew when people told the truth an' when they was lyin', even strangers. An' 'e could tell the time, an' wot the weather were gonna do."

Gracie had no idea. She tried to visualize Uncle Alf from what Minnie Maude had told her, and all she could see was a man with white hair and blue eyes who liked to make children laugh, who did a favor for Jimmy Quick, and who kept his donkey in a warm stable that smelled of hay—and pigeons. What kind of person understood evil? Good people? Wise people? People who had faced it and come out hurt but had ultimately survived?

"Mebbe," she said at length. "If 'e 'ad it, an' 'e knew wot it were, then wot'd 'e do wif it?"

Minnie Maude thought about it for so long that Gracie had just about decided she was not going to answer, when finally she did. " 'E 'ad a special place where 'e put secret things. We could look there. If 'e got 'ome wif it, 'e'd a put it there."

Gracie thought it unlikely that poor Alf had

ever reached his home, but it would be silly not to at least try. There might be something else that would give them a clue.

Minnie Maude stood up and went back to the ladder.

Gracie's stomach clenched at the thought of going down it again. It would be even worse than going up. She watched Minnie Maude's hands on the uprights. She was holding on, but her knuckles were not white. She moved as easily as if it were a perfectly ordinary staircase. Gracie would have to do the same. If Minnie Maude knew she was afraid, how could the little girl have any confidence in her? How could she feel any better, and believe Gracie could fight real evil, if she couldn't even go backward down a rickety ladder?

"Are yer comin'?" Minnie Maude called from the stable floor.

There was a flurry of wings, and another pigeon landed and strutted across the floor, looking at Gracie curiously.

"Yeah," Gracie answered, and gritted her teeth. Tucking her skirt up, she went down the steps with barely a hesitation.

"This way," Minnie Maude said, and started across the floor, kicking the straw out of the way with her scuffed boots. There was a half archway leading into another room where bales of straw were stacked on one side, and harnesses hung on hooks on the wall on the other side.

"They're extra," Minnie Maude said, swallowing back a sudden rush of tears. "Yer always need extra pieces, in case summink gets broke. Charlie'll 'ave the real harness on 'im."

Gracie looked at the worn leather, the old brasses polished thin, the rings, buckles, and bits, and felt the overwhelming loss wash over her. These were like the clothes of a person who was missing, maybe even hurt or dead. She stared at the objects, trying to think of something to say, and she noticed the scars on the whitewash of the wall. It looked as if somebody had banged against it, and then drawn something sharp for a couple of inches, digging into the stone. The white of the lime covering it was cut through and flaking.

She turned slowly. Minnie Maude was staring at it too.

Gracie's eyes went to the floor. It was flat cement, uneven, half-covered now with loose pieces of hay from the bales. There were more scuff marks, scratches, and brown stains, as if something wet had been spilled, and then stood in. Whatever it was had been smeared. Perhaps someone had slipped.

"Gracie . . . ," Minnie Maude whispered, putting out her hand. "Summink bad 'appened 'ere."

She was cold when Gracie touched her. Gracie meant to hold Minnie Maude's hand gently, but found she was gripping, squashing Minnie Maude's thin little fingers. It did not even occur to her to lie. This was not the time or the place for it.

"I know." She thought of telling her that it

might not have been Charlie's blood, but it didn't need saying. Somebody had been hurt here.

"Gold's precious," Minnie Maude went on. "Lot o' money. But it must a bin more 'n that, eh?"

"Yeah," Gracie agreed. "Summink inside it."

"A present for God?"

"Mebbe."

"Wot d'yer give God, then? In't 'e already got everyfink'?" Minnie Maude asked.

Gracie shook her head. "I dunno. Mebbe it in't fer 'im."

Minnie Maude's eyes widened. "I never thought o' that. Wot d'yer think it could be?"

"It must be summink very precious," Gracie replied. "And I think we gotta find it."

"Yeah." Minnie Maude nodded vigorously. "We 'ave."

Minnie Maude turned toward the door just as it flew open and Stan strode in, broad, bowlegged, his face twisted with anger.

"Wot yer doin' in 'ere, missie?" he demanded of Minnie Maude. Then, swinging around to Gracie, he said, "An' you don't belong 'ere neither! Leave! Out of 'ere!" He waved his arms as though to force them out.

Minnie Maude stood as if frozen.

"Go on!" Stan shouted. "In't yer got no chores ter do, yer lazy little girl? Think yer 'ere fer us ter feed yer gob while yer sit 'ere in the 'ay day-dreamin'?"

Minnie Maude started to say something, then saw his hand swinging wide to clip her round the side of the head, and ducked out of his way. She turned to stare at Gracie. "C'mon!" she warned, making for the door, and escape.

Gracie wanted to stay and argue, but she knew better. There was an anger in Stan's face that was deeper than mere temper. There was a shadow of fear in it also, and she knew that people who were frightened were dangerous. Something very bad indeed had happened in this place, and the taste of it put wings on her feet. She veered sideways and shot past his outstretched hand, through the open door, and down the path to the alleyway.

Through the back gate she nearly bumped into Minnie Maude.

"Yer all right?" Minnie Maude asked anxiously.

"Yeah." Gracie pushed her hair back and straightened her rumpled skirt, then picked a few pieces of hay from her shawl.

"Wot are we gonna do?" Minnie Maude asked.

Gracie felt as if she were jumping into a fast, icy river. The only thing worse would be being left on the bank.

"We're gonna find out exactly where Uncle Alf went the day 'e were killed," she answered, as if that had been her decision all along.

" 'Ow are we gonna do that?"

"We're gonna ask Jimmy Quick wot way 'e went, an' then foller it an' find out 'oo saw Uncle Alf the same way. They might know, cos of it bein' someone diff'rent than Jimmy."

"Then wot?" Minnie Maude's eyes did not flicker an instant.

Gracie's mind raced. "Then we'll find out where 'e were killed, exact like, an' 'oo 'e saw, an' 'oo 'e di'n't."

Minnie Maude gulped. "Then we'll know 'oo killed 'im?"

The thought was enormous, and terrifying. Suddenly it did not seem so clever at all. In fact it seemed the depth of stupidity. "No we won't," Gracie said sharply. "We'll just know where 'e might a picked up the casket . . . an' o' course where 'e couldn't've, since 'e in't bin there yet."

Minnie Maude looked hopeful. "We'll go and see Jimmy Quick." She squinted up at the sky. "We could get there now, but 'e won't be 'ome yet."

Gracie was more concerned with thinking of a good reason to go back to ask Jimmy Quick about the route he took, so they could explain why they asked.

"Wot's the matter?" Minnie Maude demanded, the fear back in her voice.

"Nuffink," Gracie said immediately, wondering why she was suddenly putting off telling the truth. "Jus' planning wot ter say, cos why we want ter know? Jimmy Quick in't silly. 'E's gonna ask. We gotta 'ave summink ter say as could be true."

"We wanna know w'ere me Uncle Alf died," Minnie Maude said, watching Gracie carefully. "I'm gonna put a flower there."

" 'Ave yer got one?" Gracie said reasonably. "I got twopence. We could buy some . . . if yer like?"

Minnie Maude nodded. "Thank yer. That's . . ." She searched for a word for the complicated emotion. "Good," she finished, unsatisfied.

Gracie smiled at her, and suddenly Minnie Maude beamed back, her whole face lit with gratitude. They had a plan.

"We'll go ter see Jimmy Quick this evening," Gracie said decisively. "If we wait till termorrer, 'e'll mebbe take us, an' we don't want 'im ter, cos we need ter ask questions it's better as 'e don't know."

Minnie Maude nodded vigorously.

"I'll meet yer 'ere, at 'alf past lights on," Gracie went on. She looked up at the lamppost just above where they stood. "Watch for the lamplighter. 'E's usually reg'lar. Yer wait, if I in't 'ere right away."

Minnie Maude nodded again.

*G*racie continued with her duties for the day, missing some out and working double speed at others. She tried not to think of the wild promises she had made to Minnie Maude Mudway. She must have lost all the sense she'd ever had! Now she was scrubbing the kitchen bench, lye stinging her hands, fingers wet and cold. The sleet outside was turning to snow, everyone else was thinking of Christmas, and she was planning to go and ask a rag and bone man what his route was, so she could look for the people who had murdered Alf Mudway for a casket! Oh—and the real purpose of the whole thing was to find a donkey, who was probably as right as rain somewhere else, and not sparing them a thought in its head. If donkeys had thoughts.

Then on the other hand, he might be wandering around alone, lost, scared stiff, knowing his master was dead, because he had seen it happen. He could be shivering, wet and frightened, not knowing what to do about it—and hungry. She imagined him, standing in the dark and the rain, ears down, tail down, slowly getting wetter and wetter. She really didn't have any choice.

Added to which, if she didn't help, then Minnie Maude would go off and do it on her own. Gracie knew that without doubt, because Minnie Maude was only eight, and had no idea what she was doing. And Aunt Bertha didn't care. Somebody had to look after Minnie Maude, just like Minnie Maude had to look after Charlie. Some things couldn't be helped, no matter how daft they were, and how much you knew better.

Which is why she kept running out at the back to see if the lamplighter had been yet, and when she saw the light in the distance, she lied to her gran that she had promised old Mrs. Dampier to run an errand for her. Mrs. Dampier never remembered anything, so she wouldn't know. Gracie slipped out of the kitchen into the rain before she could answer the inevitable questions.

Minnie Maude was waiting for her, standing huddled in the shadows, her shawl wrapped around her head and shoulders, skirts flapping damply in the gusty wind, boots soaked. But her face lit with happiness when she saw Gracie, and she darted out of the shelter of the wall and fell in step beside her without giving her time to hesitate or say anything more than " 'Ello."

" 'E'll be 'ome now," Minnie Maude said, skipping a step to match her stride with Gracie's. " 'Avin' 'is tea. We'll ask 'im."

They walked in silence, their feet echoing on the cobbles. The snow had almost stopped, and it was beginning to freeze hard in the few places where it lay. It was wise to watch for icy patches, so as not to slip. Most of the lamps were lit, and there was a yellow warmth to them, like lighted windows to some palace of the mind. There was a slight fog rising, muffling the sound of distant wheels, and every now and then the mournful bellow of a foghorn sounded somewhere down on the river.

There wasn't much to show that Christmas was only a couple of days away, just the occasional wreath of leaves on a door, some with bright berries; or someone passing by singing a snatch of a song, happy and lilting, not the usual bawdy version of the latest from the music halls. In daylight, of course, there might have been a barrel organ, but this was far too late.

They reached Jimmy Quick's gate and made their way across the yard carefully to avoid the clutter, not wanting either to knock anything over or to bash their shins on a crate or old chair.

Jimmy was not pleased to see them. He stood in the doorway, looking immense, with the kitchen candles wavering in the draft behind him and making his shadow loom and bend.

"What d'yer want now, Minnie Maude? Yer gettin' ter be a nuisance," he said angrily. "I can't tell yer nothin', 'ceptin' I'm sorry Alf's dead. I dunno wot 'appened ter 'im. I only know it in't my fault, an' yer can come as many times as yer like, it still in't. I don't owe yer a bleeding thing!"

"Course," Minnie Maude said generously. Standing behind her, Gracie could see that she was shaking, but she kept her eyes on Jimmy's. "I jus' wanted ter ask yer wot way yer goes, so I can find the place 'e died, exact like."

"Wot for?" he said with amazement. " 'E's dead, girl. Goin' starin' at a place in't gonna change nothin'."

Minnie Maude took a deep breath. "I know that. But I wanter put a flower there. 'E should a bin with us for Christmas," she added.

Jimmy Quick swore under his breath. "Yer don't never let go, do yer? I already told yer where 'e were found. Yer got 'oles in yer 'ead, yer don't remember? 'E were in Richard Street, like I said."

Minnie Maude was temporarily speechless.

Jimmy stepped back to close the door.

" 'Ow d'yer get there?" Gracie asked him.

"Yer 'ere an' all?" He peered at her as if, in the shadows, he had not seen her. "Why d'yer care?"

Gracie decided to attack. "Look at 'er!" she told him angrily. "Size of 'er. She'd make a twopenny rabbit look good. Can't go an' leave 'er ter do it on 'er own, can I? She in't got no ma, 'er aunt Bertha don't wanna know—she's got 'er own griefs—an' Stan wouldn't throw a bucket o' water on 'er if she were on fire, let alone take 'er ter Richard Street. Alf were all she 'ad. Wot's the matter wif yer?

Can't yer jus' tell 'er which way ter go?" She scowled as if she found him highly suspicious. "Summink wrong wif it, then?"

"Course there in't, yer daft little girl," he said sharply, then he rattled off a list of streets, and she closed her eyes, concentrating on remembering them, before she looked back at him and thanked him. Then she grabbed Minnie Maude by the hand and retreated into the darkness and the jumble of the yard, pulling Minnie Maude with her. She was not ready to speak yet. She needed to concentrate on memorizing the streets, before they went out of her head. She wished she could write, then they could be kept safe longer. She could bring them back anytime she wanted—days from now, weeks even. One day she would learn, then she'd be able to keep every idea that mattered, forever. That would be like owning the whole world! You could always have people talking to you, telling you their dreams, their ideas. She would do it, absolutely definitely—one day.

She repeated the street names one more time, then turned to Minnie Maude.

"We'll go termorrer," she told her. "You say the streets over an' over, too, case I forget."

"I got 'em." Minnie Maude nodded. "When termorrer?"

Gracie started to walk briskly back toward their own streets, Minnie Maude's first, then hers. They were facing the wind now, and it was colder. "Termorrer," she said.

*I*n the morning, shreds of the fog still lingered. The air was as still as the dead, a rime of ice covered the stones so that they were slick underfoot, and all the gutters were frozen over.

Gracie found Minnie Maude in the usual place, her shawl hugged around her, hands hidden under it. Every few moments the girl banged her feet on the ground to jar them into life. The instant she saw Gracie, she came forward and the two girls fell into step, walking quickly to begin their detection.

Gracie recited the streets over in her mind, trying to make a pattern out of them, so she wouldn't forget.

"I'm gonna learn ter read," she muttered to herself as they trudged along.

"Me, too," Minnie Maude added.

Cannon Street was busy with lots of carts and drays, and a sweeper to keep the manure off the main crossings at the corners. He was working hard now, his arms swinging the broom with considerable force as he got rid of the last droppings left only a few minutes before. It was difficult to tell how old he was. He was less than five feet tall, but his narrow shoulders looked strong. His trousers were too long for him, and frayed at the bottoms over his boots. His coat came past his knees, and his cap rested on his ears. When he smiled at them, they could see that one of his front teeth was broken short, and for a moment his round face gave him the illusion of being about six.

"There y'are!" he said cheerfully, standing back to show the clean path across.

Gracie wished she had a penny to spare him, but he probably had more than she did. But she had a ha'penny, and he might also have information. She gave it to him.

He looked surprised, but he took it. For an instant, she felt rich, and grown-up. "D'yer know Alf, the rag an' bone man wot got killed on Richard Street three days back?" she asked hopefully. "'E done Jimmy Quick's round."

"'E 'ad a donkey," Minnie Maude added.

The boy thought for a while, frowning. "Yeah. It'd rained summink 'orrible. Gutters was all swillin' over. 'Ardly worth both'rin'." He jerked the broom at the cobbles to demonstrate.

"Yer saw 'im?" Minnie Maude said excitedly. "Which way were 'e goin'?"

The boy frowned at her, and pointed east into the wind. "That way. Thought as 'e were orff 'is path. Jimmy'd a gorn up there." He swung around and pointed westward, the way they had come. "Still an' all, wot's it matter? Poor devil. S'pose the cold got 'im."

Minnie Maude shook her head. " 'E were done in. Somebody 'it 'im."

"Garn!" the boy said with disbelief. "Why'd anyone do that?"

"Cos 'e knowed summink," Gracie said rapidly. "Mebbe 'e see'd summink as 'e weren't meant ter."

The boy's eyes widened. "Then yer shouldn't go lookin', or mebbe yer'll know it, too! In't yer got no more sense?"

" 'E weren't yer uncle," Gracie responded, liking the sound of it, as if Alf had been hers. It gave her a kind of warmth inside. Then she thought of drawing the sweeper into it a bit more personally. "Wot's yer name?"

"Monday," he replied.

"Monday?" Minnie Maude said, and stared at him.

His face tightened a bit, as if the wind were colder. "I started on a Monday," he explained.

She shrugged. "I dunno when I started. Mebbe I in't really started yet?"

"Yeah yer 'ave," Gracie said quickly. "Yer gonna find Charlie. That's a good way ter start." She turned back to Monday. "When were Alf 'ere, an' where'd 'e go? We gotta find out. An' tell us again, but do it clear, cos we don' know this patch. It was Jimmy Quick's, not Uncle Alf's."

Monday screwed up his face. " 'E went that way, which weren't the way Jimmy Quick goes. I see'd 'im go right down there, then 'e turned the corner, that way." He jerked his hand leftward. "An' I dunno where 'e went after that."

"That's the wrong way," Minnie Maude said, puzzled. "I remembered it." She recited the streets as Jimmy Quick had told them, ticking them off on her fingers.

"Well that's the way 'e went." Monday was firm.

They thanked him and set off in the direction he had pointed.

"Were 'e lorst?" Minnie Maude said when they were on the far side and well out of the traffic.

"I dunno," Gracie admitted. Her mind was racing, imagining all kinds of things. This was later in the route. He couldn't have done all the little alleys to the west so soon. Why had he been going the wrong way? Had somebody been after him already? No, that didn't make any sense.

"We gotta find somebody else ter ask," she said aloud. " 'Oo else would a seen 'im?"

Minnie Maude thought about it for some time before she answered. They walked another hundred yards along Cannon Street, but no one could help.

"Nobody seen 'im," Minnie Maude said, fighting tears. "We in't never gonna find Charlie."

"Yeah, we are," Gracie said with more conviction than she felt. "Mebbe we should ask after

Charlie, not Uncle Alf? Most people push their own barrows, or got 'orses."

Minnie Maude brightened. "Yeah. Ye're right." She squared her shoulders and lengthened her stride, marching across the icy cobbles toward a thin man with a lantern jaw who was busy mending a broken window, replacing the small pane of glass, smiling as he worked, as if he knew a secret joke.

"Mister?" Minnie Maude jogged his elbow to attract his attention.

He looked at her, still smiling.

Gracie caught up and glanced at the window. The old pane he had removed had a neat hole in it, round as the moon.

"Wot's yer name?" Minnie Maude asked.

"They call me Paper John. Why?"

"Yer bin 'ere afore?" Minnie Maude watched him intently. "Like three days ago, mebbe? I'm lookin' fer where me uncle Alf were. 'E 'ad a cart, but wif a donkey, not an 'orse."

"Why?" The man was still smiling. "Yer lorst 'im?"

"I lorst Charlie, 'e's the donkey," Minnie Maude explained. "Uncle Alf's dead."

The smile vanished. "Sorry ter 'ear that."

"'E's a rag an' bone man," Minnie Maude went on. "Least 'e were."

"This is Jimmy Quick's patch," the man told her.

"I know. Uncle Alf did it fer 'im that day."

"I remember. 'E stopped and spoke ter me."

Minnie Maude's eyes opened wide, and she blinked to stop the tears. "Did 'e? Wot'd 'e say?"

"'E were singin' some daft song about Spillikins and Dinah an' a cup o' cold poison, an' 'e taught me the words of it. Said 'e'd teach me the rest if I got 'im a drink at the Rat and Parrot. I went, but 'e never turned up. I reckoned as 'e di'n't know the rest, but I s'pose 'e were dead, poor devil."

Minnie Maude gulped. "'E knew 'em. 'E used

ter sing it all, an' 'Ol' Uncle Tom Cobley' an' all too," she said.

"Oh, I know that one." He hummed a few bars, and then a few more.

Gracie found her throat tight too, and was angry with herself for letting it get in the way of asking the right questions. "Did 'e say as 'e'd picked up anyfink special?" she interrupted.

The man looked at her curiously. "Like wot?"

"Like anyfink," she said sharply. "Summink wot weren't just rags an' old clothes and bits o' fur or lace, an' ol' shoes or bones and stuff."

"Jus' things wot nobody wanted," the man said gently. "Bit o' china wot was nice, four cups an' saucers, a teapot wi' no lid. 'E must a just 'ad a fit, fallen off. Could 'appen ter anyone. 'E weren't no chicken."

"Yeah. I'm sure," Gracie replied, but she wouldn't have been if she had not seen the blood and the scratches at the stable, and if Stan had not been so angry. It was the prickle of evil in the air, not the facts that she could make sense of to someone else. " 'E were killed."

The man pursed his lips. "Well 'e were fine when I saw 'im, an' 'e di'n't say nuffink." He hesitated for a moment. " 'E were late, though, fer this end o' the way. Jimmy Quick's round 'ere a couple of hours sooner . . . at least."

"Yer sure?" Gracie asked, puzzled. She did not know if it meant anything, but they had so little to grasp on to that everything could matter.

"Course I'm sure," the man replied. "Mebbe 'e were lorst. 'E was goin' that way." He pointed. "Or 'e forgot summink an' went back on 'isself, like."

Gracie thanked him, and she and Minnie Maude continued along the way that he had indicated.

"Wot's 'e mean?" Minnie Maude said with a frown.

"I dunno," Gracie admitted, but she was worried. It was beginning to sound wrong already.

Why would anyone change the way he went to pick up old things that people put out, even good things? She tried to keep the anxiety out of her face, but when she glanced sideways at Minnie Maude, she saw the reflection of the same fear in her pinched expression, and the tightness of her shoulders under the shawl.

A couple of hundred yards farther on they found a girl selling ham sandwiches. She looked tired and cold, and Gracie felt faintly guilty that they had no intention of buying from her, not that they wouldn't have liked to. The bread looked fresh and crusty, but they had no money to spare for such things.

"D'yer know Jimmy Quick?" Gracie asked her politely.

The girl gave a shrug and a smile. "Course I do. Comes by 'ere reg'lar. Why?"

"Cos me Uncle Alf did it fer 'im three days back," Minnie Maude put in. "Did yer see 'im?" She forced a smile. "Wot's yer name?"

"Florrie," the girl replied. "Ol' geezer wi' white 'air all flying on top o' 'is 'ead?"

Minnie Maude smiled, then puckered her lower lip quickly to stop herself from crying. "Yeah, that's 'im."

" 'E made me laugh. 'E told me a funny story. Silly, it were, but I in't laughed that 'ard fer ages." She shook her head.

"Was 'e goin' this way?" Gracie pointed back the way they had come. "Or that way?" she turned forward again.

Florrie considered. "That way," she said finally, pointing east.

"Are yer certain?" Gracie said to Florrie. "That'd mean 'e were goin' backward ter the way Jimmy Quick'd do it. Yer real certain?"

Florrie was puzzled. "Yeah. 'E come that way, an' 'e went up there. I watched 'im go, cos 'e made me laugh, an' 'e were singin'. I were singin' along wif 'im. A man wif a long coat got sharp wif me cos

I weren't payin' 'im no 'eed when 'e asked me fer a sandwich."

"A man wif a long coat?" Minnie Maude said instantly. "Did 'e go after Uncle Alf?"

Florrie shook her head. "No. 'E went the other way."

"We'll 'ave a sandwich," Gracie said quickly, feeling rash and expansive. She fished for a coin and passed it over. Florrie gave her the sandwich, and Gracie took it and carefully tore it in half, giving the other piece to Minnie Maude, who took it and ate it so fast it seemed to disappear from her hands.

It was much more difficult to find the next person who had seen Alf and Charlie. Twice they got lost, and they were still west of Cannon Street. The wind was getting colder, slicing down the alleys with an edge, like knives on the skin. It found every piece of bare face or neck, no matter how carefully you wound a shawl or how tightly you pulled it. The wind stung the eyes and made them water, spilling tears onto your cheeks, then freezing them.

Horses and carts passed, with hooves sharp on the ice and harnesses jingling. Shop windows were yellow-bright as the light faded early in the afternoon. It was just about the shortest day, and the lowering sky made it even grayer.

Everyone seemed busy about their own business, buying and selling to get ready for Christmas. People were talking about geese, puddings, red candles and berries, spices and wine or ale, happy things, once-a-year sort of things to celebrate. There were no church bells ringing now, but Gracie could hear them in her mind: wild, joyful— there for everyone, rich or poor, freezing or warm beside a fire.

They just weren't there for Alf, or for lost donkeys by themselves in the rain, and hungry.

It was late and heavy with dusk when they found the roasted-chestnut stand, on Lower

Chapman Street. The brazier was gleaming red and warm, sending out the smell of coals burning.

" 'E'd a stopped 'ere," Minnie Maude said with certainty. "If 'e'd a come this way. 'E loved chestnuts."

Gracie loved them too, but she had already spent too much. Still, they had to ask.

"Please, mister," Gracie said, going right up to the stand. "Did yer see the rag an' bone man three days ago, 'oo weren't Jimmy Quick? 'E were Uncle Alf, an' 'e did Jimmy's round for 'im that day, cos Jimmy asked 'im ter. D'yer see 'im?"

" 'Im wot died? Yeah, I saw 'im. Why?" The man's face reflected a sudden sadness, even in the waning light.

" 'E were me uncle," Minnie Maude told him. "I wanna know w'ere 'e died, so I can put a flower there."

The man shook his head. "I know w'ere 'e died, but I'd leave it alone, if I was you."

Suddenly Gracie's attention was keen again.

"Why? D'yer reckon summink 'appened ter 'im? We gotta know, cos we gotta find Charlie."

The man's eyebrows rose. " 'Oo's Charlie?"

" 'Is donkey," Minnie Maude said quickly. " 'E's missin', an' 'e's all by 'isself. 'E's lorst."

The man looked at her, puzzled.

"We can't 'elp Uncle Alf," Gracie explained. "But we can find Charlie. Please, mister, wot did Uncle Alf say to yer? Did 'e say anyfink special?"

"Me name's Cob." Wordlessly he passed them each a hot freshly cooked chestnut. They both thanked him and ate before he could change his mind.

Then Gracie realized what he had said. Cob! Was this the same Cob that Dora and Jimmy Quick had spoken of that Alf had shown the golden casket to? She swallowed the chestnut and took a deep breath.

"Did 'e tell yer wot 'e'd picked up?" she asked, trying to sound as if it didn't matter all that much.

"Yeah," Cob replied, eating a chestnut himself. " 'E said as 'e'd got summink real special. Beautiful, it were, a box made o' gold." He shrugged. "Course it were likely brass, but all carved, an' 'e said it were a beautiful shape, like it were made to 'old summink precious. I told 'im no one puts out summink like that. It'd be cheap brass, maybe over tin, but 'e said it were quality. Wouldn't be shifted. Stubborn as a mule, 'e were."

Minnie Maude's face was alight. " 'E 'ad it? Yer sure?"

"Course I'm sure. 'E showed it to me. Why? Weren't it wif 'im when 'e were found?"

"No. 'E were all alone in the street. No cart, no Charlie."

Cob's face pinched with sadness. "Poor ol' Alf."

" 'E di'n't steal it. It were put out." Minnie Maude looked at Cob accusingly.

Gracie's mind was on something more important, and that didn't fit in with any sense. "But 'oo knew as 'e 'ad it?" she asked, looking gravely at Cob. 'E wouldn't tell no one, would 'e? Did you say summink?"

Cob flushed. "Course I di'n't! Not till after 'e were dead, an' Stan come around askin'. I told 'im cos 'e 'ad a right, same as you." He addressed this last to Minnie Maude.

"Yer told 'im as Uncle Alf got this box?" Gracie persisted.

"Di'n't I jus' say that?" he demanded.

Gracie looked at him more carefully. He wasn't really lying, but he wasn't telling the truth either, at least not all of it.

" 'Oo else?" she said quietly, pulling her mouth into a thin line. "Someone else 'ad ter know."

Cob shrugged. "There were a tall, thin feller, wif a long nose come by, asked, casual like, after Jimmy Quick. I told 'im it wasn't Jimmy that day, an' 'e di'n't ask no more. Di'n't say nuffink about a gold box."

"Thin an' wot else?" Gracie asked. "Why were 'e lookin' fer Jimmy Quick?"

" 'Ow'd I know? 'E weren't a friend o' Jimmy's, cos 'e were a proper toff. Spoke like 'e 'ad a plum in 'is mouth, all very proper, but under it yer could tell 'e were mad as a wet cat, 'e were. Reckon as Jimmy 'ad some trouble comin'."

"Jimmy, not Uncle Alf?" Gracie persisted.

"That's wot I said. Yer got cloth ears, girl?"

"Wot else was 'e like?"

"Told yer, tall an' thin, wif a long nose, an' a coat that flapped like 'e were some great bird tryin' ter take off inter the air. An' eyes like evil 'oles in the back of 'his skull.

Gracie thanked him as politely as she could, and grasping Minnie Maude by the hand, half-dragged her away along the darkening street.

"Were 'e the one?" Minnie Maude asked breathlessly. "The toff wi' the long nose? Did 'e kill Uncle Alf?"

"Mebbe." Gracie stepped over the freezing gutter, still pulling Minnie Maude after her.

It was almost fully dark now, and the lamplighter had already been through. The elegant flat-sided lamps glowed like malevolent eyes in the growing mist. Footsteps clattered and then were instantly lost. There was hardly anyone else around. Gracie imagined them all sitting in little rooms, each with a fire, however small, and dreaming of Christmas. For women it might be flowers, or chocolates, or even a nice handkerchief, a new shawl. For men it would be whisky, or if they were very lucky, new boots. For children it would be sweets and homemade toys.

They stopped at the next corner, looking at the street sign, trying to remember if the shape of the letters was familiar. Gracie wasn't even sure anymore if they were going east or west. One day she was going to know what the letters meant, every one of them, so she could read anything at all, even in a book.

It was then that they heard the footsteps, light and easy, as if whoever made them could walk for miles without ever getting tired. And they were not very far away. Gracie froze. She was thinking of the man Cob had described, tall, with a long nose. That was silly. Why would he be there now? If he had killed Uncle Alf, he must already have the golden casket.

Nevertheless she turned around to stare, and saw the long figure in the gloom as it passed under one of the lamps. For a moment she saw quite clearly the flapping coat, just as Cob had said.

Minnie Maude saw the figure too, and stifled a shriek, clasping her hand over her mouth.

As one, they fled, boots loud on the stones, slipping and clattering, jumping over gutters, swerving around the corner into an even darker alley, then stumbling over loose cobbles, colliding with each other and lurching forward, going faster again.

The alley was a mistake. Gracie crashed into an old man sleeping in a doorway, and he lashed out at her, sending her reeling off balance and all but falling over. Only Minnie Maude's quick grasp saved her from cracking herself on the pavement.

Still the footsteps were there behind them.

The two girls burst out into the open street again, lamps now seeming almost like daylight, in spite of the thickening swathes of fog. The posts looked like elongated women with shining heads and scarves of mist trailing around their shoulders. The light shone on the wet humps of the cobbles and the flat ice of the gutters. Dark unswept manure lay in the middle of the road.

Gracie grabbed at Minnie Maude's hand and started running again. Any direction would do. She had no idea where she was. It could not be very far from Commercial Road now, and from there she could find Whitechapel Road, and Brick Lane. But this part was so unfamiliar it could have been the other end of London.

Somewhere down on the river a foghorn let out its mournful cry, as if it were even more lost than they were. Gracie's breath hurt in her chest, but the footsteps were still there behind them. Minnie Maude was frightened. Gracie could feel it in the desperate grasp of her thin, icy fingers.

"C'mon," Gracie said, trying to sound encouraging. "We gotta get out o' the light. This way." She made it sound as if she knew where she was going, and charged across the road into the opening of a stable yard. She could hear shifting hooves behind doors, and she could smell hay and the warm animal odor of horses.

"We could stay 'ere," Minnie Maude whispered, her voice wavering. "It'd be warm. 'Orses won't 'urt yer. 'E wouldn't find us in 'ere."

For a moment it sounded like a good idea, safe, no more running. But they were trapped. Once inside a stable, there would be no way to get out past him. Still, even if he looked, he wouldn't see them in the dark, not if they got into the hay.

"Yeah . . . ," she said slowly.

Minnie Maude gripped her hand tighter. As one they turned to tiptoe across the yard toward the nearest stable door.

"Next one," Gracie directed, just so as not to be obvious, in case the man did come in there. Although what difference would one door along make, if he really did look for them?

Then there he was, in the entrance, the street-lamp behind him making him look like a black cutout figure without a face. He was tall, and his chin was impossibly long, way down his chest.

"Gracie . . ." His voice was deep and hollow. "Gracie Phipps!"

She couldn't even squeak, let alone reply.

He walked toward them.

Minnie Maude was hanging on to Gracie's hand hard enough to hurt, and she was jammed so close to her side that she was almost standing on top of Gracie's boots.

The man stopped in front of them. "Gracie," he

said gently. "I told you not to go after the casket. It's dangerous. Now do you believe me?"

"Mr. . . . Mr. Balthasar?" Gracie said huskily. "Yer . . . di'n't 'alf scare me."

"Good! Now perhaps you will do as you are told, and leave this business alone. Is it not sufficient for you that poor Alf is dead? You want to join him?"

Gracie said nothing.

Mr. Balthasar turned his attention to Minnie Maude. "You must be Minnie Maude Mudway, Alf's niece. You are looking for your donkey?"

Minnie Maude nodded, still pressing herself as close to Gracie as she could.

"There is no reason to believe he is harmed," he said gently. "Donkeys are sensible beasts and useful. Someone will find him. But where will he go if in the meantime this man who murdered Alf has killed you as well?"

Gracie stared at him. There was not the slightest flicker of humor in his face. She gulped. "We'll go 'ome," she promised solemnly.

"And stay there?" he insisted.

"Yeah . . . 'ceptin' we don' know w'ere 'ome is. I'm gonna learn ter read one day, but I can't do it yet."

He nodded. "Very good. Everyone should read. There is a whole magical world waiting for you, people to meet and places to go, flights of the mind and the heart you can't even imagine. But you've got to stay alive and grow up to do that. Make me a promise—you'll go home and stay there!"

"I promise," Gracie said gravely.

"Good." He turned to Minnie Maude. "And you too."

She nodded, her eyes fixed on his face. "I will."

"Then I'll take you home. Come on."

*T*he next day was just like any other, except that Gracie had more jobs to do than ever, and her gran was busy trying to make a Christmas for them all. Gracie got up early, before anyone else was awake, and crept into the kitchen, where she cleared out the stove, and tipped the ashes on the path outside to help people from slipping on the hard, pale ice. Then she laid the wood and lit the new fire. She balanced the sticks carefully and blew a little on them to help the fire take. First she put the tiniest pieces of coal on and made sure they took as well. The small flames licked up hungrily, and she put on more. It was alarming how quickly they were eaten and gone. Lots of things went quickly. One moment they were there, and the next time you looked, they weren't.

It would be Christmas in two days. There would be bells, and singing, lots of lights, people would wear their best clothes, and ribbons, eat the best food, be nice to one another, laugh a lot. Then the next day it would all be over, until another year.

The good things ought to stay; someone ought

to make them stay. The dresses and the food didn't matter, but the laughing did, and you didn't wear the bells out by ringing them. Did happiness wear out? Maybe things didn't taste so sweet if you had them all the time?

She was still thinking about that when Spike and Finn came stumbling in, half-awake. Reluctantly they washed in the bucket of water in the corner. Then, wet-haired and blinking, they sat down to the porridge, which was now hot. They left plates almost clean enough to put away again.

By the end of the afternoon, Gracie's chores were finished, and her mind kept going back to Minnie Maude. She had to be worrying about Charlie. What kind of a Christmas would it be for her if he was not found? If they went looking around the streets, just for Charlie, not asking about Uncle Alf, or the golden casket, would that be breaking their promise to Mr. Balthasar? It was the casket the toff wanted, not a donkey who really wasn't any use to him.

She did not sleep very well, tossing and turning beside her gran, listening to the wind whistling through the broken slates. She woke up in the morning tired and still more worried. It was Christmas Eve. There was no reason why she should not at least go and see Minnie Maude and ask her how she felt about things.

She made sure the whole house was tidy, the stove backed up, the flatirons put where they could cool without scorching anything. Then she wrapped herself in her heaviest shawl, with a lighter one underneath, and set out in the hard sleet-edged wind to find Minnie Maude. Although she knew what Minnie Maude would say. Donkeys had hair all over them, of course, but it wouldn't be much comfort in this weather. When she had wet hair, she froze!

Bertha was in her kitchen, her face red, and she looked flustered. She opened the door, and as soon as she saw Gracie on the step, she put out a hand and all but hauled her inside, slamming the door shut after her.

117

"Yer seen Minnie Maude?" she said angrily. "Where'd that stupid little thing go now?"

Gracie's heart beat wildly, and her breath almost choked her. There was something badly wrong; she hardly dared even think how wrong. She could see that the red marks on Bertha's face were weals from someone's hand striking her, and Bertha held one shoulder higher than the other, as if even when she wasn't thinking of it, it hurt her and she needed to protect it.

"I in't seen Minnie Maude since two days ago," Gracie answered, looking straight into Bertha's red-rimmed eyes. "We said as we wouldn't look anymore ter see wot 'appened to 'er uncle Alf, cos it were too dangerous—" She knew immediately that she had made a mistake, but there was no way to take it back. Bertha would know the moment she lied. If you weren't used to lying, and the lie mattered, it always showed in your face.

"Wot d'yer mean, dangerous?" Bertha asked,

her voice dipping very low. "Wot yer bin askin'? Wot've yer done?"

Something near the truth was best. "Where 'e were killed," Gracie replied. "Minnie Maude wanted ter put a flower there." She kept her eyes steady, trying not to blink too much. Bertha was watching her like a cat studying a mouse hole in the wall.

"Well, it don't matter," Bertha said at last. "Put it anywhere. Alf won't care. 'E's dead an' gorn. You tell 'er that. She don't listen ter me."

"I will," Gracie promised. "Where is she?"

Bertha's face was white beneath the red weals. "I thought as she'd gorn ter sleep in the stable, but she in't there. Then I thought as she'd mebbe gorn fer you."

"No! In't seen 'er since two days ago." Gracie heard her own voice touched with panic. "When d'yer see 'er terday?"

Bertha's voice was husky. "I di'n't see 'er terday."

A dark fear fluttered in the pit of Gracie's stom-- ach. "Wot did she take a miff about? Were it sum- mink ter do wi' Jimmy Quick, or the chestnut man?"

"It were summink ter do wif 'er always med- dlin'," Bertha replied. "Stan lost 'is temper wif 'er summink awful. I were afeared 'e were gonna 'it 'er, but 'e di'n't. 'E jus' lit out, white as paper, swearin' witless, an' next thing I know, she were gorn too."

Gracie was too frightened to be angry, and she could see that beneath Bertha's arrogance and self-defense, she was frightened also. There was no point in asking her for help.

"Well, if she in't 'ere, no point in me lookin'," Gracie said, as if that were some kind of reason.

Bertha opened her mouth as if to answer, then closed it again without speaking.

Gracie turned and left, walking away across the yard and out into the street again. She did not go back toward her own home; there was nothing to see that way. Where would Minnie Maude go, and, more urgently, why? What was Stan so angry about, and why was Bertha afraid? If Bertha were just afraid that Minnie Maude had been gone all night, she would have been looking for her herself, not standing around working in the kitchen.

Gracie's step slowed because she had no idea where to begin. One thing she was certain of as the wind sliced through her shawl, chilling her body, was that no one stayed out all night in this weather without a reason so harsh it overrode all sense of safety or comfort. Minnie Maude was looking for Charlie, but she must have had some idea where he was, or else there was something she was so frightened of at home that staying out alone in the icy streets was better.

What Gracie needed was to work out what Minnie Maude would have done. Something pretty urgent, or she would have waited until today, and told Gracie about it. Unless she'd thought Gracie had given up!

She stood at the curb watching the water flecked with ice running high over the gutters, as the wind whined in the eaves of the houses in the street behind her. The hooves of a horse pulling a dray clattered on the stones, wheels rumbling behind it.

Gracie had promised Mr. Balthasar not to ask any more questions about Uncle Alf's death. Minnie Maude knew that Gracie had meant it. Minnie Maude wouldn't have gone to look for Gracie; she would have gone off on her own. But where? Jimmy Quick wasn't going to tell them anything more. Even Minnie Maude wouldn't wander around the streets hoping to catch sight of Charlie. She must have gone somewhere in particular.

Which way had they gone before? Gracie looked left, and right. Minnie Maude would have gone down to the Whitechapel High Street and over into Commercial Road, for sure, then into the narrower roads with people's names, on either side of Cannon Street. If Gracie could just find those streets, she would know where to begin.

She set off briskly, and was on the far side of the goods yard before she was lost.

She looked to the left and couldn't remember any of the shop fronts or houses. She turned the other way. There was a broken gutter sticking out in the shape of a dogleg that she thought she'd seen before. That was as good a reason as any for making a decision. She went that way.

She passed an ironmonger's window with all sorts of strange tools in it, things she couldn't imagine using in a kitchen. She couldn't have been there before. If she'd seen those things, she would have remembered them.

Where on earth had Minnie Maude gone? It was Gracie's fault. She should have known better than to trust her. Minnie Maude loved that wretched donkey as much as if it had been a person, maybe more! Donkeys didn't lie to you, or swear at you, or tell you off, say that you were useless or lazy or cost the earth to keep. Maybe Charlie even loved her back. Maybe he was always happy to see her?

All right, so maybe Minnie Maude wasn't stupid to be loyal to a friend, just daft to go off without telling anyone. Except who cared anyway? Bertha? Maybe, but she didn't act like it. She was more scared than anything—maybe of Stan?

There was no point in standing there in a strange street. Gracie set off again, briskly this time. At least she would get a bit warmer. A few hot chestnuts would be a good thing right then. Maybe Minnie Maude had gone back to Cob, to see if he knew anything more? Or if not Cob, then maybe Paper John, although he hadn't said anything very helpful.

Who else might she have looked for? The crossing sweeper, Monday? Without realizing it she was walking more slowly, thinking hard, grasping for memory, and reasons. What had Minnie

Maude done that had made Stan so angry? Or was he just scared too, but would rather get angry than admit being scared? If Alf really had been killed by someone over the golden casket, then could Stan know something about it?

How did he know what Minnie Maude had been doing? She had said something, she must have. But what? Had she told him something, or asked him? Or he'd said something, and she had remembered . . . or understood—but what?

Gracie stopped in the shelter of a high building with a jutting wall. There was no point in going any farther until she worked things out. She might be going in the wrong direction, and would only have to go all the way back. The wind was harder and there were occasional pellets of ice in it. Her fingers were numb. She leaned against the wall where an uneven door frame offered her a little shelter.

Why had Minnie Maude gone? She must have had a reason, something that had happened—or something that had suddenly made sense to her. If Stan had said something, what could that be? How would he know anything about it anyway?

Or was it some meaning she'd put together, and then she'd seen a pattern?

A hawker pushed his barrow across the street, wheels bumping in the gutter, the wind in his face.

Think! Gracie said to herself angrily. *You were there all the time. Everything Minnie Maude heard, so did you! What did she understand all of a sudden?*

She was shaking with the cold, but there was no point in walking anywhere if she didn't know where to go. And the other thing, if she was really thinking as hard as she could, she wouldn't be noticing where she was, and she'd get even more lost. That wouldn't help Minnie Maude or Charlie, or anyone else.

Where had she and Minnie Maude been when they'd followed Jimmy Quick's route? What had they seen, or heard? They'd spoken to Monday, the crossing sweeper on Cannon Street. She tried to recall everything he had said. None of it seemed to matter much. Certainly it wouldn't have sent Minnie Maude out of the house, breaking her promise, and on a bitter night with ice on the wind.

Then there'd been Florrie, the peddler; and Paper John. Then there was Cob, the chestnut seller. He'd said a lot. He was the one who'd seen the toff, and Alf had actually told him about the golden casket.

But the more Gracie thought about it all, the less did she see anything in it that she hadn't seen two days before. Nobody had spoken of anything suspicious. It was exactly the same route, though backward, as Jimmy Quick always took—the same streets, the same people saw him. He had even started at about the same time. She could re-member most of the streets, only not necessarily in the same order. But Alf would have had it right,

because it made sense. One street led into another. There was only one way to go.

She tried again to remember exactly what
everyone had said. She closed her eyes and
hunched her shoulders, wrapping her shawl even
more tightly around herself, and pictured the
roasted-chestnut man. He was the only one who
had seen Alf after he'd had the casket. Cob had
looked worried, but not really downright frightened. She could see it in her mind's eye, the way
he'd stood, his expression, the way he had waved
his arms to show which way the man he'd called
the toff had come . . . except that he had been
coming the way Alf was going, not the way he had
just passed! That made no sense.

She tried it again, but with Cob waving the
other way. Except that he couldn't have. He was
standing next to the brazier, about the length of
his forearm from it. If he had waved that arm, he
would have hit the brazier, and very likely burned

himself. He might even have knocked it over. So it couldn't be right.

She tried turning him around, but that didn't work either. He had definitely pointed the way Alf was still going, not where he had been. She recited the order of the streets Jimmy had told them. Then she tried to say them backward, and got them jumbled up.

There was only one answer—Alf had done them the other way around. He had started at the end, and worked back to the beginning. The same circle—but backward.

Had someone counted on him doing it the same way as always? They would have expected him to be at a certain place at a certain time. The casket had been left for someone else. Alf had taken it without realizing it was important. Whoever it was—the toff—had gone after him to get it back, and by that time Alf had decided he wanted to keep it. Perhaps there had been a fight, and Alf had been killed because he wouldn't give it up?

Then why take Charlie? Why take the cart? And whose blood had it been on the stable floor?

It was getting colder. There was no answer that made sense of everything. The only things that seemed certain were that Alf was dead, Charlie and the cart were missing—and Alf had taken Jimmy Quick's route backward, being just about everywhere when nobody expected him.

Oh, and there was one other thing—the casket was missing, too. If it hadn't been, then the toff wouldn't still be looking for it. And worst of all, Minnie Maude was missing now too. That was Gracie's fault. She had left her alone when she knew how much the little girl cared. If she'd thought about it, instead of how tired and cold she was, and how much help her gran needed, then she would have seen ahead. She'd have gone to Minnie Maude's earlier, in time to stop her from wandering off and then getting taken by the toff.

Well, Gracie would just have to find her now. There wasn't anything else she could possibly do. She had to use her brains and think.

There was more traffic in the street, people coming and going, carts, wagons, drays, even one or two hansoms. Who had left the casket out with the old things for the rag and bone man, not expecting him to come by for hours? Why would anybody do that? For somebody else to pick up, of course. That was the only thing that made sense.

Who would that be? The toff, naturally. But who'd left it? And why? If you wanted somebody to have something, wouldn't you just give it to them? Leaving it on the side of the street was daft!

Unless you couldn't wait? Or you didn't want to be seen? Or somebody was chasing you?

Only, Alf had come along instead, and too soon. Perhaps it had been hidden inside an old piece of carpet, or inside a coal scuttle, or something like that. Then no one else would even have known it was there.

What did Alf do with it? He'd had it when he'd stopped for hot chestnuts, because Cob had seen it. Then where had Alf gone? He couldn't have had it when he was killed, or whoever killed him would have taken it away—wouldn't they?

Maybe it wasn't the toff who'd killed him?

But if somebody else had, then why? Because of the casket—it was the only thing special and different. Then what on earth was inside it that was worth so much—and was so dangerous? It must have been something very powerful, but not good. Good things, a real gift from the Wise Men for Jesus, wouldn't make people kill one another like this. Alf was dead, Bertha was frightened stiff, and Stan was angry enough to hit her in the face, probably because he was scared as well.

And Gracie was so afraid for Minnie Maude that she felt a kind of sickness in her stomach and a cold, hard knot inside her, making it difficult to breathe. Every time she thought she had made sense out of it all, it slipped away. She needed to get help. But from who? None of the people she knew would even understand, and they all had their own griefs and worries to deal with. They would just say that Minnie Maude had run off, and she'd come back when she got cold or hungry enough. They'd tell Gracie to mind her own business, look after Spike and Finn, and do as her gran told her.

She looked up and down the street as it grew busier. People hurried along the pavement, heads bent, the rain and sleet pounding. Many of the people were carrying parcels. Were they presents for Christmas? Nice food—cakes and puddings? There'd be holly with red berries, and ivy, maybe mistletoe, and ribbons, of course.

There was one person she could ask. He'd be very angry, because she had promised to stop asking questions, but this was different. Minnie Maude was gone. He could be angry later.

She straightened up, turned back the way she had come, and started walking into the wind. It stung her face and seemed to cut right through her shawl as if her shawl had been made of paper, but she knew where she was going.

Mr. Balthasar looked at her grimly. His dark face, with its long, curved nose, was set in lines of deep unhappiness.

Gracie swallowed, but the lump in her throat remained.

"Will yer please 'elp me, mister, cos I dunno 'oo else ter ask. I think Minnie Maude's in trouble."

"Yes," he agreed quickly. "I think she probably is. You look frozen, child." He touched her shoulder with his thin hand. "And wet through. I will find you something dry, and a cup of tea." He started to move away.

"There in't time!" she said urgently, panic rising in her voice. Warm and dry would be wonderful, but not till Minnie Maude was found.

"Yes, there is," he replied steadily. "A dry shawl will take no time at all, and you can tell me everything you know while the kettle is boiling. I shall close the shop so we will not be disturbed. Come with me."

He locked the door and turned around a little sign on it so people would not knock, then he found her a wonderful red embroidered shawl and wrapped it around her, instead of her own wringing-wet one. Then, while she sat on a stool and watched him, he pulled the kettle onto the top of the big black stove, and cut bread to make toast.

"Tell me," he commanded her. "Tell me everything you have done since you last spoke to me, where you went and what you have discovered."

"First day I 'elped me gran, then terday I went ter see Minnie Maude, an' she weren't at 'ome," Gracie began. "'Er aunt Bertha tol' me as she'd gorn out, after Stan shouted at 'er. 'E were real mad, an' Bertha were scared. There were red marks on 'er face where 'e'd 'it 'er." It sounded silly now that she told him, because she hadn't actually seen it and couldn't explain any of her feelings. People did hit each other, and it didn't have to mean much.

He did not point out any of that. Turning over the toast to brown the other side, he asked her how Bertha sounded, what she looked like.

"And so you went looking for Minnie Maude?" he said when she had finished. "Where?"

"I thought as she must 'ave remembered summink," she replied, breathing in the smell of the crisp toast. "Or understood summink wot didn't make no sense two days ago."

"I see." He took the toast off and spread a little butter on it, then jam with big black fruit in it. He put it on a plate, cut it in half, and passed it to her.

"Is that all for me?" Then she could have kicked herself for her bad manners. She wanted to push the plate away again, but that would have been rude too, and the toast was making her mouth water.

"Of course it is," he replied. "I shall be hurt if

you don't eat it. The tea will be ready in a minute. What did she realize, Gracie?"

"Well, we knew Alf went the wrong way," she said, picking up a piece of the toast and biting into it. It was wonderful, crisp, and the jam was sweet. She couldn't help herself from swallowing it and taking another bite.

"The wrong way?" he prompted.

She answered with her mouth full. "Jimmy Quick always goes round 'is streets in one way. Uncle Alf went the other way. 'E started at the end, an' did it backward, so 'e were always everywhere at the wrong time." She leaned forward eagerly. "That were when 'e picked up the casket, nobody were expectin' 'im even ter be there. It were put fer someone else!"

"I see." The kettle started to whistle with steam, and Balthasar stood up and made the tea. "Do you know why he did that?"

"No." Now she wondered why she didn't know, and she felt stupid for not thinking of it.

"I shall inquire," he replied. "If something caused him to, such as a carriage accident blocking a road, or a dray spilling its load so he could not get past, that might be different from his deliberately choosing the other way around. Presumably this man, the toff, went to collect the casket, and found that it was gone. How did he know that the rag and bone man had taken it?" He put up his hand. "No, no need to answer that—because all the stuff for the rag and bone collection was gone. But he caught up with poor Alf—so if Alf was going the wrong way round, how did the toff know that?" He brought the teapot to the table and poured a large mug full for her. He passed the mug across, his black eyes studying her face.

"I dunno," she said unhappily. "D'yer think as 'e worked it out? I mean that Alf 'ad gone the wrong way round?"

"How did he know it was Alf, and not Jimmy Quick, as usual?" Balthasar asked. "No, I rather think he was waiting and watching, and he saw what happened."

"Then why di'n't 'e go after 'im straigh'away?" Gracie asked reasonably. "In fact, if the casket were left there for 'im, why di'n't 'e take it before Alf even got there? That don't make no sense."

Balthasar frowned, biting his lip. "It would if he did not wish to be seen. Whoever left it there for him would know what was in it, and that it was both valuable and dangerous. It might be that the toff could not afford to have anyone see him with it."

Gracie gulped. "Wot were in it?"

"I don't know, but I imagine something like opium."

"Wozzat?" she asked.

"A powder that gives people insane dreams of pleasure," he replied. "And when they wake up, it is all gone, and so they have to have more, to get the dreams back again. Sometimes they will pay a great price, even kill other people, to get it. But it is not something to be proud of, in fact very much the opposite. If the toff is an addict, which means that he can no longer do without it, then he will do anything to come by it—but he will take great care that none of his friends know."

For a moment she forgot the toast and jam.

"Someone put it there for him, in the casket," Balthasar went on. "And he waited out of sight, to dart out and pick it up when they were gone. Only this time Alf came by before he could do that. Continue with your tea, Gracie. We have business to do when we are finished."

"We 'ave?" But she obeyed and reached for the mug.

"We have a little more thinking to do first." He smiled bleakly. "I would tell you to go home, because I believe this will be dangerous, but I do not trust that you would obey. I would rather have you with me, where I can see you, than following after me and I don't know where you are and cannot protect you. But you must promise to do as I say, or we may both be in great danger, and Minnie Maude even more so."

"I promise," she agreed instantly, her heart pounding, her mouth dry.

"Good. Now let us consider what else we know, or may deduce."

"Wot?"

He half-concealed a smile. "I apologize—what we may work out as being true, because of what wc already know. Would you like another piece of toast? There is sufficient time. Before we do anything, we must be certain that we have considered it all, and weighed every possibility. Do you not agree?"

"Yeah. An' . . . an' I'd like another piece o' toast, if you please."

"Certainly." He stood up quite solemnly and cut two more slices of bread and placed them before the open door of the oven. "Now, let us consider what else has happened, and what it means. Alf had the casket at the time he spoke to the chestnut man—Cob, I believe you called him? If we know the route that Mr. Quick normally took, then we know what the reverse of it would be, with some amendments for traffic. Hence we know where Alf is most likely to have gone next. And we know where his body was found."

"Yeah, but it don't fit in, cos 'oo's blood is it on the stable floor? An' 'oo fought there an' bashed up the wall? An' why'd 'e take Charlie an' the cart as well?" She drew in her breath. "An' if 'e killed Alf an' took the casket, wot's 'e still looking for? That's stupid. If I done summink wrong, I don't go makin' a noise all over the place. I keep me 'ead down." She colored with shame as she said it, but right then the truth was more important than pride.

"You have several good points, Gracie," Mr. Balthasar agreed. "All of which we need to address." He turned the toast over and filled her mug with fresh, hot tea.

"Thank you," she acknowledged. The heat was

spreading through her now, and she looked forward to more toast and jam. She began to realize just how cold she had been.

"I think it is clear," he continued, sitting down again, "that the toff does not have the casket, or at the very least, he does not have whatever was inside it. If he did, he would not only, as you say, keep his head down, he would be enjoying the illicit pleasures of his purchase."

She did not know what "illicit" meant, but she could guess.

"So where is it, then? 'Oo's got it?" she asked.

"I think we must assume that Alf did something with it between speaking to Cob and meeting whoever killed him presumably the toff. Unless, of course, it was not the toff who killed him but someone else. Although to me that seems rather to be complicating things. We already have one unknown person . . ."

"We 'ave? 'Oo?"

"Whoever passed that way just before Alf, and

left the casket," he replied. "Have you any idea who that could be?"

She felt his eyes on her, as if he could will her to come up with an answer. She wished she could be what he expected of her, and even now she wished she could think of something that really would help Minnie Maude.

"Is it someone 'oo knew where Charlie's stable is?" she asked, wondering if it was silly even as she said it. "Cos somebody 'ad a fight there. We saw the marks, an' the blood on the floor."

"Indeed. And do you know if it was there before Alf went out with Charlie the day he was killed?" he asked with interest.

She saw what he was thinking. "Yer mean if it weren't Alf or Charlie, then it 'ad ter be ter do wi' the casket?"

"I was assuming that, yes. What does this Stan do for a living, Gracie? Do you know?"

"Yeah. 'E's a cabbie . . . "

Mr. Balthasar nodded slowly.

"An' 'e's mad, an' scared," she added eagerly. "D'yer think Minnie Maude worked that out too?" Her eyes filled with tears at the thought of what violence might have happened to Minnie Maude, if Stan were the one who had left the casket for the toff.

"I think we had better finish our tea and go and speak to Cob," Balthasar answered, rising to his feet again. "Come."

"I gotta get me own shawl, please?" she said reluctantly. Compared with the thick red one, hers was plain, and wet.

"I will return it to you later," he replied. "This one will keep you warm in the meantime. Come. Now that we have so many clues, we must make all the haste we can." And he strode across the wooden floor and flung open the back door, grasping for a large black cape and swinging it around his shoulders as he went.

Outside in the street he allowed her to lead the way, keeping up with her easily because his legs were twice the length of hers. They did not speak, simply meeting eyes as they came to a curb, watching for traffic, then continuing.

They found Cob on his corner, the brazier giving off a warmth she could feel even when she was six or seven feet away.

Balthasar stood in front of Cob, half a head taller and looking alarmingly large in his black cape. He seemed very strange, very different, and several people stared at him nervously as they passed, increasing their pace a little.

"Good afternoon, Mr. Cob," Balthasar said gravely. "I must speak to you about a very terrible matter. I require absolute honesty in your answers, or the outcome may be even worse. Do you understand me?"

Cob looked taken aback. "I dunno yer, sir, an' I dunno nothin' terrible. I don't think as I can 'elp yer." He glanced at Gracie, then away again.

"I don't know whether you will, Mr. Cob. You may have black reasons of your own for keeping such secrets," Balthasar answered him. "But I believe that you can."

"I don't 'ave no—" Cob began.

Balthasar held up his hand, commanding silence. "It concerns the murder of a man you know as Alf, and the abduction of Minnie Maude Mudway."

Cob paled.

Balthasar nodded. "I see you understand me perfectly. When Alf left you, on the day he died, which way did he go?"

Cob pointed south.

"Indeed. And it was two streets farther than that where someone caught up with him and did him to death. Somewhere in that distance Alf gave the casket to somebody. Who lives or works along those streets, Mr. Cob, that Alf would know? A pawnshop, perhaps? A public house? An old friend? To whom would such a man give a golden casket?"

Cob looked increasingly uncomfortable. "I dunno!" he protested. " 'E di'n't tell me!"

"How long after Alf spoke to you did this gaunt gentleman come by?"

Cob moved his weight from one foot to the other. "Jus' . . . jus' a few moments."

"Was he on foot?"

"Course 'e were," Cob said derisively. "Yer don't go 'untin' after someone in a carriage!"

"Hunting," Balthasar tasted the word. "Of course you don't. You don't want witnesses if you catch him, now, do you?"

Cob realized that he had fallen into a trap. "I di'n't know 'e were gonna kill 'im!" he said indignantly, but his face was pink and his eyes too fixed in their stare.

Gracie knew he was lying. She had seen exactly that look on Spike's face when he had pinched food from the cupboard.

"Yer mean yer thought as the toff, all angry an' swearin', were one of 'is friends?" she said witheringly. "Knows a lot o' rag an' bone men, does 'e?"

"Listen, missy . . . ," Cob began angrily.

Balthasar stepped forward, half-shielding Gracie. He looked surprisingly menacing, and Cob shrank back.

"I think you would be a great deal wiser to give an honest answer," Balthasar said in a careful, warning voice. "How long after Alf was here did the toff come and ask you about him?"

Cob drew in breath to protest again, then surrendered. " 'Bout five minutes, I reckon, give or take. Wot diff'rence does it make now?"

"Thank you," Balthasar replied, and taking Gracie by the arm, he started off along the street again.

"Wot diff'rence does it make?" Gracie repeated Cob's question.

"Five minutes is quite a long time," he replied. "I do not think he would have run. That would draw too much attention to himself. People would remember him. But a man walking briskly can still cover quite a distance in that time. Alf would be going slowly, because he would be keeping an eye out for anything to pick up."

"Then why di'n't 'e catch up wif Alf sooner?" Gracie asked.

"I think because Alf stopped somewhere," Balthasar answered. "Somewhere where he left the casket, which is why he didn't have it when the toff killed him. And that, of course, is why the toff also took Charlie and the cart, to search it more carefully in private. He could hardly do it in the middle of the street, and with poor Alf's dead body beside him." He stopped speaking suddenly, and seemed to lapse into deep thought, although he did not slacken his pace.

Gracie waited, running a step or two every now and then to keep up.

"Gracie!" he said suddenly. "If you were to kill a rag and bone man, in the street, albeit a quiet one, perhaps a small alley, and you wished to take away the man's cart in order to search it, what would you do to avoid drawing attention to yourself and having everybody know what you had done?"

She knew she had to think and give him a sensible answer. She had to try not to think of Minnie Maude and the trouble she was in; it only sent her mind into a panic. Panic was no help at all.

"Cos I di'n't want nobody to look at me?" she pressed, seeking for time.

"I don't care if they look," he corrected. "I don't want them to see."

"Wot?" Then suddenly she had an idea. "Nobody sees rag an' bone men, less they want summink. I'd put 'is 'at on an' drive the cart meself, so they'd think I was 'im!"

"Magnificent!" Balthasar said jubilantly. "That is precisely what a quick-thinking and desperate man would do! In fact, it is not necessarily true that he was killed where his body was found. That too could have been carried a short way at least, and left somewhere to mislead any inquiry. Yes, that is truly a great piece of imaginative detection, Gracie."

Gracie glowed with momentary pride, until she

thought of Minnie Maude again. Then it vanished. "'As 'e got Minnie Maude?" she asked, afraid of the answer.

"I don't know, but we will get her back. If he took her, it is because he still doesn't have the casket, so he will not harm her until he does. We must find it first."

"Well, if the toff don't 'ave it, then Alf must a given it ter someone else between Cob an' wherever 'e were killed."

"Indeed. And we must find out where that is. It is unfortunate that we know so little about Alf, and his likes and dislikes. Otherwise we might have a better idea where to begin. Perhaps we should assume that he is like most men—looking for comfort rather than adventure, someone to be gentle with him rather than to challenge him. Tell me, Gracie, what did Minnie Maude say to you about him? Why did she like him so much? Think carefully. It is important."

She understood, so she did not answer quickly,

knowing her response would dictate where they would begin to look, and it might make the difference in terms of finding Minnie Maude in time to save her. It was silly to think Minnie Maude couldn't be hurt. Alf was dead—and they knew the toff was out there. She could well believe that the powder he was addicted to had driven him mad to the point where he had tasted evil, and now could not rid himself of it.

" 'E were funny," she said, measuring her words and still skipping the odd step to keep up with him. " 'E made 'er laugh. 'E liked 'orses an' dogs, an' donkeys, o' course. An' 'ot chestnuts."

"And ale?"

"Cider." She struggled to recall exactly what Minnie Maude had said. "An' good pickle wif 'am."

"I see. A man of taste. What else? Did she ever speak of his friends, other than Jimmy Quick? Tell me about Bertha."

"I think as Bertha is scared."

"She may well have reason to be. Who is she

scared of, do you think? Stan? Someone else? Or just of being cold and hungry?"

She thought for a few moments. "Stan . . . I think." She thought back further, into her own earlier years, to when her father was alive. She remembered standing in the kitchen and hearing her mother's voice frightened and pleading. "Not scared 'e'd 'it 'er, scared o' wot 'e might do that'd get 'em all in trouble," she amended aloud.

"And Bertha is frightened and tired and a little short of temper, as she has much cause to be?"

"Yeah . . ."

"Come, Gracie. We must hurry, I think." He grasped her hand and started to stride forward so quickly that she had to run to keep up with him as he swung around the corner and into a narrower street, just off Anthony Street—the way Jimmy Quick's route would have taken them. They were still two hundred yards at least from where Alf's body had been found. Balthasar looked one way, then the other, seeming to study the bleak fronts of the buildings, the narrow doorways, the stains of soot and smoke and leaking gutters.

"Wot are yer lookin' fer?" she asked.

"I am looking for whatever Alf was seeking when he came here," Balthasar replied. "There was something, someone, with whom he wanted to share this casket he had found. Who was it?"

Gracie studied the narrow street as well. There was no pavement on one side, and barely a couple of feet of uneven stones on the other. Yet narrower alleys that led into yards invited no one. The houses had smeared windows, some already cracked, and recessed doorways in which the destitute huddled to stay out of the rain.

"It don't look like nowhere I'd want ter be," she said miserably.

"Nor I," Balthasar agreed. "But we do not know who lives inside. We will have to ask. Distasteful, but necessary. Come."

They set out across the road and approached the old woman in the first doorway.

Later, they were more than halfway toward the arch and gate at the end of the road when they found something that seemed hopeful.

"Took yer long enough," a snaggletoothed man said, leaning sideways in the twelfth doorway. He regarded Gracie with disfavor. "I 'ope yer in't expectin' ter sell 'er? Couldn't get sixpence for that bag o' bones." He laughed at his own wit.

"You are quite right," Balthasar agreed. "She is all fire and brains, and no flesh at all. No good to customers of yours. I imagine they like warm and simple, and no answer back?"

The man looked nonplussed. "Right, an' all," he agreed slowly. "Then wot der yer want? Yer can't come in 'ere wif 'er. Put people off."

"I'm looking for my friend, Alf Mudway. Do you know him?"

"Wot if I do? Won't do me no good now, will it! 'E's dead. Yer wastin' yer time." The man stuck out his lantern jaw belligerently.

"I know he is dead," Balthasar replied. "And I

know he was killed here. I am interested that you know it too. I have friends to whom that will be of concern." He allowed it to hang in the air, as if it were a threat.

"I dunno nuffink about it!" the man retaliated.

"One of my friends," Balthasar said slowly, giving weight to each word, "is a tall man, and thin, as I am. But he is a little fairer of complexion, except for his eyes. He has eyes like holes in his head, as if the devil had poked his fingers into his skull, and left a vision of hell behind when he withdrew them."

The color in the man's face fled. "I already told 'im!" he said in a strangled voice. "Alf come in 'ere ter see Rose, an' 'e went out again. I di'n't see nuffink! I dunno wot 'e done nor wot 'e took! Nor the cabbie neither! I swear!"

"The cabbie?" Balthasar repeated. "Just possibly you are telling the truth. Describe him." It was an order.

" 'E were a cabbie, fer Gawd's sake! Cape on for the rain. Bowler 'at."

Gracie knew what Balthasar had told her, but she spoke anyway.

"Wot about 'is legs?" she challenged. She knocked her knees together and then apart again. "Could 'e catch a runaway pig?"

Balthasar stared at her.

"Not in a month o' Sundays," the man replied. "Bowlegged as a Queen Anne chair."

Balthasar took Gracie by the arm, his fingers holding her so hard she could not move without being hurt. "We will now see Rose," he stated.

The man started to refuse, then looked at Balthasar's face again and changed his mind.

The inside of the house was poorly lit, but surprisingly warm, and the smell was less horrible than Gracie had expected. They had been told that Rose's was the third room on the left.

"I'm sorry," Balthasar apologized to her. "This may be embarrassing for you, but it will not be safe to leave you outside."

"I don' care," Gracie said tartly. "We gotta find Minnie Maude."

"Quite." Unceremoniously Balthasar put his weight against the door and burst it open.

What met Gracie's eyes was nothing at all that she could have foreseen. What she had expected, after Balthasar's words, was some scene of lewdness such as she had accidentally witnessed in alleys before, men and women half-naked, touching parts of the body she knew should be private. She had never imagined that it would be a half-naked woman lying on the floor in a tangle of bedclothes, blood splashed on her arms and chest, staining the sheets, bruises all over her face and neck.

Balthasar said something in a language she had never heard before, and fell onto the floor on his knees beside the woman. His long brown fingers touched her neck and stilled, feeling for something, waiting.

"Is she dead?" Gracie said in a hoarse whisper.

"No," Balthasar answered softly. "But she has been badly hurt. Look around and see if you can find me any alcohol. If you can't, fetch me water."

Gracie was too horrified to move.

"Gracie! Do as I tell you!" Balthasar commanded.

Gracie tried to think where she should look. Where did people keep bottles of whisky or gin? Where it couldn't be seen. In the bottom of drawers, the back of cupboards, underneath other things, in bottles that looked like something else.

Balthasar had Rose sitting up, cradled against his arm, her eyelids fluttering as if she were going to awaken, when Gracie discovered the bottle in the bottom of the wardrobe, concealed under a long skirt. She uncorked the top and gave it to him.

He said nothing, but there was a flash of appreciation in his eyes that was worth more than words. Carefully he put the bottle to Rose's lips and tipped it until a little of the liquid went into her mouth. She coughed, half-choked, and then took in a shaky breath.

"Rose!" he said firmly. "Rose! Wake up. You're going to be all right. He's gone and no one is going to hurt you again. Now breathe in and out, slowly."

She did so, and opened her eyes. She must have known from his voice that he was not whoever had beaten her. He had a slight foreign accent, as if he came from somewhere very far away.

"Rose," he said gently. "Who did this to you, and why?"

She shook her head a little, then winced at the pain. "I dunno," she whispered.

"It is too late for lies," he insisted. "Why?"

"I dunno." Tears slid down her cheeks. "Some geezer just went mad an' . . ."

Gracie bent down in front of her, anger and fear welling up inside her. "Course yer know, yer stupid mare!" she said furiously. "If yer don't tell us about the casket, an' 'oo took it, Minnie

Maude's going ter be killed too, jus' like Alf, an' it'll be on yer 'ead. An' nobody's never gonna fergive yer! Now spit it out, before I twist yer nose off."

Balthasar opened his mouth, and then changed his mind and closed it again.

Rose stared in horror at Gracie.

Gracie put her hand out toward Rose's face, and Rose flinched.

"A' right!" she squawked. "It were a toff with mad eyes, like a bleedin' lunatic. Proper gent, spoke like 'e 'ad a mouth full of 'ot pertaters. 'E wanted the gold box wot Alf gave me, and when I couldn't give it to 'im, 'e beat the 'ell out o' me." She started to cry.

Gracie was overcome with pity. Rose looked awful, and must have been full of pain in just about every part of her. Balthasar had wound the end of a sheet around the worst bleeding, but even the sight of so much scarlet was frightening. But if the toff had Minnie Maude, then obviously he could just as easily do the same to her, or worse. And Alf was already dead.

"Why di'n't yer give 'im the box?" Gracie demanded, her voice sharp, not with anger but with fear. "Wot's in it worth bein' killed fer?"

"Cos I don't 'ave it, eedjit!" Rose snapped back at her. "Don't yer think I'd 'ave given 'im the bleedin' crown jools, if I'd 'ave 'ad them?"

Gracie was dismayed. "Then 'oo 'as?" she said hollowly.

"Stan. Cos them Chinamen came to 'is place and beat the bejesus out of 'im for the money, 'E came 'ere jus' before. I reckon the bastard knew that lunatic were be'ind 'im, an' 'e went out the back. Then a few minutes after, this other geezer came in the front an' started in on me as soon as I din' give 'im the box."

"That is not the complete truth," Balthasar said quietly. "It makes almost perfect sense. Clearly Alf gave you the box, just before he was killed. At the time, no one else knew that, but Stan worked it

out. I daresay he knew Alf well enough to be aware
of his association with you, so it was only a matter
of time before he came here. We may assume that
the toff was aware of this also, but not where you
were, and therefore he followed Stan."

"'Ow'd 'e know about Stan?" Rose looked at
him awkwardly. Her cheek where she had been
struck was swelling up, and one eye was rapidly
closing. In a day or two the bruises would look
much worse.

Balthasar glanced at Gracie, then back to
Rose. "I think we can deduce that Stan was the
one who placed the casket and its contents on the
road near where the toff was waiting for the op-
portunity to pick it up. He hid in order that whoever dropped off the box would not see him. His
addiction is not something he would care to have
widely known, or his association with such people.
When his addiction is under control, I daresay he
is a man of some substance, and possibly of re-
pute, and would then look much like anyone else.

We are seeing him when he has been deprived of his drug and is half-insane for the need of it."

Gracie shivered involuntarily. It was a thing of such destructive force that the evil of it permeated the room. "If 'e were followin' Stan, Minnie Maude weren't wif 'im, were she?" She swung around and stared accusingly at Rose. "Well, were she?"

"No! 'E were by 'isself!"

Gracie looked at Balthasar, desperation swelling into panic inside her. "If the toff's got 'er, why'd 'e chase after Stan? Where is she now? Is she . . . dead?"

Balthasar did not lie to her. "I don't think so. All the toff wants is the casket. He needs what is inside it as a drowning man needs air. Minnie Maude is the one bargaining piece he has. He will return to get her before he goes to where he expects to find Stan, then he will offer a trade— Minnie Maude for the casket."

Gracie gulped. "And Stan'll give it to 'im, an' Minnie Maude'll be all right?"

"I hope so. But we must be there to make sure that he does, just in case he has it in mind to do otherwise." He looked at Rose. "We will send for a doctor for you." He took a coin out of his pocket. "Where would Stan go, Rose?"

She hesitated.

"Do you want this ended, or shall we all come back here again?" he asked.

"Oriental Street, down off Pennyfields, near Lime'ouse Station," she said, her eyes wide with fear. "There's a stable there . . . it's—"

"I know." Balthasar cut her off. He put the shiny coin into her hand. "Pay the doctor with this. If you choose to spend it other than on your well-being, or lack of it, it is your own fault. Take care!" He stood up and went to the door. "Come on, Gracie. We have no time to waste."

At the entrance he told the snaggletoothed man to send for a doctor, or he would risk losing good merchandise. Then, outside in the alley, Balthasar marched toward the larger road, swung to the right, and continued on at such a pace that Gracie had to run to keep up with him. At Commercial Road East he hailed a cab, climbed up into it, pulling her behind him, and ordered the driver to go toward Pennyfields, off the West India Dock Road, as fast as he could.

" 'Ow can we catch up wif 'im?" Gracie asked breathlessly as she was being thrown around uncomfortably while the cab lurched over icy cobbles, veered around corners, and jolted forward again. She was pitched from one side to the other with nothing to hang on to. " 'E must be ages ahead of us."

"Not necessarily," Balthasar insisted. "Stan will be ahead of us, certainly, but he does not know anyone is following him."

"But the toff'll catch up wif 'im long before we do!" She was almost pitched into his lap, and scrambled awkwardly to get back straight on her own seat again. If this was what hansoms were like usually, then she was very glad she didn't ride in them often. "'E could kill 'im too, ter get the casket. Then wot'll 'appen ter Minnie Maude?"

"I don't think Stan will be so easy to kill," Balthasar answered grimly. "He must know what is in the casket, and be used to dealing with the kind of men who trade in opium, and who buy it. The toff will know that, which is why he will take Minnie Maude with him. Stan will have to see her alive before he passes over anything." He touched her arm gently. "At least until then, Minnie Maude will be safe. But that is why we must hurry. Stan is a very frightened man, and the toff is a very desperate one."

Gracie turned and looked out the window. The houses were strange to her. Long windows had cracks of bright yellow light behind them, curtains drawn against the moonlit sky. She could see nothing beyond, as if the windows were blind, closed up within themselves. Maybe everyone inside the houses was all together, drinking tea by the fire, and eating toast and jam.

"Where are we?" she asked a few minutes later.

"We are still on Commercial Road." He rapped on the front wall of the cab with his fist. "Turn left into Pennyfields, just before you get to the West India Docks Station. Halfway along it is Oriental Street. Now hurry!"

"Right you are, sir!" the cabby answered, and increased speed again.

Gracie looked out of the window again. There seemed to be traffic all around them, carriages, other cabs, a dray with huge horses with braided manes and lots of brass, a hearse, carts and wagons of all sorts. They were barely moving.

"We gotta go faster!" she said urgently, grasping Balthasar's arm. "We won't get there in time like this!"

"I agree. But don't panic. They are stuck just as we are. Come, we shall walk the rest of the way. It is not far now." He pushed the door open and climbed out, passing coins up to the startled driver. Then, grasping Gracie by the arm again, he set off, head forward, pushing his way through the crowds.

Gracie wanted to ask him if he was certain he knew where he was going, but the noise was a babble like a field full of geese, and he wouldn't have heard her. It was hard enough just to keep hold of him and not get torn away by the people bumping and jostling their way, arms full of bags and boxes. One fat man had a dead goose slung over his shoulder. Another man had his hat on askew and a crate of bottles in his arms. There was a hurdy-gurdy playing somewhere, and she could hear the snatches of music every now and then.

She lost count of how far they went. She felt banged and trodden on with every other step, but if they could just find Minnie Maude in time, the rest was of no importance at all.

Here in the crowd it was not so cold. There was no space for the wind to get up the energy to slice through your clothes, and the shawl Mr.

Balthasar had given her was much better than her own. Her boots were sodden, but perhaps it was as well that her feet were numb, so she couldn't feel it every time a stranger stepped on them.

She did not know how long it was before they were gasping in a side alley, as if washed up by a turbulent stream into an eddy by the bank.

"I believe we have not far to go now," Balthasar said with forced optimism.

She followed him along the dark alley, their footsteps suddenly louder as the crowd fell behind them. Ahead the cobbles looked humpbacked and uneven, the little light there was catching the ice, making it glisten. The doorways on either side were hollow, the dim shadows of sleeping people seeming more like rubbish than human forms. In a hideous moment, Gracie felt as if the sleepers were waiting for someone to collect them—someone who never came.

Ahead there was a sound of horses shifting

weight, hooves on stone, a sharp blowing out of breath. It was impossible to see anything clearly. Lights were as much a deception as a help, a shaft of yellow ending abruptly, a halo of light in the gathering mist, a beam that stabbed the dark and went nowhere.

"Tread softly," Balthasar whispered. "And don't speak again. We are here, and both Stan and the toff will be here soon, if they are not already. Please God, we are soon enough."

Gracie nodded, although she knew he could not see her. Together they crept forward. He was still holding on to her so hard she could not have stayed behind even if she had wanted to.

Foot by foot they crept across the open space, through the wide gates and into the stable yard. Still they could see only tiny pools of light, the edge of a door, a bale of hay with pieces sticking out of it raggedly, the black outline of a cab and the curve of one wheel. There was a brazier alight. Gracie could smell the burning and feel the warmth of it more than see it. A shadow moved near it, a man easing his position, turning nervously, craning to catch every sound. She had no idea if it was Stan or not.

Balthasar kept hard against the wall, half-hidden by a hanging harness, its irregular shape masking his and Gracie's beside him. The tightening grasp of his hand warned her to keep still.

Seconds ticked by. How long were they going to wait? Somewhcre ten or twelve yards away a horse kicked against the wooden partition of its stall with a sudden, hollow sound, magnified by the silence and the cold.

Stan let out a cry of alarm and jerked around so violently that for a moment his face was lit by the coals of the brazier, his cheeks red, his eyes wide with fear.

Nothing else moved.

Gracie drew in her breath, and Balthasar's fingers tightened on her arm.

From the shadows at the entrance a figure materialized, long and lean, its face as gaunt as a skull, a top hat at a crazy angle over one side of the brow. Deep furrows ran from the nose around the wide mouth, and the eyes seemed white-rimmed in the eerie light as the brazier suddenly burned up in the draft.

Stan was rigid, like a stone figure. From the look on his face, the man in the doorway might have had death's scythe in his hands. But it was nothing so symbolic that stirred beside the figure's thin legs and the skirts of the man's black frock coat. It was Minnie Maude, her face ash-pale, her hair straggling in wet rats' tails onto her shoulders. He had hold of her by a rope around her neck.

Gracie felt the cold inside her grow and her own body tighten, as if she must do something, but she had no idea what. She felt Balthasar's grip on her arm so hard it brought tears prickling into her eyes. She pulled away, to warn him, and he loosened it immediately.

"You did not deliver my box," the toff said quietly, but his perfect diction and rasping voice filled the silence, echoing in the emptiness of the stable. Somewhere up in the loft there would be hay, straw, probably rats. "Give it to me now, and I will give you the girl. A simple exchange."

"I left it fer yer," Stan retorted with a naked fear one could almost smell. "In't up ter me ter 'old yer 'and while yer sneak out an' pick it up. In fact, yer'd prob'ly cut me throat fer seein' yer if I did."

"I would have preferred that we not meet," the toff agreed with a ghastly smile. His teeth were beautiful, but his mouth twisted with unnameable pains. "But you have made that impossible." He gave a quick tweak to the rope around Minnie Maude's neck. "I have something that belongs to you. I will trade it for what you have that belongs to me. Then we will part, and forget each other. I imagine the men who supply you, and pay you whatever pittance it is, are not happy with you."

Stan's breath wheezed in his throat, as though

the whole cage of his chest were too tight for him. "I in't got it!"

"Yes, you have! Those who supply it want their money, and I want what is in my box. You want the child." He made it a statement, but there was an edge of panic in his voice now, and his eyes were wild, darting from Stan to the shadows where the light from the lanterns flickered.

Gracie was motionless, afraid that even her blinking might somehow catch his attention.

"Yer've always 'idden," Stan argued. "Now I've seen yer, wot's ter say yer won't kill me, like yer killed Alf?"

The toff drew in a quick breath. "So you do have it. Good. This is a beginning. You are quite right. I will kill to get what I need. With regret, certainly, but without hesitation." He pulled Minnie Maude a little closer to him, using the rope around her neck. She looked very thin, very fragile. One hard yank could break the slender bones. The end of her life would be instantaneous.

176

Balthasar must have had the same conviction. He let go of Gracie's arm and stepped forward out of the shadows.

"Do not lie to the man, Stanley." He spoke quietly, as if he were merely giving advice. If he was afraid, there was nothing of it in his voice, or in the easy grace with which he stood. "Alf gave it to Rose, perhaps as a gift. He had no idea what was inside it, simply that it was pretty. When you realized where it was, you took it from her, as he"— he gestured toward the toff, "knew you would. He followed you and beat that information out of Rose. He will not pay the suppliers until he has his goods, as you well know, which is why you are afraid of them. They will surely hold you accountable, possibly they already have. I imagine it is your blood on your stable floor, which is why you are terrified now."

Stan was shaking, but he kept his eyes on the toff, never once turning to look at Balthasar behind him. "An' 'e'll kill me if I do," he said. " 'E di'n't never want ter be seen. I 'ave ter leave it where 'e can watch me put it, then go, so 'e can creep out an' get it in private, like. Only that damn' Alf did Jimmy Quick's route all arse about-face, an' took it before 'e could come out."

"Yes, I had deduced that," Balthasar answered.

A slight wind blew through the open doors, and the lantern light wavered again.

"Give it to me, or I'll kill the girl!" the toff said more sharply. His patience was paper-thin, the pain of need twisting inside him.

"Then you will have nothing to bargain with!" Balthasar snapped, his voice the crack of a whip. "Stanley has the box, and he will give it to you."

The toff's eyes shifted from one man to the other, hope and desperation equally balanced.

The silence was so intense that Gracie could hear the horses moving restlessly in the stalls at the far side of the partition, and somewhere up in the loft there was the scrabble of clawed feet.

They waited.

Gracie stared at Minnie Maude, willing her to trust, and stay still.

Stan's eyes were fixed on the toff. "If I give it yer, 'ow do I know yer'll let 'er go?"

"You know I'll kill her if you don't," the toff replied.

"Then yer'll never get it, an' yer can't live without it, can yer!" Stan was jeering now, had become ugly, derisive, as if that knowledge gave him some kind of mastery.

The toff's body was shaking, the skin of his face gray and sheened with sweat where the lantern light caught him. He took a step forward.

Stan wavered, then stood his ground.

Minnie Maude whimpered in terror. She knew the toff was mad with need, and she had no doubt he would kill her, perhaps by accident if not intentionally.

"Give it to him," Balthasar ordered. "It is of no use to you, except to sell. There is your market standing in front of you. If he kills Minnie Maude, you can never go home! Have you thought of that? You will be a fugitive for the rest of your life. Believe me, I will see to it."

Something in his tone drove into Stan's mind like a needle to the bone. His shoulders relaxed as if he had surrendered, and he turned away from the toff toward the nearest bale of straw. He pushed his hand into it in a hole no one else could see, and pulled out a metal box about eight inches long and four inches deep. Even in the dim and wavering light the gold gleamed on the finely wrought scrollwork, the small fretted inlays, and the elaborate clasp. Gracie had never seen anything so beautiful. If it wasn't a gift for the Christ child, it should have been.

The toff's eyes widened. Then he hurled himself at it, his hands out like claws, tearing at Stan, kicking, gouging, and butting at him with his head, top hat rolling away on the floor.

Stan let out a cry of fury, and his heavy arms circled the man, bright blood spurting from Stan's nose onto the man's pale hair. They rocked back and forth, gasping and grunting, both locked onto the golden casket.

Then with a bellow of rage Stan arched his back, lifted the toff right off his feet, whirled him sideways, and slammed him down again as hard as he could. There was a crack, like dry wood, and the toff lay perfectly still.

Very slowly Stan straightened up and turned not to Minnie Maude but to Balthasar. "I 'ad ter do it! You saw that, di'n't yer." It was a demand, not a question. "'E were gonna kill us all." When Balthasar did not answer, Stan turned to Minnie Maude. "'E'd a killed you, an' all, fer sure."

Minnie Maude ran past him, evading his outstretched arms, and threw herself at Gracie, clinging on to her so hard it hurt.

It was a pain Gracie welcomed. If it had not hurt, it might not have been real.

"Yer stupid little article!" she said to her savagely. "Why di'n't yer wait fer me?"

"Just wanted to find Charlie," Minnie Maude whispered.

"I 'ad ter!" Stan shouted.

"Possibly," Balthasar replied with chill. "Possibly not." He held out his hand. "You will give me the casket."

Stan's face hardened with suspicion. He looked at Balthasar, then at Gracie and Minnie Maude standing holding on to each other.

"Like that, is it? Give it ter you, or you'll kill both of 'em, eh? Or worse? Do wot yer bleedin' want ter. I don' need two little girls. Blood's on yer 'ands." There was almost a leer on his face. "I should a known that's wot you were. Thought for a moment you was after saving Minnie Maude. More fool me."

Could that really be what Balthasar had wanted all the time—the gold casket, and the poisonous dreams inside it?

Balthasar looked at Stan as if he had oozed up out of the gutter. "I will give the opium back to those who gave it to you," he replied icily. "To save your life—not because you deserve it, but it is still a life. I will tell them it was not your fault, you are incompetent, not dishonest. You would be well advised not to seek them out again. In fact, it would be to your advantage if they did not remember your name, or the place where you live."

Stan stood with his mouth open, halfway between a gape and a sneer.

"As for the casket," Balthasar continued, "I shall give that to Gracie and Minnie Maude. I think they have earned it, and its owner no longer has any use for it." He glanced down at the toff, his face gaunt, oddly vacant now, as if his tortured spirit had left it behind.

"If you go immediately," Balthasar went on, still speaking to Stan, "you may not be found to blame for this, and the police do not need to know that you were here. Nor do the gentlemen who deal in opium."

" 'Ow do I know I can trust yer?" Stan asked,

but the belligerence was gone from his face and he spoke quietly, as though he would have liked an answer he could cling on to, one to save his pride.

"You don't," Balthasar said simply. "But when the police do not trouble you, and you never see or hear from the opium dealers again, you will know then."

Stan gave him the casket.

Balthasar opened it very carefully, but there was no secret catch to it, no needles to prick or poison. Inside was a fine silk bag full of powder, which he took. He put it into the pocket on the inside of his coat. Then he examined the box carefully, blew away any suggestion of powder or dust from every part of it, and wiped it with his handkerchief. He held it out to Gracie.

"I know that all you wanted was to save Minnie Maude, but I think you have earned this. You and Minnie Maude will decide what is best to do with it. But it is very precious. Do not show it to people or they may take it, although it has nothing inside it now."

Gracie reached out slowly, afraid to touch it, afraid even more to hold it in her hands.

"Take it," he repeated.

She shook her head, putting the tip of one finger gently on the shining surface. It was smooth, and not really cold. "It shouldn't be fer me," she said huskily.

"What would you like to do with it?" he asked.

"When I first 'eard about it, I thought it were a present—cos it's Christmas. Yer know—like wot the Wise Men brought for Jesus."

"Gold for the king, because He is king of all of us," he agreed. "Frankincense because He is priest, and myrrh because He is the sacrifice that redeems all of us from the death of the soul. Is that what you would like to do with it?"

She nodded. "Yeah. But I don't know 'ow. An' it's empty."

"Christ will know what it cost you to get it," he

told her. "And it doesn't matter a great deal where you go. Christmas is everywhere. But I do know of a place where some people are holding a very special Christmas Eve party, with a nativity scene. I can't take you, because I have to get rid of this poison, back to the people who own it, before they find Stan and take their price in his blood. But I can show you the direction to go."

"Wot's that wot you said?"

"A nativity scene? It is people creating a little play, like the first Christmas all over again. It's very special, very holy. Come." He looked at Minnie Maude. "Are you able to come too? It has to be done tonight, because this is Christmas Eve. This is the night when it happened in the beginning and created a whole new age, an age of hope, and a new kind of love."

Minnie Maude nodded slowly, gripping on to Gracie's hand.

"Can you walk a little?" Balthasar asked anxiously. "I can get you a hansom cab to ride in, but you will still have to walk at the far end."

"I in't got no money fer an 'ansom," Gracie told him. "I could pay for an omnibus, if there is one, mebbe?"

"I shall pay for it, and tell him exactly where to go. But I think you had better wrap up the casket in the edge of your shawl. We do not want to draw people's attention to it."

She took the casket from him and obediently wound the end of the red shawl around it until the box was completely hidden. "I'll bring the shawl back to yer after Christmas," she promised.

"If you wish," he said solemnly. "And I shall return you your own one, clean and dry. But if you prefer this one, we can leave matters as they are."

It was a wonderful thought. This one was warmer, and far prettier. But it must also have been expensive. She resisted the temptation. "That wouldn't be fair."

"As you wish. Now come. It is late and there is no time to spare. In less than an hour it will be Christmas Day."

*T*he ride in the hansom did not seem so long this time. Minnie Maude sat very close to Gracie, and once or twice Gracie even thought she might be asleep. They rattled through the dark streets of the East End back through the heart of the city toward the West End and the nice houses. All the lamps were lit and the wind had blown away the earlier fog. Gracie could see wreaths of leaves on doors, lighted windows, carriages with patterns and writing on the doors. Horse brasses gleamed. There was a sound of jingling, laughter, and people calling out cheerfully. Somewhere voices were singing.

"I'll be back fer yer," the cabby said when he stopped. "It's that 'ouse there." He pointed. "Yer stay there till I come fer yer, you 'ear."

"Yes, sir." Gracie clasped the casket in one arm, and Minnie Maude's skinny little hand in the other. Normally she would not have dreamed of pushing her way into a grand house like this, but she had a present to give to Jesus, and Mr. Balthasar had told her that this was the place to do it.

She and Minnie Maude walked over the cobbles and into the stables at the back of the big houses. There were lots of people around, all wearing smart clothes, ladies with fur muffs and woolen cloaks, and gentlemen with curly fur collars on their coats. No one seemed to mind them coming in.

"Wot are they all doin' 'ere?" Minnie Maude whispered. "They're just standin' around out 'ere in the stable."

"I dunno," Gracie replied. "But Mr. Balthasar said it were 'ere, so it must be."

There was a slight noise behind them and a ripple of excitement. The group nearest the entrance moved apart to allow passage through, and in the next moment a man in a long robe appeared. It was very plain, like pictures Gracie had seen from the Bible. The man had curly hair all over the place, as if he had forgotten to comb it. He was smiling, and he had a brownish-gray donkey by the halter. It had long ears and a pale nose, and on its back rode a young woman with hair like polished chestnuts. She was smiling too, as if she knew something so wonderful she could hardly contain the happiness of it.

The people standing in the stable yard held up their lanterns, and they all cheered. The donkey stopped by the open stable door, and the man helped the young woman down. She was clearly with child and she moved a little awkwardly, but she turned to touch the donkey gently and thank it for carrying her.

Gracie watched as if seeing a miracle. She knew what was going to happen next, as though she had already seen it before. In a few minutes the bells would ring for midnight, and it would be Christmas. Then Jesus would be born. There would be angels in the sky, shepherds coming to worship, and Wise Men to bring gifts. Would it still be all right to give hers?

She gripped Minnie Maude's hand more tightly and felt her fingers respond.

Then the bells started, peal after peal, wild and joyous, the sound swirling out over the rooftops everywhere.

The stable doors opened, and the young woman sat in the straw with a baby in her arms, the man behind her. There were a couple of horses, who probably lived there, and the donkey.

Three men came from the back of the scullery doorway, dressed up like shepherds, carrying big staffs with curly tops. The bystanders were quiet, but they were all smiling and holding one anothers' hands.

Next came the three Wise Men, each dressed more gorgeously than the one before. They had robes of reds and blues and purples. One had a turban wound around his head, another a gold crown. They all knelt before the baby and laid gifts on the ground.

Minnie Maude poked Gracie in the side. "Yer gotter give ours!" she urged. "Quick, or it'll be too late."

"Ye're comin' too!" Gracie dragged her forward, unwrapping the gold casket as she went and holding it out in front of her. Even here, among all this wealth and splendor, it shone with a beauty unsurpassed.

Gracie stopped in front of the young woman. "Please, miss, we'd like ter give this to the Baby Jesus. It oughter be 'is." Without waiting for permission, she put it down on the straw in front of her, then looked up. "It in't got nuffink in it," she explained. "We in't got nothing good enough."

"It is perfect as it is," the young woman replied. She looked Gracie up and down, then looked at Minnie Maude, and her eyes filled with tears.

"Nothing could be more precious." She was about to add something more when the donkey came forward through the straw and pushed his nose against Minnie Maude, almost knocking her off balance.

She turned and stared at him, then flung her arms around him, burying her face in his neck.

"Charlie!" she sobbed. "Where yer bin, yer stupid thing? I 'unted all over fer yer! Don't yer never do that again!"

"I'm sorry," Gracie said to the young woman. "She thought 'e were lorst."

"Well, he's found again," the young woman replied gently. "Tonight we are all found again." She turned to the man. "Thomas, I think we should see that these two girls have something hot to eat, and to drink." Then she looked at the donkey and smiled. "Happy Christmas, Charlie."

A Christmas Odyssey

*D*edicated to all who look upward

*H*ENRY RATHBONE LEANED A LITTLE FARTHER forward in his armchair and regarded his visitor gravely. James Wentworth had an air of weariness in his face that made him look older than his sixty-odd years. There was something close to desperation in the way his hands fidgeted, clenching and unclenching on his knees.

"What can I do?" Henry asked gently.

"Perhaps nothing," Wentworth answered. As he spoke, the logs in the fire settled deeper, sending up a shower of sparks. It was a bitter night, ten days before Christmas. Outside, the icy wind moaned in the eaves of this pleasant house on Primrose Hill. Beyond, the vast city of London prepared for holiday and feasting, carols, church bells, and parties. There was not long to wait now.

"You say 'perhaps,'" Henry prompted him. "So possibly there is something to be done. Let us at least try." He gave a brief smile. "This is the season of hope—some believe, of miracles."

"Do you?" Wentworth asked. "Would you pursue a miracle for me?"

Henry looked at the weight of grief in his friend's face. They had not met in more than a year, and it seemed that Wentworth had aged almost beyond recognition in that time.

"Of course I would," Henry replied. "I could not promise to catch it. I cannot even swear to you that I believe in such things."

"Always honest, and so literal," Wentworth said with a ghost of amusement in his eyes.

"Comes from being a mathematician," Henry answered. "I can't help it. But I do believe there is more to be discovered or understood than the multitude of things that we now know all put together. We have barely tasted the realm of knowledge that lies waiting."

Wentworth nodded. "I think that will suffice," he accepted. "Do you remember my son, Lucien?"

"Of course." Henry remembered him vividly: a handsome young man, unusually charming. Far more than that, he was filled with an energy of mind and spirit, an insatiable hunger for life that made other people think of new horizons, even resurrect old dreams.

Pain filled Wentworth's eyes again and he

looked down, as if to keep some privacy, so as not to be so acutely readable.

"About a year ago he began to frequent certain places in the West End where the entertainment was even more . . . wild, self-indulgent than usual. There he met a young woman with whom he became obsessed. He gambled, he drank to excess, he tasted of many vices he had not even considered previously. There was an edge of violence and cruelty in his pursuits that was more than the normal indulgence of the stupidity of a young man, or the carelessness of those with no thought for consequences."

He stopped, but Henry had not interrupted him. The fire was burning low. He took two more logs from the basket and placed them on the embers, poking them to stir up the flames again.

"Now he has disappeared. I have tried to look for him myself," Wentworth continued. "But he evades me, going deeper into that world and the darkness of those who inhabit it. I . . . I was angry in the beginning. It was such a waste of the talent and the promise he had. To begin with, when it was just overindulgence in drinking and gambling, I forgave him. I paid his debts and even saved him from prosecution. But then it grew far worse. He became violent. Had I gone on rescuing him, might I have given him to believe that there is no price to be paid for cruelty, or that self-destruction can be undone at a word, or a wish?" His hands gripped each other, white-knuckled. "Where does forgiveness eventually become a lie, no longer an issue of his healing but simply my refusal to face the truth?"

"I don't know," Henry said honestly. "Perhaps we seldom do know, until we have passed the point. What would you like me to do?"

"Look for Lucien. If I go after him myself, I only drive him deeper into that terrible world. I am afraid that he will go beyond the place from where he could ever return, perhaps even to his death." He looked up, meeting Henry's eyes. "I realize how much it is I ask of you, and that your chances of success may be slight. But he is my son. Nothing he does changes that. I deplore it, but I shall not cease loving him. Sometimes I wish I could; it would be so much easier."

Henry shook his head. "Those of us who have loved don't need an explanation, and those of us who haven't would not understand it." His smile was rueful, with a little self-mocking in it. "I study science and logic, the beauty of mathematics. But without those things that are beyond explanation, such as courage, hope, and above all, love, there can be no joy. I'm not even sure if there could be humor. And without laughter we lose proportion, perhaps in the end even humanity."

He became serious again. "But if I am to look for Lucien, I need to know more about him than the charming young man I met, who was apparently very well able to hide the deeper part of himself from superficial acquaintances, perhaps even from those who knew him well."

Wentworth sighed. "Of course you must. That is still not to say that I find it easy to tell you." He sighed. "Like most young men, he explored his physical appetites, and to begin with I did not find his excesses worrying. I can remember being somewhat foolish myself, in my twenties. But Lucien is thirty-four, and he has not outgrown it. Rather, he has indulged more dangerous tastes: drugs of different sorts that release all inhibitions and to which it is all too easy to become addicted. He enjoys the usual pleasures of the flesh, but with young women of a more corrupt nature than most. There is always the danger of disease, but the woman he has chosen is capable of damage of a far deeper sort."

For a few moments Wentworth stared into the flames, which were now licking up and beginning to devour the new logs. "She offers him the things he seems to crave most: a feeling of power, which is perhaps the ultimate drug, and of being admired, of being able to exercise control over others, of being regarded as innately superior."

Henry did not argue. He began to see the enormity of what his friend was asking of him. Even if he found Lucien Wentworth, what was there he could say that might tempt him to come back to the father he had denied in every possible way?

"I'll try," he said quietly. "But I have little idea how to even begin, let alone how to accomplish such a task."

"Thank you," Wentworth replied, his voice hoarse. Perhaps he was finally facing the reality that to try at all was little more than a kindness, driven by pity rather than hope. He rose to his feet as if exhaustion all but overwhelmed him. "Thank you, Henry. Call if you have anything to tell me. I shall not disturb you to ask." He put one hand in a pocket and pulled out a piece of paper. "Here is a list of the last places that I know he frequented. It may be of use."

*H*enry Rathbone awoke the following morning wishing that he had not promised Wentworth that he would help him. As he sat at the breakfast table, eating toast and marmalade without pleasure, he admitted to himself that it was a lack of courage that had made him agree to it. Even if Henry found him, Lucien Wentworth was not going to come home. He did not want to. His father might be spared a good deal of distress simply by not knowing for certain what had happened to him.

But Henry had given his word, and now he was bound to do his best, whatever that might turn out to be. How should he begin? He had had a good deal of fun in his own university days, which were now at least thirty-five years behind him. He had sat up all night talking, certainly drunk more beer than was good for him, knew some women of a sort his mother didn't even imagine existed, and learned some very bawdy songs, most of which he still remembered.

But he had grown out of it before he was thirty. It was all a hazy memory now, which was not even worth exploring. What compelled Lucien was something entirely different. It was a hunger that fed upon itself and that, in the end, would devour everything.

He spread out the sheet of paper Wentworth had given him, the list of places he had found Lucien in the past. But by his own admission Lucien was no longer likely to be in such places. He had sunk deeper than mere drunken brawling and abuse, or even the simple womanizing many young men indulged in at the better-known brothels.

Many of his own friends had sons who had disappointed them, one way or another, but a good man did not ask questions about such things, and if he accidentally learned of them he affected not to have. He certainly did not repeat it to others.

*H*enry's own son, who was perhaps London's most brilliant barrister, had been both admired and deplored, depending upon whom he had represented most recently. He had also, at times, behaved in ways that Henry found difficult to understand, and would certainly not have wished to discuss with anyone outside the family—except perhaps Hester Monk. It had never been a matter of overindulgence. Actually he wondered at times if it might not have been better for Oliver to have let himself go occasionally, even at the cost of an error or two!

Once, Henry had hoped Oliver would marry Hester, but he had realized some time ago that it would not have made Hester happy. She needed a man of more will and passion, like William Monk. Whether or not Hester would have made Oliver happy he was less certain. He thought perhaps she might have, but of course it was far too late now.

However, Hester might be able to advise Henry in his quest for Lucien, and he could be honest with her. There would be no need for any pretense, which would be exhausting, and in the end also self-defeating.

Hester had been a nurse in the Crimea during that wretched war, which was now—at the end of 1865—a decade gone into history. On her return home, she had initially dreamed of reforming nursing in England, in line with Florence Nightingale's beliefs. However, the world of medicine was powerful, and unready for such advances. Hester had been obliged to seek one position after another in private nursing. Then she had married Monk, and found it difficult to work so far from home. As his work prospered, she had opened the clinic in Portpool Lane where she and others nursed women of the street who could find no other medical care for their most desperate needs. The funds came from charitable donations. Through these experiences, Hester might well have access to the kind of knowledge that Henry now needed.

With a little spring in his step he increased his pace along the wet, windy street and hailed a hansom cab.

"Portpool Lane, if you please," he requested, climbing up and seating himself comfortably. It was not a long ride, even though the traffic was growing denser as the light faded in the winter afternoon.

"Right y'are, Guv," the driver said briskly, urging his horse forward along the Strand, and then left up Chancery Lane.

The street lamps were being lit already. It was not long until the shortest day of the year, and they traveled in the murk of smoke and drifting rain. Henry could hear the clatter of hooves, the jingle of harness, and the hiss of wheels on the wet cobbles.

"Happy Christmas!" a man called out cheerfully, his voice rising above the cries of peddlers and curses of those caught up in tangles of traffic.

"You too!" came back the reply.

"Get on, yer fool!" someone else yelled out, caught behind a slow-moving dray, and there was a roar of laughter.

"Happy Christmas to you too!"

They turned right briefly up High Holborn, and then left on Gray's Inn Road. Just past the square Henry rapped with his cane to catch the driver's attention. "This will be excellent, thank you. I can walk the rest of the way."

"Right, sir," the driver said with some surprise. "'Appy Christmas, sir."

Henry paid him, adding a rather generous tip, prompted by the well wishes, even though he knew they were given for precisely that purpose.

He crossed the road to the entrance of Portpool Lane and stepped onto the narrow path with confidence. The street lamps were few, and the vast dark mass of Reid's Brewery dominated the farther end, but he knew his way.

*I*nside the clinic, Squeaky Robinson was sitting at the table going over the accounts. It was his profession to keep the books—not that it had always been so. In the previous incarnation of the building he had owned it, and run it as a very successful brothel. He had been tricked out of its ownership by William Monk and Oliver Rathbone, Sir Oliver, as he now was.

The loss of it meant that Squeaky, in his later middle years, had become homeless and penniless in the same instant. What was worse, he even stood in some danger of going to prison. That was a fate he had managed to avoid all his life, from childhood pocket-picking, with great skill—none of your ordinary stuff—right through his whole career until he owned this warren of buildings and made a handsome profit from them.

But those days were over, and he greatly preferred not to think of them. He was now a perfectly respectable man, keeping the books and managing the offices of the Portpool Lane Clinic for Hester Monk, who was a lady of spirit, considerable intelligence, and formidable will.

His attention was on the next column of figures when the door opened and a tall, lean gentleman came in, closing it behind him to keep out the bitter weather. Squeaky used the word "gentleman" in his mind, because years of experience had taught him to estimate a man's social standing at a glance, and also to make a pretty accurate guess as to his intentions. In the past, his life had occasionally depended on that, and old habits died hard. This man he judged to be a gentleman by nature, possibly middle-class by birth, and a scholar by occupation. This estimate he drew from his unpretentious but well-cut clothes, his mixture of modesty and confidence, and the very slight stoop of his shoulders.

"Mornin' sir," he said curiously. "Can I help you?"

"Good morning," the man replied pleasantly. His voice reminded Squeaky of someone, but he could not recall who. "My name is Henry Rathbone. I would very much like to speak with Mrs. Monk. If she is here, would you be good enough to ask her if that is possible?"

Of course: He must be Sir Oliver's father. That was the resemblance. Now why would he be here to see Miss Hester? Squeaky regarded him more closely. He had a mild, agreeable face, but there was nothing passive about those blue eyes. A very clever man, Squeaky judged, possibly very clever indeed, but—at the moment—also a worried man. Before he let him in to see Hester, Squeaky would like very much to know what he wanted so urgently that he came all the way from wherever he lived to a place like Portpool Lane.

"She's helpin' patients right now," he replied. "We had a bad night. Big catfight down Drury Lane, knives an' all." He saw the gentleman's look of pity with satisfaction. "Mebbe I can help? In the meantime, like."

Rathbone hesitated, then seemed to come to some decision. "It is advice I need, and I believe Mrs. Monk may be able to guide me toward someone who can give it to me. When might she be free?"

"Is it urgent?" Squeaky persisted.

"Yes, I'm afraid it is."

Squeaky studied the man even more closely. His clothes were of excellent quality, but not new. This suggested that he cared more for substance than appearance. He was sure enough of himself not to have any hunger to impress. Squeaky looked into the clear blue eyes and felt a twinge of unease. He might be as gentle as he seemed, but he would not be easy to fool, nor would he be put off by lies. He would not have come to Hester for medical help; he would most certainly have his own physician. Therefore it was help of some other sort that he wanted: perhaps connected with the clinic, and the kind of people who came there.

"Mebbe I can take a message to her?" Squeaky suggested. "While she's stitching and bandaging, like. Is it about the kind o' folk what come here?" It was a guess, but he knew immediately that he had struck the mark.

"Yes, it is," Henry Rathbone admitted. "The son of a friend of mine has sunk into a most dissolute life, more so than is known to any of my own acquaintances, even in their least-attractive pursuits. I want to find this young man, and attempt to reconcile him with his father." He looked a little self-conscious, perhaps aware of how slender his chances were. "I have given my word, but I do not know where to begin. I was hoping that Hester might know at least the areas where I could start. He is apparently concerned with a deeper level of vice than mere gambling, drinking, or the use of prostitutes."

Squeaky felt a sharp stab of alarm. This sounded like a story of grief that Hester would get caught up in much too much. Next thing you know, she'd be helping him, making inquiries herself. What really worried Squeaky was not just the harm she could come to, but the ugly things about his own past that she might learn. As it was, she might guess, but there was a great deal about himself that he had managed to keep from her, in fact to even pretty well wipe out of his own memory.

"I can help you," he said quietly, his heart thumping in his chest so violently he feared it made his body shake. "I'd be the one she'd ask anyway. I know that kind o' thing. Some things a lady doesn't need to find out about, even if she has nursed soldiers an' the like."

Henry Rathbone smiled very slightly. "That would be good of you, sir. I'm afraid I don't know your name."

"Robinson. Most folks call me Squeaky." He felt faintly embarrassed explaining it, but no one ever used his given name. He had practically forgotten the sound of it himself, nor did he care for it. "I'd be happy to oblige. Tell me what you need, an' I'll make a few inquiries as to where you can begin."

*W*hen Henry Rathbone had gone, Squeaky closed his account books, which were perfectly up-to-date anyway. He locked them back in the cupboard in his office where he kept them, and went to look for Hester.

He found her upstairs. Her long, white apron was blood-spattered, and as usual, her hair poked out where she had pinned it back too tightly and it had worked its way undone. She looked up from the clean surgical instruments she was putting back in their cases.

"Yes, Squeaky? What is it?"

His mind was already made up. She must not have any idea what he intended, or, for that matter, that Henry Rathbone had called to see her. Hester was clever, so he would need to lie very well indeed for her to believe him. In fact it might be better not to hide the fact that he was lying, but just to fool her as to which lie it was.

"I need to go away for a little while, not quite sure how long," he began.

She looked at him coolly, her blue-gray eyes seeming to bore right into his head.

"Then we shall have to manage without you," she said calmly. "We are well up-to-date with most things. I'm sure Claudine and I will be able to take care of the money and the shopping between us."

Squeaky wondered why she did not ask where he was going, and what for. Was it because she had already decided that she knew? Well, she didn't!

"A friend of mine is in trouble," he started to explain. "His son has gone missing and he's afraid he's in danger." There now, that was the truth— almost.

A momentary sympathy touched her face, and then vanished.

"Really? I'm sorry."

She didn't believe him! That hurt, particularly because Squeaky was doing this just to protect Hester from herself. He knew the kind of place Lucien Wentworth was likely to have ended up in, and that was a part of the underworld that even Hester didn't imagine, for all her experience. This was all his own fault. He had broken the first rule of successful lying—never answer questions that people hadn't asked you!

"It's Christmas," he said, as if that explained everything.

She smiled with extraordinary sweetness, which made him feel worse.

"Then go and help him, Squeaky. But remember to come back. We should miss you very badly if you didn't."

"It's . . ." he began. How could he explain it to her without her wanting to help? And she couldn't. It was a dark world she shouldn't ever have to know about. Weren't war and disease enough without her seeing all about depravity as well?

She was waiting.

"It's my home here," he said abruptly. "Of course I'll be back!" Then he turned and walked away, furious with himself for his total incompetence. All this respectability had rotted his brain. He couldn't even tell an efficient lie anymore.

Downstairs and outside he caught a hansom south toward the river. He begrudged the expense, but there was no time to waste with buses, changing from one to another, and even then not ending up where you really wanted to be.

It might take him some time to find Crow, the man whose help he needed. Crow had intended to be a doctor, but various circumstances, mostly financial but not entirely, had cut short his studies. Squeaky had considered it indelicate to ask what those circumstances were, and he had no need to know. As it was, Crow's medical knowledge was sufficient for him to practice, unofficially, among the poor and frequently semi-criminal who thronged the docksides both north and south of the river around the Pool of London. He took his payment in whatever form was offered: food, clothes, sometimes services, sometimes a promise both parties knew could not be kept. Crow never referred to such debts again.

It took Squeaky the rest of the afternoon, a conversational supper of pork pie at The Goat and Compasses, and then more walking and questioning, to find Crow in a tenement house just short of the Shadwell Docks. Since he wanted a favor, Squeaky waited until Crow had seen his patient and collected his fee of sixpence—which was insisted upon by the patient's father—and the two of them were free to walk out onto the road beside the river.

Crow turned up the collar of his long, black coat and pulled it more tightly around himself against the icy wind coming up off the water. He was tall—several inches taller than Squeaky— and at least twenty-five years younger. Today he had a hat jammed over his long straight black hair, but in the lamplight Squeaky saw the same wide smile on his face as usual. He seemed to have too many teeth, fine and strong.

"You must want something very badly," he remarked, looking sideways at Squeaky. "And it isn't a doctor. You've got plenty of those much nearer Portpool Lane. You look agitated."

"I *am* agitated," Squeaky snapped. He told Crow about Henry Rathbone's visit to the clinic and his request for help in finding Lucien Wentworth. As they strode in the dark along the narrow street in the ice-flecked bitter wind, the cobbles slick under their feet, he also told him about the sort of indulgence that Lucien Wentworth had apparently sunk into.

Crow shook his head. "You can't let Hester go looking into that!" he said anxiously. "Don't even imagine it."

"I'm not!" Squeaky was disgusted, and hurt. Crow should have known him better than to even have thought such a thing. "Why do you think I'm looking for you, you fool?"

Crow stopped in his tracks. "Me? I don't know places like that. I've treated a few opium addicts, but for other things—slashes, broken bones, not the opium. As far as I know, there isn't anything you can do for it."

Squeaky felt a wash of panic rise inside him. He couldn't do this alone. He knew enough about the underworld of self-indulgence to be aware of its labyrinthine depths and dangers. What on earth had possessed him to begin this? He should have told Henry Rathbone that the whole thing was impossible. For that matter, Rathbone should have told Lucien's father that in the first place. Squeaky was really losing his grip. Respectability was an idiot's calling.

"Right!" he said tartly. "I'll go back and tell Hester I can't do it."

"You didn't tell her anything about it in the first place," Crow pointed out, but there was no smile in his eyes.

"And how do I tell Mr. Rathbone that I can't do it?" Squeaky said sarcastically. "Without her knowing, eh? She's clever, that one. She can read a lie like it was writ on your face. She'll know, whatever I say."

Crow thrust his hands into his pockets. His hands always seemed to be bare, whatever the weather. Squeaky looked at him. "Why don't you get someone to pay you with a pair o' gloves?" he said pointedly.

Crow ignored the remark. "Are you saying obliquely that you will tell Hester I refused to help?"

"Obliquely? Obliquely? You mean sideways?" Squeaky said crossly. "Why can't you say it straight out? And no, I'm not saying it sideways, I'm telling you plain that she'll know, 'cause if she were in my place, you'd be the person she'd ask. Which comes to my point. You want me to tell her you won't help, or you want to tell her yourself?"

Crow shook his head. "You haven't lost your touch, Squeaky. You're a hard man."

"Thank you," Squeaky said with unexpected appreciation.

Crow glared at him. "It wasn't a compliment! What do we know about this Lucien Wentworth, apart from the fact that his father is wealthy and seems to have let him have a lot more money than is good for him?"

Squeaky shrugged and started to walk again, talking half over his shoulder as Crow caught up with him. He repeated what Henry Rathbone had told him about Lucien's weakness for physical pleasure, his need to feel a sense of power, to feel admired, to feel—as it might appear to his deluded and immature mind—loved.

Behind them a string of barges went downriver with the ebbing tide, their riding lights bright sparks in the wind and darkness. To the south a foghorn sounded mournfully.

Crow's expression grew grimmer as he tramped beside Squeaky. Finally they turned inland and slightly up the slope, leaving the sounds of the water behind them. The thickening gloom of the winter night lay ahead. Lamps shone one after another along the narrow street, angular beacons toward the busier High Street.

"It's going to be a long night," Crow said as they reached the crossroad. They waited for the traffic to clear, and then hurried over, their boots splashing in the gutter and then crunching on the cobbles already slicked with ice. "And we may not find anything."

Squeaky wanted to tell him to stop complaining, but he knew that Crow was right, so he said nothing for several minutes.

"Let's have a drink first," he suggested finally. He thought of offering to pay for both of them, but that was a bad habit to start.

*I*t was, as Crow had said, a very long night. They began with extremely discreet inquiries in the Haymarket. The area was notorious for the prostitutes who patrolled its pavements so openly that no decent woman went there, even if accompanied by her husband. However well-dressed she was, she would be likely to be taken for a lady of the night. In this area such women might be indistinguishable from ladies of society, especially those whose taste was a little daring.

"I don't know what we'll learn here," Crow said, watching a couple of young women quite openly sidle up to a group of theatergoers.

"Do you know which theaters are fashionable right now for tastes a bit sharper than usual?" Squeaky asked challengingly.

"My patients don't come up this way," Crow admitted. "East End music halls are more their line, if they've a few pence to spare."

"Then shut up, and watch," Squeaky retorted. "And follow me."

They tried to find places selling more than alcohol, entertainment, and the chance to pick up a prostitute.

Their first three attempts were abortive, but the fourth led them to a very small theater off Piccadilly where the drama on stage was overshadowed by the exchanges in the many private boxes and on the narrow stairs. The lighting was yellow and very dim, making most of the people look sallow and a little sinister. Heaven only knew what they looked like in daylight.

Squeaky watched and waited. He did not know the names of the current young dandies who indulged themselves. Their dull eyes were half-focused, lids drooping. Opium, he thought to himself.

He studied one young man closely, and, brushing past him, felt the quality of the cloth in his jacket sleeve. Yes, definitely money there. He hoped he had not lost his childhood art of picking pockets. There was often very good information to be had from the contents of a gentleman's pocket—his name and address from his card, if nothing else.

Squeaky knew that moving unnoticed in places such as these would require a little money, and he had no intention whatsoever of financing it himself. His money was earned with proper work these days, and deserved to be spent respectably. Better to pick pockets without Crow's noticing, though. You never knew what his peculiar aversions might be. There was no accounting for taste, or superstition.

From that theater they learned of others, more daring. The first cost them even to gain entrance.

From the outside it looked like a perfectly ordinary public house.

"Don't look worth the trouble," Squeaky said disparagingly, regarding the chipped pillars and peeling plaster with distaste.

"An affectation, perhaps?" Crow suggested. Then he hurried over to explain. "A suggestion to the eye of the more sordid appetites catered to within?"

Squeaky was amused, not so much by the idea as by the wording Crow chose. He shrugged and paid for their entry.

"Ye're right," he said generously as soon as they were through the archway and down the steps into the main room. It was crowded with people, all of them with glasses or goblets in their hands, except the two almost-naked women who were practicing the most extraordinary and vulgar contortions on a makeshift stage, to the hoots and jeers of the onlookers.

"They'll be needing me professionally," Crow observed, wincing at a particularly unnatural-looking move.

Squeaky made no comment. He began to methodically talk to one person after another, asking questions, learning little.

It took them over an hour to learn that Lucien was known here, but had not been seen in more than a month.

They moved on to another place where they learned nothing, and then a farther tavern that at first seemed very helpful. However, in the end the man they found there turned out not to be Lucien, merely some other lost youth bent on finding oblivion.

By four in the morning Squeaky was tired and cold. His head ached. And his feet were sore. He realized all the reasons he had been willing to give up the pursuit of temporary pleasure in favor of a warm bed in the Portpool Lane clinic, and only the very occasional night awake chasing around after other people's needs. Even then, his time was not spent outside in the rain and the freezing wind, with his feet wet and water sliding down his neck from the rain. Being inside a low-ceilinged room and among the confusion of loud voices was not much better. He had forgotten how he disliked stupid laughter and the crush of bodies in narrow spaces, the smell of stale smoke and drink. Even the music had less appeal than it used to.

They entered a cellar deep below a tavern. The yellow gaslight made the stone walls look even more pitted and stained. They did at least serve good brandy. Apart from warming Squeaky's body a bit, the drink encouraged him to think that this was the kind of place that might attract a man like Lucien Wentworth, who was raised to know the quality of brandy and partook only of the best.

It was actually Crow who began the conversation with a nearby stranger that finally yielded the first scent of Lucien.

"Clever," Crow observed amiably to the man nearest him. They were both looking at a provocatively dressed young woman who was miming an obscene joke to the delight of onlookers.

"Cost yer," the young man remarked. "But they all do."

"I prefer something a bit . . ." Crow hesitated. "Unusual."

The young man looked him up and down as if assessing his taste. "You'da liked Sadic." He sighed wistfully. He was so slight as to be almost emaciated. The bones of his wrists looked fragile when his shirtsleeves slid back. "She was beautiful."

"Really . . ." Crow had difficulty pretending interest. Squeaky realized he had no idea what kind of woman Crow liked. The subject had never arisen.

"Face pale as a lily," the young man went on dreamily. "Hair like black silk. And sea-blue eyes, bright as deep water in the sun."

Squeaky let his mind wander. This was all a waste of time.

Crow was still pretending to be interested. "She sounds different," he said, regarding the young man closely. You pursued her? Was she all you imagined?"

The young man lifted one bony shoulder. "No idea. She only had time for Lucien."

That caught Squeaky's attention, and he sat upright too quickly. The young man turned to stare at him, breaking the thread of his remembrance.

Crow glared at Squeaky.

Squeaky scratched himself, as if it had been a sudden itch that had disturbed him. "Too bad," he commiserated. He caught Crow's eye and decided to say no more.

"Is she still around here?" Crow asked casually.

"What?"

"The girl with the sea-blue eyes."

"Oh, Sadie? Haven't seen her." The young man

fished in his pocket, but apparently did not find what he was looking for. He furrowed his brow. "I'm getting out of here. This is becoming tedious. Do you want to come to Potter's with me?"

"Sounds like a good idea," Crow agreed, without asking Squeaky. "I'd like to hear more about Sadie. You make her sound special, something new."

"Won't do you any good." The young man rose to his feet, and swayed a little. Crow caught him by the arm, steadying him. "Obliged," the young man acknowledged the assistance, letting out a belch of alcoholic fumes. Don't bother with Sadie. I told you, she went with Lucien."

"Where to?" Crow asked him, still holding his arm.

"God knows." The young man waved a hand in the air.

"We aren't on conversational terms with God," Squeaky put in acidly. "I ask, but he doesn't bleedin' answer."

The young man started to laugh and ended with a hacking cough.

Crow patted him on the back. It was a useless gesture, but one that allowed him to keep a firm hold on his arm and prevent him from collapsing altogether as he guided him toward the way out.

The journey to Potter's was made erratically along footpaths slick with ice. Holding on to each other was a way to maintain balance as well as to make sure that they did not lose the young man, and that he did not pass out in one of the many doorways. He might well freeze to death if he did.

"Fool," Squeaky muttered under his breath. Now that he was not making money out of other people's vices, he had a far less tolerant view of them. "Fool!" he repeated as the young man stumbled. He would have fallen flat on the ice-covered paving stones if Crow and Squeaky had not yanked him to his feet again.

When they finally reached Potter's they found that the place was dimly lit, mostly by tallow candles in a variety of holders. Despite the lateness of the hour it was still full of people. Some were drinking, while others lounged in corners quietly smoking what Squeaky knew from past experience was tobacco liberally laced with other substances, possibly opium derivatives of some sort. The air was heavy and rancid with the stench of smoke, alcohol, sweat, and various other bodily odors.

Crow wrinkled his nose and shot a grim look

at Squeaky. Squeaky tried to smile but knew it looked sickly on his face.

They were offered brandy, and bought some to try to revive the young man. He seemed to be falling asleep, or possibly into a kind of stupor.

The sharp spirit going down his throat stirred him, at least temporarily. "What?" he said abruptly. "What did you say?"

"You were telling us about Sadie," Crow prompted him. "How beautiful she was, and how much fun."

"Yes, Sadie." He repeated the name as if rolling the flavor around his mouth. "What a woman. Skin like . . . like . . ." He could not think of anything adequate. "So alive," he said instead. "Always laughing, dancing, making jokes, kissing someone outrageously, places you wouldn't believe."

"Lucien . . ." Crow put in.

"Oh yes, him especially," the young man agreed. "He would do anything for her, and did." A slow, dreamy smile spread across his face. "She dared him to swallow a live fish . . . eel, I think it was. Revolting."

"Did he?" Squeaky asked.

The young man looked at him with disgust. "Of

course he did. Told you, he'd do anything for her. Admired her." There was envy in his face. "Said she made him feel like a god—or a fallen angel, maybe. Can you see it?" He smiled a little vacantly. "Spiraling down from the lip of heaven in an everlasting descent to the fires of hell and the dark underlight of those who have tasted all that there is and know everything that the universe can hold." He began to laugh. It was a strange, shrill sound broken by hiccups.

One of the candles on the cellar wall guttered and went out.

There were several moments of silence before he spoke again. "And of course there was Niccolo," he added. "Never knew if she actually wanted him, or if she just used him to make Lucien mad with jealousy. Either way, it worked."

"Niccolo?" Crow repeated the name. "What was he like? Who was he?"

The young man stared blankly.

"Who was he?" Crow repeated with exaggerated patience.

"No idea." The young man seemed to lose interest. Squeaky fetched more brandy, but it didn't help. Their informant was beginning to drift off into a stupor.

"Who was Niccolo?" Squeaky said, his voice edged with threat.

The young man stared at him and blinked. "Sadie's lover," he replied, giggling in a falsetto voice. "Sadie's other lover." He started to laugh again, then slowly slid off the chair and fell in a heap on the floor.

Crow bent down as if to pick him up, or at least to try.

"Leave him," Squeaky ordered. "He's probably as well off there as anywhere else. You won't get anything more out of him. We need to find this Sadie. Can't be too many as look like her. C'mon."

It was now past five in the morning, and there was hardly anyone left sober enough to give them any answers. They went out into the early morning darkness and the bleak easterly wind. Crow started to turn down toward the river, and his home.

"No yer don't!" Squeaky said sharply. "We in't finished yet."

Crow snatched his arm away. "There's nobody else awake at this hour, you fool!" he said impatiently. "It's pointless looking now. Not that there's much point at any time. I want some breakfast, then to sleep."

"So do I. Come to the clinic and we'll get both."

"Yes? And how are you going to explain all this to Hester?" Crow asked witheringly.

"I'm not." Squeaky was disgusted with Crow's lack of imagination. "I'm not going to tell her anything. We'll get a good breakfast, then find a couple of rooms there with no one in them, and she won't know." Then another thought occurred to him. "It's warm there, and only a mile away."

Crow gave in, pretending it was a favor to Squeaky. Then he gave one of his flashing grins, which was a mark of his good nature and slightly eccentric sense of humor. "Come on then. I suppose it's really not a bad place at all."

The following evening was much easier. They now knew exactly who they were looking for. Additionally, contacts whom Squeaky had used in the past could be persuaded to yield a little information in return for promises of unquestioning medical help for things, such as unexplained knife wounds or even the odd gunshot.

Sadie's name was recognized by several people they asked in taverns and small theaters of the more louche kind. It seemed she was as great a beauty as the young man the previous evening had suggested, although she did not apparently sing or dance. But, far more arresting than mere physical perfection, she was said to possess a wild energy, imagination, and laughter that fascinated more men than just Lucien Wentworth, although they all seemed agreed that he was the most obsessed with her. He had already come close to killing a man who had tried to claim her forcibly.

"At each other's throats over 'er, they were," one raddled old woman told them, where they found her in a busy and very expensive brothel off Half Moon Street. "Stuck a knife in 'is guts, that Lucien did. Daft bastard." She sucked at her few teeth where the taste of whisky still lingered. "E'll kill somebody one day. If 'e din't already."

Squeaky silently provided some more.

"Ta'," she said, grasping hold of it with gnarled hands, lumpy and disfigured by gout. "Ever seen dogs fight? Like that, it was. Sneerin' an' teasin' at each other. An' she loved it. Food an' drink it were to 'er. The sight o' blood fair drove 'er wild. Eyes bright as a madwoman, and a glow on 'er skin like she were lit up inside."

"Where is she now?" Crow asked her, controlling his voice with difficulty.

"Dunno." She shook her head.

"Did the man live?" he asked. "The one Lucien knifed?"

"Never 'eard," she said with a shrug. "Prob'ly."

Squeaky looked at the swollen hands. "Where'd he go, this Lucien?" He tried to imagine the pain. He reached out and put his thin, strong fingers over hers. "I s'pect you know, if you think about it," he suggested.

"No I don't," she told him. "Places best not talked about. I don't know nothing." She nodded. "Safer that way."

"Wise to be careful who you talk to," Squeaky agreed. "Best if you just talk to me, an' him." He nodded toward Crow. Then very slowly he tightened his grip on her hand, squeezing the swollen joints.

She let out a shriek of pain. Her lips drew back in fury, showing stumps of teeth.

"Oh, how careless of me," Squeaky said in mock surprise. "Gout, is it? Very painful. So they say. You'll have to leave off the strong drink. Where did you say they went, then? I didn't hear you right." He allowed his hand to tighten just a fraction.

She let out a string of abuse that should have curdled the wine, but she also named a couple of public houses. One was off an alley to the south of Oxford Street, and the other to the north, in a tiny square behind Wigmore Street.

She looked at him with venom. "They'll eat you alive, they will. Go on, then, I dare yer! Think yer know it all? East End scum, y'are. Know nothing. East End's kid's stuff, all there up front. West End's different. They'll drown yer, an' walk away whistlin'. Find yer body in the gutter next mornin', an' nobody'll give a toss. Nobody'll dare ter."

"She's right," Crow said warningly as they went outside again into the icy street.

"An' what do you know about the West End?" Squeaky dismissed him.

Crow blinked. For a moment Squeaky thought he saw something quite different in the blue eyes, as if he had once been the sort of man who knew such places. Then the idea seemed absurd, and Crow was just the same amiable "would-be" doctor he'd known for years.

"We better tell Mr. Rathbone that we can't find

what happened to Lucien Wentworth," Squeaky said aloud. "He could've gone anywhere—Paris even, or Rome."

"There's no need to give up," Crow argued. "We've a fair chance of finding him."

"Course we have!" Squeaky responded. "An' what damn good will that be? Best if his father never hears the kind o' company he kept. If he went to these places—an' I have heard of them, no matter what you think—then he isn't coming back. They don't need to know that."

Crow was silent for several moments. "Is that what you would want?" he said finally.

Squeaky was indignant. "How the hell do I know? As if I had children what should've been gentlemen."

"I think we should tell them the truth," Crow replied thoughtfully. "At least tell Mr. Rathbone the truth. Let him decide what to tell Lucien's father."

"Soft as muck, you are!" Squeaky shook his head. "And about as much use. What'll he want to know that for? Tell him Lucien's gone to Paris, and he'll stop looking."

"Then don't tell him," Crow replied. "I will."

*L*ate in the afternoon, only eight days before Christmas now, Squeaky and Crow together alighted from the hansom cab on Primrose Hill. They walked by the light of the street lamp across the pavement and up the path to Henry Rathbone's house. It had taken a certain amount of inquiring to find out where he lived, and they were later than they had intended to be. Squeaky felt nervous, and—in spite of the fact that Crow hid it well—he knew that he did too. This was a quiet neighborhood and eminently respectable. They were both ill-fitting strangers here. Added to that, they carried with them news that would not be welcome. It was really a message of defeat.

Squeaky hesitated with his hand on the brass knocker. He was furious with himself for being such a coward. He had never been in awe of anyone when he was a businessman, selling women to those who wanted or needed to buy. He had despised them and was perfectly happy that they should know it. It was a straight exchange: money for the use of a woman.

Well, maybe it was not quite that simple, but

close enough. There were never any questions of honor or embarrassment in it. Violence, now and again, of course. People needed to be kept to their side of the arrangement. They tended to slip out of it if you allowed them to. Let yourself be taken advantage of once and it would happen again and again.

"Are you going to knock, or stand there holding that thing?" Crow asked peevishly.

Squeaky picked it up and let it fall with a hard bang.

"Now look what you made me do!" he accused, turning to glare at Crow.

The door swung open, revealing a calm-faced butler.

"Good afternoon, gentlemen. How may I be of service to you?"

Squeaky swallowed and nearly choked.

"We would like to speak to Mr. Henry Rathbone, if you please," Crow answered, while Squeaky tried to collect himself and regain his composure.

The butler blinked and looked confused.

"Mr. Rathbone asked Mr. Robinson here to perform a service for him," Crow continued. "We have come to report our findings so far, and see what Mr. Rathbone would like us to do next."

"Indeed?"

The butler still seemed uncomfortable. It was hardly surprising. Squeaky was lean and snaggle-toothed, and had long gray hair falling onto his collar. Crow had a charming smile with far too many teeth. His hair was black as soot, as was his bedraggled coat with its flapping tails. And— simply because he had had no time to return home and put it down—he still had his doctor's Gladstone bag with him.

Squeaky drew in his breath to try a better explanation.

Perhaps because of the length of time they had been on the step, Henry Rathbone appeared in the hall behind the butler. He recognized Squeaky immediately.

"Ah, Mr. Robinson. You have some news?" He looked at Crow. "I am afraid I do not know you, sir, but if you are a friend of Mr. Robinson, then you are welcome."

"Crow. Doctor, or almost," Crow said a little sheepishly. There was a note of longing in his voice, as if the "almost" had cost him more than he wanted to admit.

"Henry Rathbone. How do you do, sir? Please come inside. Have you eaten? If not, I can offer you toast, a very agreeable Belgian pâté, or Brie, and perhaps some apple tart and cream. Hot or cold, as you prefer."

Crow could not keep the smile from lighting his face.

Squeaky wanted that supper so badly he could taste it in his mouth already. Guilt at the news he brought overwhelmed him, but only for a couple of seconds.

"Thank you, Mr. Rathbone," he replied quickly, just in case Crow had any other ideas. "That would be very nice indeed." He took a step forward into the hall as the butler pulled the door wider to let him pass.

They sat next to the fire in the sitting room. Squeaky was fascinated first by the number of books in the cases in the walls, and then by the delicate beauty of the two small paintings hung over the mantel. Both were seascapes with an almost luminous quality to the water. He felt Rathbone's eyes on him as he stared, and then the heat of embarrassment burned up his face.

"Boningtons," Henry said quietly. "They've always held a particular appeal for me. I'm glad you like them."

"Yes." Squeaky had no idea what else to say. He

was even more out of his depth than he had expected to be, and it made him highly uncomfortable. Suddenly he did not know what to do with his hands, or feet.

Crow cleared his throat and stared at Squeaky.

Henry looked at him, waiting.

Squeaky plunged in. Better to get it over with. "Thing is," he began tentatively. "Thing is . . . we found word of Mr. Wentworth."

Henry leaned forward eagerly. "You did? Already? That's a most excellent start."

Squeaky felt the sweat prickle on his skin. He was making a complete pig's ear of this. He didn't even mean to be deceptive, except for the best of reasons, and here he was doing it. Respectability had put him out of practice of saying anything the way he meant it.

"Thing is," he began again. "His father's right, he's picked up with some very bad company indeed. Woman called Sadie, a real bad lot. Seems he's lost his wits over her. Got tangled up with a rival, and now there in't anything daft enough or bad enough he won't do to impress her. Even damn near killed someone."

He drew in a deep breath. "Mr. Rathbone, he in't going to come back as long as she'll give 'im

the sort of attention he wants, an' she's playin'
him off against this other young fool, clear as day
to anyone with eyes in their heads. It's a world
you don't know, sir, an' don't want to."

Henry looked sad, but not surprised. "I see," he
said quietly. "It seems to be as bad as his father
feared." He looked across at Crow. "Do I assume
that you agree, Doctor?"

Crow blushed, not for the question, but for the
courtesy title to which he had no right. He faced
him squarely. "Yes sir. I'm afraid he's sunk to the
kind of place people don't come back from. It isn't
just the drinking, although that'll get to you in
time. It's the violence. It seems this young woman
thrives on it. The sight and smell of blood excites
her, the idea that men will kill each other over her."

"Are you saying that we shouldn't try?" Henry
asked him.

Squeaky drew in his breath to tell him that
that was exactly what they were saying, then he
saw Crow's face and changed his mind.

"Yes sir," Crow answered gravely. "It's the
man's own heart that's keeping him there. I . . . I
suppose if we can find him, we could tell him that
his father wants him back, but I don't think it'll
make any difference. I'd say, sir, that he's best not

to know what's become of his son. What he imagines would be bad, but once you've seen something for real, there's no escaping it ever. There's things you don't want to see."

"Lots of things," Henry agreed. "But that is not a reason to turn away. Perhaps if we could persuade Lucien that there is a way back, then . . ."

Squeaky leaned forward. "He doesn't want to come back! There's no one keeping him there except himself. Crow's right, Mr. Rathbone."

"I suppose he is," Henry murmured. "But I have given Mr. Wentworth my promise. If you would be kind enough to tell me the best direction in which to begin, I shall do so. And perhaps any other advice . . ."

Squeaky could not bear it. This man was a babe in the woods. He had not the faintest idea what he was dealing with. He would be robbed and probably killed within the first couple of hours.

"You can't," he said simply. "You'd be done over an' left in the gutter. Maybe even knifed, 'specially if Lucien knows you're after him. I can't let you . . . sir."

"I am not doing it from choice, Mr. Robinson,"

Henry replied gently. "I have promised an old friend that I will do all I can. I have not yet done that. Please, give me whatever advice you have, and allow me to reimburse you for the trouble you have taken so far, and any expense you may have incurred."

"We didn't go to any expense," Squeaky said with an honesty he knew he would regret later. He saw Henry's disbelief in his eyes. "I relieved one or two gentlemen of their wrongful earnings," Squeaky explained without a flicker. "Used 'em to buy a little information. And no trouble neither. So you don't owe us at all." He made to rise to his feet, but Crow did not follow him, so he sat back down again. "And a very good supper too," he added.

Crow took a deep breath, as if to steady himself, then he spoke quickly.

"If you're determined to go an' see for yourself, then I'll come with you. I know the way better than you do."

Squeaky cursed himself. He should have seen that coming. He knew Henry Rathbone was a fool, but he should have realized that Crow was too.

"You neither of you know a damn thing!" he said furiously. "Like sending kittens into a dogfight! I'll come with you." He wanted to add a whole lot more, but there didn't seem to be any point, and every time he opened his mouth he got himself into more trouble.

"Thank you, Mr. Robinson," Henry said with a beautiful smile.

*T*he three of them set out a short while later. This time they took a hansom at Henry Rathbone's expense, and alighted in Oxford Street.

Once they had agreed that they were all going, they had discussed practical plans over tea and fruitcake. Since they were now aware of the kind of woman they were looking for, and her name, as well as that of her other lover, Niccolo, they had clear places to start.

"Off Oxford Street," Squeaky said knowingly. "Nothing cheap. This woman likes money an' class. No fun in getting a couple o' drunkards rolling around on the floor. You can see that any-where."

Henry winced.

Squeaky saw it. "You sure you want to find this Lucien?"

"I am," Henry replied, his voice low.

Crow said nothing, but he was clearly unhappy. He did not argue with Henry. Possibly he even understood, in his own way.

Squeaky rose to his feet. "Then we'll get started."

They went to one public house after another, following the trail of those who had seen or heard of Sadie, or the names Lucien and Niccolo. The songs were ever bawdier as the night went on. In the galleries above the makeshift stages, prostitutes stalked up and down until they attracted the attention of a customer. Then they disappeared into one of the many side rooms provided for the purpose.

There was much drink flowing, mostly whisky and gin. And, with the right request, and accompanied by the right money, laudanum, opium, and various other, stronger substances such as cocaine were available to enhance the vividness of the experience, or to block out a grief that might intrude upon pleasure.

Henry Rathbone masked his distaste, but it was obvious that it was with great difficulty. Then as the evening wore on, Squeaky saw in his eyes a look that he knew was pity.

Crow asked questions, but Squeaky realized how acutely he was watching the people he saw, understanding the pasty skins, the scabs no paint or powder could disguise. A feeling of hopelessness settled over him.

It was near Piccadilly, in a narrow, gaslit old music hall, toward morning, when they met Bessie. She was perhaps fourteen or fifteen. It was hard to tell because she was thin and narrow-chested, but her skin was still blemishless and had some natural color. She was fetching and carrying drinks to people for the barman, who was pouring out and taking money as fast as he could. Bessie wove her way through the crowd with a certain grace, but in spite of her air of innocence, she seemed quite capable of giving back as good as she received in any exchange. One man who ventured to touch her caught a full glass of cider in his lap. He leapt to his feet in fury, to much laughter and jeering from those around him.

"Yer lookin' fer Lucien?" she said in answer to Henry's question. "'E in't 'ere no more. Gone after that Sadie." The expression on her face was not so much disgust as a weary kind of sorrow. "Yer'd think a man like that'd know better, wouldn't yer?"

"You know him?" Henry said quickly.

She shrugged a thin shoulder in an oddly adult gesture. "Talked with 'im some. Listened to 'im, more like. See'd 'ow 'is face lit up when 'e told us about 'er. Think she was like Christmas come. More like bleedin' 'alloween, if you ask me. Let the devils out that night, din't they? God knows wot yer'll meet with." Then her face was wistful. "But she were pretty, in a mad sort o' way."

"Do you know where they went?" Henry asked her. "I am a friend of his father's, and I would dearly like to give him a message."

She shook her head. "I can guess, sort o'," she admitted. "I in't never been there meself, but I 'eard." She hesitated.

"What?" Crow asked quickly.

"I dunno." She snatched the tray on which she carried the glasses and pushed her way back into the crowd.

Crow swore under his breath.

"Do you think she knows something?" Henry asked dubiously. "She's only a child."

Squeaky got up off his seat and forced his way between two men with glasses full of whisky. One slopped over and he swore with low, sustained fury. Squeaky ignored them, and the group of painted women beyond them, flirting desperately. A man and a woman in a red dress argued over the price of opium, another two over cocaine. Squeaky caught up with Bessie again as she neared the barman.

"What were you going to say about Lucien?" he demanded. "You know where we could look." He wondered whether to offer her money, or if it would insult her. She certainly must need it, but those who were the most desperate were also at times the most easily insulted. "We need your help," he finished. If she asked for money, he would give it to her—Henry Rathbone's money, of course.

She looked him up and down, her lips pursed. "'E won't go with yer," she told him.

"I know that," he replied. "But Mr. Rathbone don't. He's . . . a bit innocent, like. He won't stop until he finds out for himself."

Bessie shook her head. "In't goin' ter do any good. But I can 'elp yer, if yer want."

"Show us?"

She hesitated, a flicker of fear crossing her thin, soft face.

"We'll look after yer. Yer won't come to no harm," Squeaky promised rashly, aware even as he said it that he was speaking wildly out of turn.

"I s'pose," she agreed, looking down at the floor, then suddenly up at him, her eyes bright and afraid.

Squeaky cursed to himself. He really was losing his grip.

*O*ver the next two nights Squeaky went with Henry, Crow, and Bessie deeper and deeper into the squalid world of illicit pleasure. In New Bond Street they turned into an alley westward and immediately found themselves on steps down into a garishly lit cellar where both men and women were lying around, some on makeshift beds, others simply on the floor.

Henry stopped a few paces in, his mouth pulled down at the smell.

"Don't stop," Squeaky warned him. "It's opium, an' sweat, an' sex. Don't take no notice."

Henry started moving obediently. A little ahead of them a man in a black coat reeled on wobbly legs, laughing at nothing. To his left someone was weeping; in the red light it was impossible to tell if it was a man or a woman. It was hard for him to think of this as a place of pleasure, and yet these people had come here willingly, at least to begin with.

He watched a man rocking back and forth, his face distorted as in his mind he clung to an ecstasy so brief, so illusory it slipped from him even as they watched.

Bessie led them, occasionally faltering. Often she looked back to make certain they were all there, as if she feared suddenly finding that she was alone, and somehow betrayed. At times she clung to Squeaky, gripping his thin hand so her hard, strong little fingers dug into his flesh. He found it painful, and yet the couple of times she let go, he was hurt, as if she had stopped needing him.

"Squeaky, you're losing your wits," he said to himself with disgust. "You always thought being respectable was stupid. Now you know for certain."

To Henry Rathbone it was a descent into a kind of hell that was not just visual. The noise of it, and the stench of body fluids and stale alcohol were almost worse. His stomach clenched at the sight of ground-in filth mixed with the harsher stench of sewage. Voices were loud, angry, then whining. Ahead of him someone laughed hysterically and without meaning.

To Crow it was a series of sicknesses. A man shambled across the floor with the gait of the drunkard and collapsed sideways. His nose was swollen and broken-veined, the skin of his arms flaccid. Crow recoiled without meaning to, and knocked into another man who turned on him. His face was scabbed and ulcerated, yellowed with jaundice, the whites of his eyes the color of urine.

The nightmare grew worse.

Crow bumped into a couple who seemed to have no control of their limbs, and little awareness of where they were, their eyes vague, unfocused.

The man, no more than thirty years old, reached to grasp a bottle, only to have it slip from his fingers and smash on the floor.

Two old men engaged in disjointed conversation, then became lost, as if the ideas behind it escaped them into the fog.

Crow knew the reasons. He knew that those who drank to oblivion seldom ate. Their bellies were bloated, and yet they were starving. Perhaps that was the core of it all: their dreams and their senses were frantically consuming but never fed.

Then in all the babble and moaning someone

mentioned Lucien's name. Crow spun around. An old woman with unnaturally bright hennaed hair was telling Henry very clearly that she had seen Lucien, only two days ago.

"Pretty, 'e were, an' gentle spoke," she said with a toothless grin. "Twenty years ago, in me prime, I'd 'ave 'ad 'im."

Crow thought her prime was more like forty years ago, or even fifty, but he did not interrupt.

"Who was he with?" Henry asked her patiently.

"Another pretty feller," she replied. "But got a nasty eye. Looked at yer like rats, 'e did. Ol' Roberts 'ates rats. Breaks their necks if he catches 'em." She held up both her hands and twisted them sharply, as if she were wringing the water out of laundry. She made a clicking sound with her tongue, to imitate the breaking of bone.

"Were they friends, these two?" Henry asked her with as much patience as he could manage.

"Nobody's friends." She looked at him witheringly. "Particular these two weren't. After the same bint ter lie with, weren't they!"

"Sadie," he guessed.

"Mebbe. Long-legged piece, with black 'air."

"Where will I find them?" He was blunt at last.

She cackled with laughter.

"Where will I find them?" he repeated, with an edge of annoyance.

. She blinked. "Wot?"

"Where are they, yer stupid mare?" Squeaky interrupted angrily.

She turned to him, her eyes suddenly focusing. "Go an' ask Shadow Man," she hissed. "See if 'e'll tell yer. Go an' get 'is soul back fer 'im."

There was a moment's silence. One or two people close to them pulled back a step or two.

"Who is Shadow Man?" Henry asked.

"Shadwell, 'is name is. The devil, I call 'im." She stared at him, then her face seemed to contort into a kind of convulsion, and she started to shiver violently.

Henry turned to Crow. "Can you help her, man? She's having some kind of a fit. Can't you . . ." His voice trailed off.

"No one can help her," Crow answered. "Her demons are inside her own head. Come on. We've one more place to try tonight. It's not far from here."

"Are you sure?"

"Had enough?" Crow looked at him with some sympathy.

Henry lifted his chin a little. "No. If we've more

to try, then we'll try them. Word is bound to spread. How much deeper is there to go?"

"There are tunnels under the river," Squeaky answered. "Old ones, before they rebuilt the sewers. Believe me, we're not at the bottom yet. Although the real bottom may be up a bit from there."

Henry stared at him, confused.

"There's a bottom of despair," Squeaky replied. "And a bottom of power, an' cruelty. We haven't even touched the places where people do things to each other like some of those paintings by that German feller, or Dutch he was maybe. Pictures of torture, an' things with animals you wouldn't even think of."

"Lucien wouldn't . . ." Henry began, then stopped. "Or perhaps he would. As you said, the real demons are in your own mind. If they conquer, perhaps anything of other people's pain may be illusory to you."

Squeaky was not certain what he meant. The demons he knew were real enough: cold, hunger, disease, fear, and even at times loneliness. That wasn't illusory.

"Who's this Shadwell?" Crow asked, looking at each of them in turn. "Do you think that's just the drink talking in her?"

"No," Bessie interrupted them for the first time, shaking her head violently. "'E's real."

"Have you seen him?" Henry asked her.

She put her hands up to her face, her eyes wide with fear. "No! I don't look. But I 'eard. 'Is voice is soft, like 'e got summink in 'is throat an' 'e can't speak proper. But you can 'ear 'im anyway."

Squeaky looked sideways at her. "Yer sure you ain't making that up?"

"Course I'm sure! 'E's real! I'll show yer where 'e's bin, but I won't take yer there." She put out her hand, and—cursing himself again—he took it.

She led them through freezing alleys. The steady dripping of eaves left long icicles hanging like glittering daggers above them in the sporadic lamplight. The air was bitter with the acrid smell of old chimneys and open drains.

They turned into a tiny square and through an archway into a whorehouse. The madame eyed them grimly.

"I apologize," Henry said hastily. "We appear to be lost."

The woman let out a gale of laughter, and belched from the depths of her huge stomach. "Yer got no money, get out. That way!" She jabbed her fingers to the left.

They escaped obediently down steps, along a somber passage and up again into a noisy hall that was apparently the entrance to a very large house. It was initially quiet, except for a sudden shout that made them all start and then move closer together, as if in the face of some unseen threat.

A man appeared in the doorway, leaning on a stick to support himself. He was Squeaky's height, but skeletally thin. His face was pale, as if it were painted with white lead, and his eyes were odd colors, one lighter than the other, and both ringed with black. He was dressed in old-fashioned breeches to the knee and a velvet frock coat, all in a faded lavender. He could have stepped out of a previous century. He surveyed them.

"Nothing for you here," he said, pronouncing his words with pedantic care. "Trying to get lost, are you?" He addressed the question to Henry Rathbone.

"We are looking for a friend," Henry replied, matching courtesy for courtesy. "We think he may have come this way, and perhaps you have seen him?"

"I see everyone, my dear." The man took a step closer, and Squeaky was aware of a draft of cold air in the room. "Sooner or later," the man added with a twitch of his lips that was not quite a smile. "What does your friend look like?"

"In his early thirties, dark-haired, slender, unusually handsome." Henry struggled to think of something unique about Lucien. "His eyes are actually dark hazel, not brown, and he speaks with a slightly husky voice." Was he making a fool of himself, by being so detailed? What would this odd-looking man notice about anyone else's appearance?

"Oh, yes," the man said with a sigh as if some deep emotion filled him. "He came this way, with Sadie, of course, with dear, fickle, dangerous Sadie. Such fun, on her good days. Or perhaps one should say 'nights.' Cruel sometimes, but then aren't we all?" He looked directly at Bessie, who shivered and stepped backward, closer to Squeaky.

Without thinking, Squeaky put his arm around her, and then wondered what on earth he was doing. He was going soft! His emotions were rotting along with his wits.

"Where can we find them?" Henry asked, still facing the man in his absurd lavender velvet. Squeaky marveled at his persistence. If he was afraid, there was nothing of it in his face, his calm blue eyes. Only looking at his hands did he see that they were stiff, as though he had to concentrate to keep them hanging at his sides, apparently casually. What a strange man he was, completely incomprehensible. Squeaky wanted to despise him—and yet he found that he could not.

This whole adventure was a very bad idea. He should have had more sense, and sent Henry Rathbone and his dreams on his way. That would have been best for everyone—even this spoiled, self-indulgent young man in his descent to hell. Let him go, if that was what he wanted. He wasn't coming back; anyone but a fool knew that.

The lavender-coated man turned slowly on his heel, keeping his balance with difficulty, and pointed to a small door to his left. "That way," he whispered. "And down, always down."

"Thank you, Mr. . . ." Henry said.

"Ash," the man replied with a bow. "Lionel Ash."

"Thank you, Mr. Ash."

Crow went first. They had opened the door, and were through it before Mr. Ash called after them. "Be careful of the blood! Don't slip on it."

Crow froze.

Henry turned back. "What blood?" he said grimly, a flicker of annoyance in his face.

"At the bottom of the stairs," Mr. Ash answered. "On the floor. Terrible mess."

"Whose blood?" Squeaky lunged toward Ash and gripped him by the throat, his strong fingers pressing into the scrawny, completely unresisting flesh.

"My, haven't we got a nasty temper!" Ash said, seeming quite unaffected by having his neck squeezed till Squeaky could feel the sinews and the bones of his spine. Squeaky tried to yank Ash off his feet, and found him unaccountably heavy.

"Whose blood?" he hissed.

"Why, the ones who were killed there, stupid!" Ash answered. "Heartless, it was." He gave a violent shudder, as if he were seized with some kind of convulsion. Then, just as quickly, he went completely limp. Suddenly he seemed to collapse and tears streamed down his white cheeks. "So much blood," he whispered. "So much."

Crow swore under his breath. He glanced at Bessie, then at Henry Rathbone, his brow furrowed.

"You had better let him go," he advised Squeaky,

nodding toward Ash in his ridiculous lavender coat. "He can't tell us anything if he can't breathe."

Squeaky loosened his grip, then pushed Ash hard against the wall. "Who was killed?" he said between his teeth.

Ash straightened his velvet coat. His eyes were narrow, like slits in the paper-white of his face.

"The handsome young man, and the woman with so much black hair," he replied. "Isn't that who you were looking for?"

Henry's shoulders sagged, and the anger and hope drained out of his eyes. "You said he'd gone down." He shook his head.

"Oh yes, far, far down, places most people don't even know about," Ash agreed. "Dream, maybe, in the silent reaches of the night, and wake up sick with a cold sweat. Down there where the shadows move in shadows!" He gave a little giggle that was almost a sob. "Shadow Man."

Suddenly Henry was angry. "Your nightmares are no more real than any other drunkard's or opium addict's. They're paper devils of your own making. Is Lucien alive or dead?"

"A good philosophical question." Ash's attention was now completely focused on Henry, as though Crow and Squeaky were not real, and

Bessie was half a creature of this world anyway. "At what point do we step across that slender, eternal line, eh?"

"When our hearts stop beating and our eyes cloud over," Henry snapped.

"Ah—hearts." More tears slid down Ash's face. "Who knows where their hearts are, or ever were? Eyes can be cloudy in more ways than one. Who sees? Who doesn't?"

Squeaky was losing his patience again. He grasped Ash by the collar of his velvet coat and jerked him around. "I think we'd better take him with us," he said to Henry. "He's a bit slow to give a straight answer." He yanked him a couple of steps farther toward the door, and the collar of his velevet jacket tore, leaving the lapels crooked and a rent down the collar's back seam.

Ash's face contorted with fury. It was still totally colorless because of the strange cosmetic he had smeared over it, but his dark lips were pulled back from small teeth, yellow and sharp. "You'll pay for that!" he snarled. "You Philistine! You sniveling animal! Go find your Lucien." He jabbed long-nailed fingers toward the door. "And be careful he doesn't tear your heart out, too!"

Crow slammed the door open and grabbed

Bessie by the hand. Squeaky followed them onto a short landing, Henry behind them, then down the narrow stone steps. There was a faint light from a lantern on the wall, and at the bottom, where it widened by several feet, there were dark stains. It was impossible by the look of them to know what they were, but in his mind he had no doubt that they were human blood.

Henry stood still, regarding the silent stone walls and floor, breathing in the stale smells: mud, candle tallow, something metallic, a sourness like body waste, old terror, and despair.

"Was Lucien the victim, or did he kill Niccolo and Sadie here?" His voice shook a little. He was giving words to his own worst fear, and Squeaky knew it as certainly as if he had known the man for years. He did not want to know him. He did not want to be forced into liking him, even admiring him. Rathbone was a dreamer and a fool. He had no grip on the realities of the world at all. He was like some child—far more so than Bessie, who at least knew what to expect of life.

Squeaky wanted to say something clever, but knew that whatever he said had to be the truth. He looked at Crow, but Crow was inspecting the floor and the lower parts of the walls. There appeared to be scratches on the stone and spatters of blood—if it was blood. Somebody had been horribly injured here—probably bled to death. Who had moved the body, and why?

"Are you sure you want to do this?" Crow turned to Henry. "If it was Lucien who was killed here, his father isn't going to want to hear that. If it was he who killed Niccolo or Sadie, he's going to want to hear that even less. Wouldn't you rather just tell him we tried, but we lost the trail? He doesn't need to know different."

"Of course I'd rather tell him that," Henry said quietly. His eyes stared into the darkness ahead of them, where the passageway seemed to go upward again, but at a slope rather than by steps. "But I'm not a very good liar."

"Then I'll do it for you," Squeaky offered. "I'm excellent."

Henry laughed quietly. "That's very kind of you, Mr. Robinson, but it wouldn't help, not in the long run. James Wentworth is my friend. I owe him a better answer than a lie."

"Why?" Squeaky said reasonably. "He did something for you that you got to pay back?"

"Not as simple as that," Henry answered. "But yes, I suppose so. Friendship. Being there over the years, knowing when to speak and when to keep silent. Sharing things because they mattered to me, even though not to him. Telling me about funny and interesting things he'd learned. Being open about his failures as well as his successes."

Squeaky had a glimpse of something new and perhaps beautiful. It was annoying, but he felt as if he had arrived somewhere just after the party was over. The music had stopped, but he could hear its echo.

Crow stood up. His face was masklike in the sallow light from the one lantern on the wall. "I'm pretty certain at least two people were killed here," he said quietly. "Very violently indeed. One here, where this blood is." He pointed to the largest stain on the ground. "Then it looks as if two people fought." He looked at splashes and smears, which were apparently trodden in several times by feet that seemed to have slipped and twisted on the edge of a larger stain. "And the other one was killed, or at least seriously injured, here. That effigy with the white lead face was right about that. Whether Lucien was one of the victims or not we need to find out."

"Yes," Henry agreed quietly. "Of course we do. And I suppose if he wasn't, we need to know what has happened to him, and . . . and if the victims were Sadie and Niccolo, then we need to know who killed them."

Squeaky was about to say that it could only have been Lucien, then changed his mind. Poor Henry had had enough for the moment. He must be exhausted, hungry, and cold, and none of them knew what time it was, or more than roughly even where they were.

Crow pushed his hands into his pockets. "We need to find someone else who knows Lucien and can tell us something of what happened here. To judge by how sticky the blood still is, it wasn't very long ago."

"What do you mean by 'not long ago'?" Squeaky said with a tremor in his voice. "An' where's the body anyway? That much blood, someone's dead, but how do we know if it was a man or a woman, let alone that it was Lucien?"

"We don't," Henry replied. "That's why we must find proof of this. Someone moved it. Where to, and why? And what is this place?"

"It's the passage between two clubs, of sorts," Squeaky answered, looking around them at the stained walls, some brick, some stone. "Or maybe more than two. I'll shake the bleedin' truth out of someone." He set off toward the light, then past it, and found a fork to the right. There was a whole network of tunnels under London that he knew about. Indeed, in the past he had used them himself. He had forgotten how dark they were, and he had intentionally forgotten the smell. It washed back on him now as if the years between had been erased and he was again a young man, hot-tempered, desperate, and greedy, buying and selling anything, especially people. It was more than distaste he felt, more than a clogging stench in his nose and throat.

Bessie was pulling on his coattails. He wanted to turn round and slap her away. She trusted him, and she had no right to. It was stupid, as if she were trying to remind him of all those other girls that he had put into the trade, faces he couldn't even remember now.

He stopped abruptly and she collided with him, hands still clinging on to the stuff of his coat.

"Stop it!" he snarled at her. "Don't follow me like . . ." He was going to say 'like a dog,' but that was too harsh, even if it was apt. She looked just like a loyal, trusting, stupid little dog that expected him to treat it right.

She let her hands fall, still looking at him,

which made him feel as if she had kicked him in the pit of his stomach.

"Like . . . like I could look after you," he finished. "Someone's got to find out what happened to the corpse. In't fit for you to see. Stay with Mr. Rathbone."

"I seen corpses," she told him, putting out her hand and taking hold of his coattails again. "I'll 'elp yer."

He blasphemed under his breath, and felt Henry Rathbone's eyes on him, even though he was farther from the light and his figure was only a shadow behind them.

"Aren't yer going on, then?" Bessie asked. "Yer in't given up, 'ave yer?"

Squeaky swore again, turning around to continue his way along the passage and up more steps to a door. Beyond it were sounds of music and laughter.

"No, I in't given up," he answered her at last. "But we've got to think what to do now. If Lucien's dead, that's the end of it."

"If it wasn't Lucien, then who was it?" Henry asked. "And even more important, who killed him, or her?"

"You mean, was it Lucien?" Crow said softly.

He looked at Henry. "Do you want to know that? What are we going to do if it was?"

Henry was silent for several moments. No one interrupted his thoughts.

"That may depend on the reasons," he answered at last, hope struggling in his voice, in what they could see of his face in the dim light. "Maybe it was self-defense. In a place like this that is imaginable."

Squeaky was torn between pity and the urgent desire to tell Henry not to be so naive. This was getting more ridiculous by the moment.

"Lucien wouldn't kill nobody less 'e 'ad ter," Bessie said at last. "If . . . if it weren't 'im as were killed."

"Right, Bessie," Henry agreed warmly. "We need to find anyone at all who has seen him in the last few hours—two or three, let us say. Please lead on, Mr. Robinson. If we can find Sadie, she may well know."

Squeaky bit back the words on the edge of his tongue, and started forward again.

They went from one tavern or doss-house to another all through the night and well into the cold, midwinter daylight. They shook people awake to ask about Lucien or Sadie. They threatened and promised. Squeaky lied inventively, while Henry persuaded—often with a few coins or a ham sandwich that he bought from a peddler—but no one would admit to knowing anything about murder. Even a hot cup of coffee from a stand on the corner of one of the alleys elicited nothing useful.

They found people huddled in doorways, covered with old clothes or discarded packing and newspapers, sometimes too drunk to even be aware of their freezing limbs. All questions about Lucien or Sadie were met with vacant stares. For most that was also true for any mention of Shadwell. The two or three who reacted did so with blank denial and with shivering more than was warranted by the cold of the icy morning.

They stopped at last for a hot breakfast at a tavern off Shaftesbury Avenue. There was a good fire in the hearth. Although the room was dirty and everything smelled of smoke and spilled ale, they sat at a scarred wooden table and ate bacon, eggs, and piles of hot toast, and drank fresh tea. Bessie managed to consume more than the other three together.

"What do we know?" Henry asked, looking at each of them in turn. "Somebody was killed at the bottom of those steps. There was too much blood for those wounds not to have been fatal." He turned questioningly to Crow.

"Yes," Crow agreed. "From the way it was placed, it could have been two people. Or it could have been one dead and one badly injured. It looked as if they had been dragged, but where to? Where are they now?"

"Why move them anyway?" Henry asked. "That's a question to which we need the answer. Buried decently, or just disposed of? Hidden to conceal who killed them, or who they were?"

"Or that they were killed at all," Crow added. "Except that they didn't wash away the blood. They could have done something about that."

"Rats'll get rid of that, in time," Squeaky pointed out.

Crow's face registered his distaste, but also a sudden spark of interest. "Then it can't have been there long," he observed. "No one we spoke to admitted to having seen anything at all." He leaned forward a little over the table. "Is that indifference, even to the bribe of food? Or are they too afraid to answer anyone? Is this man Shadwell's power so great?" He looked at Henry and Squeaky in turn. "Or is it that the murderer never came aboveground into the world in which we have been asking?"

Henry shivered, his face bleak with exhaustion, and the weight of the terrible new way of existence that had never entered his imagination before now. "I suppose there is nothing with which the police can help us?" he asked, but there was no hope in his eyes.

Squeaky nearly dropped his mug of tea, saving it with difficulty. "Damn." It would have ruined his bread and bacon. "Never!" He also narrowly avoided using the language that sprang to his mind. "We don't want the police in this," he said fervently. "If it's Lucien who's dead we don't want his father to find out this way. Then all the world'll know." He saw the alarm and the pity in Henry's face and how no more explanation was necessary.

"We have to know whether it was him or not," Henry said quietly. "How can we do that?" He looked first at Squeaky, then at Crow.

It was Bessie who answered, her mouth still full of toast.

"In't no use lookin' fer the corpses. If it's Shadwell wot done it, 'e'll put 'em where the rats'll get 'em. Rats are always 'ungry, an' bones all look the same."

Crow stopped eating, as if he could not swallow the bacon in his mouth.

Henry closed his eyes, then opened them again slowly. "Have you any idea where else we should look, Bessie?" he asked.

"'We can't find Sadie, we could look fer 'oo owned 'er,'" she replied. She took another piece of toast and bit into it, then wiped her hand across her chin to rub away the excess butter. "She's a fly piece, an' all, but worth summink. 'Ooever 'e is, 'e's goin' ter be as mad as 'ell if she's dead. Yer gotta look after yer property, or anybody'll take it from yer. 'E's gonna make sure as 'ooever did this pays fer it, so's it don't 'appen again. Keep respect, like."

She was suddenly conscious of the three men staring at her. She lowered her eyes and rubbed her sleeve across her chin, just in case there was still butter there. She wasn't used to food like this. In fact, she wasn't used to having her own food at all, specially set out for her alone, on a separate plate.

Squeaky knew she was right. He was annoyed that he hadn't thought of that himself. He should have! He really had to get out of Portpool Lane; his brain was curdling.

"Course," he agreed a little sourly. "That's the one thing we know. She were the woman dead, so someone's going ter be mad as hell, 'cause he's been robbed. By all accounts she were something real special. Drove men mad for 'er. Who knows how many more, before Lucien."

"Excellent," Henry approved wryly. "A little sleep, and then we shall begin again. That is, if you are all still willing? I would be extremely grateful for your help."

"Course," Bessie said immediately.

"Yer'd help anyone on two legs, fer a piece o' toast an' jam," Squeaky said with disgust.

She gave him a radiant smile. "'E don't 'ave ter 'ave two legs," she corrected him.

Henry and Crow both laughed aloud. Henry patted her gently on the shoulder. "I suggest we find somewhere with a place to sleep, reconvene at dusk for something to eat, and then continue on our way."

Crow turned to Bessie. "I'll find you somewhere." He stood up. "Come on."

She rose also and followed him obediently, leaving Squeaky feeling oddly alone. Crow was out of line: Squeaky was the one looking after her, not him. He did not notice Henry Rathbone's smile.

*T*hey spent the greater part of the following night asking discreet questions of pimps, tavern-keepers, barmen, and other prostitutes. Again they bribed, flattered, and threatened. No one admitted to having seen Sadie, and it began to look more and more likely that she, and not Lucien, had been the victim. Unless there had been two corpses, and that was still unclear.

Some time toward morning the four of them sat in the corner of a public house in an alley off St. Martin's Lane, eating steak and kidney pudding with a thick suet crust and plenty of gravy. Outside the sleet was falling more heavily. Hail-stones rattled on the window behind them. In the yellow circle of the lamplight on the pavement they could see the white drift of them filling the cracks between the cobbles.

"Cor! Sadie were a blinder, eh?" Bessie said with growing respect at what they had learned of her. "That Shadow Man must be ready ter tear the throat out o''ooever done 'er in." She shivered. "I'm glad I in't 'im. I reckon as 'e's goin' ter die 'orrible."

"I'm afraid you are right," Henry agreed. "But if it is she who was killed, it is hard to have much pity for him. If he were caught he would most certainly be hanged."

Bessie looked at Henry with a sudden gentleness. "It's a shame, 'cause Lucien were nice. I 'ope it weren't 'im. But if it were, 'e'll get worse, yer know. They always do."

"Yes, I imagine they do," he conceded softly.

Squeaky felt a sudden and overwhelming rage take hold of him. Damn Lucien Wentworth, and all the other idle, idiotic, self-absorbed young men who betrayed the love and privilege that was theirs and broke people's hearts by throwing away their lives. They had been given far more than most people in the world, and they had destroyed it, smeared filth over it until there was nothing left. It was a kind of blasphemy. He saw that for the first time, and it overwhelmed him. The whole idea of anything being holy had never occurred to him before.

"Do we agree that it is almost certainly Shadwell who owned her?" Crow asked, eating the very last of his pudding.

"Accounts conflict," Henry answered. "But at least some of the lies are clear enough to weed out. Shadwell seems to inspire a great deal of fear in people, which would suggest that he is the ultimate power in this particular world. Whoever is responsible for Sadie's death will be running from him, and he will be pursuing them." Without asking he refilled everyone's glass with fresh ale.

"But is it Lucien who killed her, or not?" Crow asked, directing his question at no one in particular.

"We will take Bessie's advice," Henry asserted. "We will look for whoever else is seeking the killer, because Shadwell will need to have vengeance for her death, even if only to preserve his own status. His resources will be immeasurably better than ours."

Squeaky sighed, his mind searching for an excuse to end this futile chase. Whatever they discovered, it wasn't going to be good. Either Lucien was dead, and in a way that his father would have nightmares about for the rest of his life, even if that wasn't long, or else Lucien had murdered the woman who had apparently betrayed him, if you could use that word for such a creature. Only an idiot, or a man drugged out of his wits, would have trusted her anyway. Squeaky had known many women of that sort. He had bought and sold them himself, not so very long ago. Well, none as beautiful as Sadie seemed to have been, but women anyway, some of them pretty enough. But he wasn't going to offer any advice on the subject because he would much rather Henry Rathbone didn't know that. Or Crow either, for that matter.

And if Lucien were still alive, then the situation was even worse. They'd have to lie. They could never tell his father about this. Better he think him dead.

"You know . . ." he began. Then he looked at Henry's face and realized he would be wasting his breath to argue.

*T*hat evening they began to descend even deeper into the world of addiction and despair. The broad streets of the West End of London were glittering bright on the surface. They walked along Regent Street and into the Haymarket, passing theaters of the utmost sophistication. Bessie lagged behind, staring at the notices, the lights, the fashions. Several times Squeaky had to yank at her hand to drag her along.

The lamps were lit, and the gleam off of them caught the pale drifts of snow, touching it with warmth.

"Come on!" Squeaky said sharply, but Bessie was watching the carriages clattering up and down the center of the street, or swiveling around to look at people walking arm in arm, men with greatcoats on, women in capes trimmed with fur.

They turned off Piccadilly into an alley, and within twenty yards there were fewer lights, and in the shadowed doorways prostitutes plied their trade, ignoring those huddled within feet of them, half asleep, sheltering from the icy wind and the sleet.

Crow led the way down the steps from the pavement into a cellar, and through that into a deeper cellar. He began asking questions, discreetly at first, full of inventive lies.

"Looking for my sister," he explained, then described Sadie as well as he could, from other people's words.

A gaunt-eyed drunkard stared at him vacantly. "Don't know, old boy. Won't care," he drawled. "Got anything fit to drink?"

Crow passed by him, and Squeaky, still holding Bessie by the hand, spoke to a fat man with a face raddled and pockmarked with old disease.

"Lookin' fer a man who owes me money," he said grimly, then described Lucien. "I don't sell my women for nothing."

But the answer he received was equally useless.

They wasted little more time there before going out the back into a half-enclosed courtyard, then down more steps into a subterranean passage leading toward the river. Here there were more rooms indulging darker tastes. Even Bessie seemed disturbed. Squeaky could feel her fingers digging into his flesh, gripping him as if he were her lifeline.

Henry said nothing, perhaps too appalled to find words. They saw men and women, and those who might have been either, in obscene costumes, practicing torture and humiliation that belonged in nightmares.

Bessie shivered and leaned her head against Squeaky's shoulder.

Patiently Squeaky described Sadie and was greeted with raucous laughter from a man with hectic energy as if fueled by cocaine. His limbs twitched, and he seemed to find it difficult to contain his impatience.

"You too?" the man said, then laughed again.

"Someone else looking for her?" Squeaky said immediately.

"Yes! Oh yes! The long black hair, the beautiful eyes. Sadie—Sadie!"

"Who?" Squeaky urged.

Suddenly the man stood still, then he started to shiver.

"Who?" Squeaky lowered his voice. "Tell me, or I'll slit yer throat!"

Henry drew in his breath to protest, then changed his mind.

"Shadwell," the man replied very softly. Then he swiveled around, pushed his way between two men sharing a bottle, and disappeared.

Squeaky looked around at the vacant stares of the opium and laudanum addicts, the rambling half conversations of the drunkards, and gave up. He jerked his hand to direct them onward, and gripped Bessie more tightly as they followed a short, heavy man out into the alley.

Squeaky saw these people now with deepening disgust precisely because he had seen them all before. He had just forgotten the sheer and useless misery. Suddenly respectability, whether it dulled your wits or not, had a sweetness nothing else could match. It was like drinking clean water, breathing clean air.

Standing here in this filthy alley, he wanted to turn and run, escape before it caught hold of him again, or before he woke up and realized that everything he had now was just a dream. Hester Monk would despise him if she ever saw this. The thought of that made the sweat break out on his body in a way no physical fear ever had.

He hurried on, asking questions discreetly, in roundabout fashion, as if looking for pleasure himself.

It was obvious that Henry Rathbone found it repugnant to see people's misunderstanding as to his intent, but he offered no explanation. The distaste, the embarrassment lay in his eyes and the faint pulling of his mouth, almost impossible to read in the garish light of gaslamps. Squeaky saw it only because he knew it was there.

They did not mention Lucien's name, only his description, and regrettably there were many young men of excellent family and considerable means, even in the most depraved places, where any kind of sexual pleasure was for sale, the more bizarre the more expensive.

In one wide tunnel close to the river, laughter echoing along its length, magnified again and again, water dripping down the walls, Henry mentioned Shadwell again, as if it were half a joke. It was met with sudden silence. The blood drained from the skin of the man they were talking to, or perhaps it was a woman. In the flickering light and under the paint it was hard to tell. His naked shoulders were pearly white, blemishless, and without muscles, but his forearms were masked by long pink gloves, up to the elbow. Crow had seen such things before, but Henry was clearly uncomfortable. Still, he refused to let anything stop him in his quest.

"If you would be good enough," Henry persisted.

The man—or woman—froze. There was music playing somewhere, strident and off-key.

"You heard wrong," he said. His voice shook. "Someone's playin' you for a fool. I have to go." And with a surprisingly hard shove, he knocked Henry off balance so that Squeaky only just prevented him from falling.

Crow seized the man by the arm. "No names, just which way?" he demanded.

But it was no use. The fear of Shadwell was greater than anything Crow or Squeaky could call up.

They heard word of Lucien in several places, or at least of someone who might have been him. On the other hand, such a person might have been anyone, even Niccolo, Sadie's other lover.

"Why yer wanna know?" a short, monstrously fat man demanded, waddling around the bench in a brothel entrance to stare at them. His face was red, with a bulbous nose, crazed over its surface with broken veins. His flesh wobbled as he moved, and Bessie backed away from him, pushing herself hard against Squeaky's side.

The fat man looked her up and down, his eyes almost level with her throat. He lowered his gaze to her chest. "What d'yer want for 'er? There's some as like skinny bints, like they was children."

"She's not for sale," Henry snapped. "Touch her, and Mr. Robinson will break your fingers." He said it with perfect seriousness.

Squeaky drew in his breath to protest vigorously, then realized that perhaps if the man did touch Bessie, he would indeed be delighted to do something like that, or something even more personal.

The fat man stepped back, his eyes hot, his large hands clenched. Then, moving with surprising speed, he darted behind his bench again. His other hand plunged into the space between it and the wall, and came out brandishing the long, thin blade of a sword. The light glittered on its polished steel. It made a whiplike sound as he sliced it through the air.

Henry had nowhere to retreat; he was already against the wall. The little color in his face drained away as he realized his situation. Crow moved away, to distract the fat man's attention, but it was Squeaky who seized the hat stand by the door. Swinging it round like a long staff, he cracked it over the fat man's head, who crashed down, blood pouring from his scalp.

Henry stared at the widening pool in horror.

Squeaky dropped the stand and grabbed Henry by the arm, leaving Bessie to follow. "Come on!" he ordered. "Out of here!"

"But he's injured!" Henry protested. "Shouldn't we . . ."

Squeaky swore at him. Ignoring his protest, he half-pulled him off his feet, dragging him to the door and out into the alleyway. It was pitch-dark and he had no idea where they were going. It was important to simply get away from the brothel and the fat man bleeding on the floor.

They walked rapidly, crowding each other in the dark, ice-slicked alley, tripping over debris, and hearing rats scuttle away. They kept moving until they had gone at least a quarter of a mile, then finally stopped in an empty doorway sheltered from the wind, and well out of the light of the solitary street lamp.

"Thank you," Henry said quietly. "I'm afraid I was taken by surprise. A foolish thing to have allowed. I apologize."

"It's nothing." Squeaky spoke casually, but a sudden warmth welled up inside him. He was ridiculously, stupidly pleased with Henry's gratitude. For a moment he felt like a knight in shining armor.

They continued their pursuit. The winter day and the bitter cold of night were almost indistinguishable in the cellars and passages between one smoky, raucous room and another.

After half a dozen abortive leads as to where Niccolo and Sadie might be, they came to a small abandoned theater. A score of people lay on the floor half asleep. Some gave at least the impression of being together, clinging to each other's body warmth. One man lay alone, huddled over in pain, his arms wrapped around himself defensively. His dark hair was matted, but still thick.

Crow picked his way across the floor and bent down beside him. Squeaky saw, from where he stood a dozen feet away, that the sleeping man's face was gaunt, but still handsome in the dark, sensitive way Niccolo had been described to them.

Crow shook his shoulder. "Niccolo?" he said sharply.

The man stirred.

"Niccolo?" Crow shook him harder and the man pulled away with a gasp of pain.

Bessie started forward from Squeaky's side. "It in't Niccolo, that's Lucien!" she said urgently. "'E's 'urt." She clambered over the bodies, some cursing her, and bent down beside Crow. "Yer gotta do summink," she demanded. "'Ere! Lucien! It's me, Bessie. We come to 'elp yer."

Lucien stirred and half sat up, grunting with the effort, holding his left arm to his side. "Who the hell are you?" His speech was slurred but it still held the remnants of his origins, the home and the privilege to which he had been born.

The eagerness died out of Bessie's face. "Don't yer remember me?"

Lucien groaned.

"Of course he does," Crow said with sudden anger. "He's just half asleep, and he's hurt."

"Yer gonna 'elp 'im," she urged Crow.

Without answering, Crow pulled the coat Lucien was wearing away from him and looked at the wound. His shirt was matted with blood on the right side of his chest.

Lucien winced and swore. "Leave me alone!" he said with a burst of real fury. "Get out."

Henry stepped over a couple of sleeping figures and went to Crow and Lucien. He reached down and took Lucien's arm. "Stand up," he ordered. "Before we can help you, we need to get somewhere clean, where we can see what we're doing."

"I don't want your bloody help!" Lucien snapped. "Who the hell are you anyway?"

"My name is Henry Rathbone. Stand up."

Something in the authority of his tone made Lucien obey, but sullenly.

Squeaky also stepped forward. He could see

other people beginning to stir. A lone figure in the farthest archway was standing upright, one arm bent a little as if holding something, perhaps a weapon.

"We got ter get out of here," he said tersely to Henry and Crow. "You bring him." He gestured toward Lucien. "Give him a clip around the ear if he makes a fuss." He snatched Bessie's hand and almost pulled her off her feet. "C'mon."

They could not go far. Lucien was weak, and they had no idea how deep his wound was or how long ago he had sustained it. It was bitterly cold outside, and a steady, hard sleet was turning back to a soaking rain. Here in the passages and alleys so narrow that the eaves met overhead, the pall of smoke in the air was made worse by the fog blowing up from the river, so even at midday the light was thin and pale.

"We need to find somewhere to look at this," Crow said grimly. "And something to eat," he added.

They searched for more than an hour, asking for a room, space, anything private. All the time Crow and Bessie supported Lucien, who was rapidly growing weaker, and stumbling every few yards.

At last they found a back room in a pub. After a good deal of hard bargaining, threats from Squeaky, and money from Henry, they were shown to one small, dirty room with candles and a wood-burning stove, for which fuel was extra. Squeaky went to buy food and to find the nearest well to fill a bucket of water. Bessie swept the floor after very neatly stealing a neighbor's broom. She returned it with a charming smile, saying she had found it in the alleyway.

Crow and Henry did what they could to help Lucien. Crow, who still had his Gladstone bag with him, took out a length of clean bandage and a small bottle of spirit.

"This is going to hurt," he told Lucien. "But it'll hurt a hell of a lot more if you get gangrene in it. That could kill you."

Lucien glared at him. "What the hell do you care? Who are you, anyway? Who are any of you?"

"I'm a doctor," Crow replied, measuring the spirit out into a small cup.

"I'm not drinking that," Lucien told him.

"You're not being offered it," Crow replied. "It's to clean your wound. It'll sting like fire." Without hesitating he jerked Lucien's protective arm away from the wound and placed an alcohol-soaked bandage on it.

Lucien screamed. His voice choked off as he gagged and gasped for breath.

Bessie stared at Crow. Her face was ashen, but she said nothing.

Henry felt sick. He could barely imagine the pain. He looked at the wreck of a man lying on a pile of rags on the floor, the messy knife wound in his side now exposed, and he remembered the youth he had known a dozen years ago.

Crow's dark face was tense, his concentration on the tools of his art: the scalpel, the forceps, the needle and thread. He was an extraordinary young man, not much more than Lucien's age. Henry realized that he had spent the last four or five days in Crow's company, and yet he knew almost nothing about him. He did not even know his full name, much less where he came from, who his family were, or even where he lived.

He watched now as Crow bent to clean and stitch the gash in Lucien's side. His hands were lean and strong: beautiful hands. And his face was unusual: too mercurial to be handsome, too many teeth—that enormous smile. He was also skilled.

Henry wondered why he had not qualified as a doctor, but it would be grossly insensitive to ask, inexcusably so. He maintained his silence, simply handing him the instruments as he was asked for them.

It took a little while, and when Crow was finally satisfied, Lucien lay back on the rags, exhausted. "Thank you," he said with a gasp.

"What happened?" Crow asked.

"Someone stuck me with a knife," Lucien replied. "What the hell does it look like?" He was still speaking between gritted teeth.

"It looks like you were caught in a fight," Crow told him. "What happened to the person who stabbed you?"

"Why?" There was a faint flicker of a smile. "You want to go bandage him too?"

Crow ignored the question. "Are you injured anywhere else? Is there anything more I can do?"

"No." Lucien hesitated. "Thank you."

Crow put his instruments away and closed his bag. "I rather thought the other person might be dead—was it a man or a woman? Or one of each? Which was how they managed to strike back at you."

Lucien stared at him, moving a little so he

faced him, his eyes wide, his face fallen slack with amazement.

Crow waited, looking expectantly for an answer.

Slowly Lucien lay back, relaxing against the rags with a wince as his muscles pulled against the bandage.

"I didn't kill anyone," he said wearily. "It was a stupid fight over cocaine. Some idiot thought I had his and he attacked me."

"And did you?" Crow raised his eyebrows.

"I don't even use the damn stuff! I like opium . . . now and then." His eyes looked somewhere far away. "I'm drunk on life, on laughter and passion, on dreams of the impossible, on Sadie, and something that seems like love, or at least seems like not being alone." His voice dropped. "How in hell would you know what I'm talking about." It was a dismissal, not a question.

"No idea," Crow replied, his sarcasm barely discernible. "The rich are the only ones who have any idea what loneliness is, or loss, or the sense of having failed. The rest of us are too busy with hunger, cold, and disease, and finding somewhere to sleep for the night—or at least to lie down."

Lucien stared at him, and Crow stared straight back. Very gradually something in Lucien changed.

"I'm sorry," he said gently. "That was stupid. I despise self-pity. Most of all in myself."

Crow gave him one of his dazzling smiles. "So do I," he agreed.

Squeaky returned with food and water. Bessie portioned it out and carefully fed Lucien his share before eating her own.

When they were finished Henry turned to Lucien. "I came at your father's request," he stated simply. "He wants me to ask you to come home, but before that is possible, we need to clear up the matter of the murder of Sadie, or Niccolo."

Outside the wind was rising, rattling the windows.

Lucien gave a harsh bark of laughter. "Clear it up! You mean explain it? Somehow make it all right?" His mouth twisted with contempt. "You're an idiot. Go back and tell my father you couldn't find me. It's true enough. You have no idea who I am now, or what happened to the Lucien Wentworth you thought you knew."

"I intend to find out," Henry replied.

Lucien turned away. "You wouldn't understand."

"Don't be so incredibly arrogant," Henry said

sharply. "Do you think you are the first young man to indulge himself and throw away the life he was given? To tell other people that they wouldn't understand is to give yourself a uniqueness you don't possess. You are desperately and squalidly ordinary. The only thing different about you is that you had more to throw away than most of us."

Now Lucien was angry. "And what the hell would you know about it? You comfortable, complacent, self-satisfied . . ." He trailed off.

"Self-pity again?" Henry inquired.

"Self-disgust," Lucien replied quietly. "Go back and tell my father that you couldn't find me. It's not a lie. You couldn't find the son he wants back. That man died a year ago."

"Who killed him? You? Or Sadie?"

Lucien gave an abrupt laugh. "Very good. I did. Sadie only helped."

"Where did you meet her?" Henry asked.

"At the theater, with friends. She came to the party afterward." He smiled briefly and for a moment he was lost in another time. "God, she was beautiful! She made every other woman in the room seem half-alive, leaden creatures without color, as if they lived in the shadows."

"Like Shadwell," Henry remarked.

Lucien's eyes widened. "Don't even whisper his name," he said very quietly. "There was nothing of that in Sadie then. She was just . . . so alive. It was as if she could see the magic in everything. And she liked me. You think that's my delusion, my vanity? It isn't. There were loads of other men there with titles, and more money than I'll ever have."

Henry said nothing.

"She liked me," Lucien repeated, but his voice wavered a little this time, the certainty gone.

"Of course," Henry agreed. "And it is very pleasant to be liked."

For an instant there was a devastating loneliness in Lucien's face, then anger. "She didn't ask for anything," he said sharply. "Never money. She was more fun than any other woman I've known. She knew how to dress, how to dance, how to be funny and wise and more original than anyone else. She made the rest of them look like cows! Half asleep most of the time. Never saying anything except placid agreement, whatever they think you want them to say. I wouldn't be surprised to see most of them chewing the cud!"

"And she found you equally interesting," Henry

observed, a slightly dry amusement in his voice. "That must have been most agreeable for you."

"It was," Lucien snapped. Then suddenly he seemed to crumple, and sweat broke out on his forehead.

Crow looked across at Henry, frowning a little.

"Where is Sadie now?" Henry asked. "Is she the one who was murdered, or was it Niccolo?"

"I don't know. I think it was Niccolo," Lucien replied.

"If you don't know, that means you haven't seen either of them."

"Yes," Lucien agreed hoarsely. "I don't know!"

Henry allowed his gaze to wander around the cold room again, with its dark walls, its filthy windows now rattling in the wind.

"Your father would welcome you home," he said, looking at Lucien again.

The color burned up Lucien's face. "I can't come," he said very quietly, avoiding Henry's eyes.

"Why not?" Henry asked.

"Shadwell—Shadow Man," Lucien replied. "I . . . I do things for him. I owe him."

There was silence for a few minutes. Squeaky put another piece of wood in the stove. They'd be lucky if it lasted the night. Outside the rain was running down the gutters and dropping from the eaves. Bessie sat next to Squeaky, close to him for warmth.

"Did you kill Sadie?" Henry asked Lucien.

Lucien's eyes opened wide. "No!"

"Or Niccolo?"

"No! I can't think of any reason you should believe me, but I haven't killed anyone, at least . . . at least not directly. God knows what I've caused indirectly. Poor Sadie. It was a hell of a mess." His face pinched with remembered pain, and his eyes seemed to see the memory as if it were more real than Henry himself, or Crow sitting on the floor a few feet away.

"But you saw it?" Henry challenged.

"Only the blood," Lucien replied.

"What is it you do for Shadwell?" Henry asked.

"Bring people here—young ones with money."

Lucien started to shudder. His body seemed to slip out of his control, and his teeth rattled.

Henry took off his coat and wrapped it around Lucien, folding it over his thin body with gentleness. Then he sat back on the ground again, looking oddly vulnerable in his shirtsleeves.

Bessie looked at him anxiously, but Squeaky put out his hand to stop her from interrupting.

If Henry was cold, he gave no sign of it.

"Bring people here to indulge their tastes, and then they find that they are addicted, and have to come back again and again? And if they become troublesome, who deals with them then?"

"I don't know," Lucien stammered through his teeth. "Shadwell himself, maybe."

"Was Sadie troublesome? Was she no longer doing what he wanted of her?" Henry persisted.

Lucien stared at him. Then he closed his eyes and turned away. "She always did what he wanted. She couldn't afford not to."

"Why not?"

"Don't be so damn stupid!" Lucien gave an abrupt, painful laugh that ended in choking. When he caught his breath again he went on. "He gave her the pretty things she liked, and the cocaine she needed."

"So then why did he kill her?"

"I don't know. Maybe it wasn't him."

"Niccolo?"

"I don't know. He could be dead too." Lucien gulped. "Maybe it was that verminous little toad in the lavender velvet."

"Ash. Why would he kill them?"

"I don't know."

Henry waited.

Lucien sighed. He looked away, avoiding Henry's eyes. "I've crossed a few people, made enemies. If Niccolo is dead, whoever killed him probably thought it was me. We looked rather alike. In the half light of that passage, and if he was with Sadie . . ." He stopped. His face filled with regret and a peculiar kind of pain that was extraordinarily honest, without self-pity, as if he could see his loss with new clarity. "We were always headed to destruction, she and I."

Crow looked at Henry, his expression anxious.

Henry nodded and moved away, allowing Lucien to rest, at least for a while.

*B*essie was looking after Lucien, who was lying close to the stove. Henry Rathbone sat in the corner with Squeaky and Crow, who were huddled in their coats. They were saving the last few pieces of wood for the early morning.

"What do we look for now?" Henry asked, a note of desperation in his voice.

"Pick him up an' carry him out," Squeaky said

impatiently. "Before he gets us killed. Let his father deal with it."

Crow gave him a black look. "And of course this Shadwell will just let that happen! Next thing they know, the police will come to Wentworth's door looking for Lucien for the murder of whoever it was who was knifed to death at the bottom of those stairs."

Henry straightened up. "Then we need to know who it was, and who killed them."

"And if it was Lucien?" Crow asked him.

Henry bit his lip. "Then we find out how . . . and why, and decide what to do about it." He was sitting with his back against the wall, the candlelight accentuating his features. Rathbone looked appallingly tired, and yet there was no anger in his face, no bitterness that Squeaky could see. Of course he was a fool. Without Squeaky and Crow to look after him he would have come to grief in minutes. He would have been robbed blind, possibly killed if he had put up any resistance. He seemed to believe anything he was told, no matter how obviously a lie.

And yet there was a kind of courage in him that Squeaky had to grudgingly admire. And in spite of the stupid situation Henry had gotten them all into, Squeaky also rather liked him. That was another thing that had gone badly wrong lately: Since Squeaky had become respectable he had gone soft. Was this age catching up with him? Or cowardice? He had always been careful, all his life; to do otherwise would have been stupid. But he was never a coward! All his values had slithered around into the wrong place! Everything was out of control!

"Makes sense," Squeaky said at last. "If it's Sadie who's died, can't see why he would kill her. Seems to have been fascinated with her. She's the reason he got into this cesspit anyway. Likes his pleasures, that one. See it in his face when he talks about her. You get dependent on something, the bottle or the opium or whatever, then you don't destroy it. Those things make you act like an idiot, but they get to be the most important things in the world to you. You never, ever forget to keep them safe. You'd poke your mother's eyes out before you'd risk losing them."

"What if Sadie preferred Niccolo, and Lucien killed her in jealousy?" Henry asked.

"He'd kill Niccolo," Squeaky answered. "Taking her back. That's property. You don't smash something that's yours. It would just be stupid. Slap her around a bit, maybe," he conceded, remembering a few such acts of discipline from his brothel days. "Not where it shows, of course. Don't spoil the goods. So if it's him who's dead, we're in trouble."

Henry's face twisted with bitter amusement and understanding.

Squeaky blushed. He had not meant to give himself away so clearly. He would rather Henry merely guessed at his former life, rather than know it for certain. He wondered whether to try to improve on what he had said, then knew he would only make it worse.

"Do you think he is telling the truth?" Henry pressed. "And he really doesn't know who's died?"

"Not sure I'd go that far!" Squeaky protested. "Not . . . not entirely. He's bound to lie about some things."

Henry smiled.

Squeaky realized that he had just given himself away again. Now Henry would know that Squeaky always lied, at least a bit. Damn! Being respectable was a pain, and hard work!

Henry turned to Crow. "And you?"

"I've no need to lie," Crow said with a grin,

glancing at Squeaky, then away again. He straightened his face, suddenly very sober. "And I don't think Lucien has either. He's pretty well lost, whatever he says. No point really. Whether he did kill either one of them or not, he's going to get blamed for it. Personally I think it was probably that disgusting little vampire in the lavender coat. He looks like something risen from the dead. I should think he likes knives."

"I believe him too," Henry said quietly.

"Hey, just a minute!" Squeaky protested. "I didn't say I believed him. I just . . ." His mind raced. "What if Sadie told Niccolo to go to hell, and he killed her? Then Lucien comes along, sees her dead an' covered in blood, an' he slices him up? Ash had nothing to do with it."

Henry thought about it for several moments. "Then why would Lucien not admit that?" he asked. "Such an act would be justified, to the people here. And it seems they are all he cares about. This is his world—at least until we can get him out of it."

"Out of it?" Squeaky said incredulously. "Look at him! He's drunk an' he's taking God knows what else to keep him awake, or asleep, make him laugh, or see what he wants to see, feel something like being alive, God help him. He belongs here. Hell don't let go of people, Mr. Rathbone. Not that most people are willing to climb out of it, even if they could—an' they can't."

"First we have to find out if he killed either of the two victims, and if he did not, then who did."

"You asked us if we believe him that he didn't kill either of them," Crow interrupted. "And you say you do."

"I do," Henry agreed. "It is not a certainty, of course, but I shall treat it as such, unless circumstances should make that impossible. Therefore we must proceed on the assumption that someone else killed whoever it was—even both of them." He looked at Crow again. "What is your opinion of Mr. Ash?"

"Syphilitic," Crow said simply.

Henry was surprised. "You know that so easily?"

Crow smiled, but there was no pleasure in his expression. "He moved very little, but his hand slipped on the cane, as if he were not sure whether he gripped it or not, as if he could not really feel his fingers. His feet were the same. That curious, slightly stamping gait is peculiar to advanced stages of damage to the nerves. He is probably more than a little insane."

"Then he might well have been violent," Henry concluded.

"Why would he kill them?" Squeaky asked. "Even a creature like that has to have a reason."

"You are quite right," Henry agreed. "But one thing makes me wonder about the cane. Ash is quite small, and you say he has the signs of advanced syphilis?" He looked at Crow. "The cane in his hand slipped from his grasp. We saw it. Do you believe he could have attacked a healthy young man or woman and escaped completely unhurt himself?"

"Not likely," Crow conceded.

"Lucien," Squeaky said sadly. "He killed Niccolo, his rival for the girl, probably taking him by surprise—knife in the back. Then when she found them he attacked her too. That's where he got injured himself." He looked at Henry's downcast face and felt guilty for having spoken the truth when he knew it would hurt him. "You can't do anything for him."

Crow pulled his coat tightly around his shoulders. He had been staring at the ground, but now he turned to Henry. "We should put together all the evidence we can," he said, looking from Henry to Squeaky and back again. "Even here, there has to be reason in things. There are a lot of questions we haven't answered yet. What do we know about this Niccolo? Who was he and where did he come from? Did he and Lucien know each other before meeting here? In fact, did Lucien bring Niccolo here? Or the other way round?" He stopped for a moment, looking from one to the other.

"Was it for women, or opium?" he went on. "Some kind of torture, or sexual appetite? Was Niccolo a sadist? A masochist? Did he love Sadie, or was he just using her?"

Henry smiled at him. "Thank you, Dr. Crow," he said gravely. "You are a voice of hope where there seems to be very little otherwise. Your suggestions are excellent. As soon as we have had a little sleep—if such a thing is possible in this place—we shall find something fit to eat, for ourselves and Lucien and Bessie, then continue our investigation." He looked at Crow, then at Squeaky, his face grave. "If you are still agreeable to helping, of course?"

Crow shrugged. "I'm curious," he said. "I'll help."

Henry waited for Squeaky.

Squeaky felt trapped. He should have resented

it, yet against all reason or sense, he was vaguely flattered to be included. He certainly would have been hurt had Henry not asked him. But he had to put up some sort of resistance, even if only to salvage the shreds of his reputation.

"Won't do any good," he said yet again. He gestured toward where Lucien was lying curled over on his unwounded side, either asleep or unconscious. "What else are you going to do with him anyway? If he killed Sadie and Niccolo, are you going to expect his father to take him in and cover it up? They may have been rubbish, but they were still people. And who'll he kill next, eh? Have you thought of that?"

"Yes, Mr. Robinson, I have," Henry said in little more than a whisper. "Nobody comes out of a place like this without paying a price, and I am not imagining that Lucien can do so either. I want to help him, not to excuse him. It is not a physical thing, to climb out of hell, as you put it; it is an ascent of the spirit. It will be long and extremely painful, and there is a cost to be paid. It is a steep climb—a toll road if you like—and each stretch of it will exact a price. But I imagine you know that."

Squeaky was stunned. He stared at Henry's

ashen face with its clear blue eyes, and saw no evasion in it, no soft, easy forgiveness. Was Henry referring to Squeaky's own ascent from a place not as unlike this as he would wish to imagine it, until he was now positively decent? Or very nearly. Hester Monk treated him as if he were honest. Of course she probably kept a very good check on him, although he had never caught her doing so. That was a painful thought too. He very much liked having her trust. It was worth quite a lot of discomfort to keep it.

Henry was still watching him.

It occurred to Squeaky that in helping Lucien Wentworth, he might be proving that the way up was possible, proving it to Henry Rathbone, and more than that, to himself.

"Course I'll help," he said tartly. "You need me. I know a lot of things you don't."

Henry smiled, extraordinarily sweetly. "For which I am grateful," he accepted. "Now let us rest until it is time to begin."

They slept briefly, then set out to find some hot food, and perhaps pies and ale they could bring back for Lucien and Bessie. They left the alleys and walked along Piccadilly into Regent Street. It was dry now and bitingly cold, with frost and here and there a dusting of snow, which contributed to the decorations of colored ribbons and wreaths of holly and ivy on shop doors.

"Happy Christmas!" a stout woman called out cheerfully, passing sweets to a child.

"And to you!" a gentleman returned. "Happy New Year to you!"

Someone was singing "God rest ye merry gentlemen" and other voices joined in.

The traffic was heavy, the clatter of hooves and the jingle of harnesses loud.

Squeaky rolled his eyes, and said nothing.

"Happy Christmas," Henry replied to a passerby.

After another hundred yards they found a tavern serving hot food that had a good fire in the hearth. Henry paid for them all, including provisions to take back to Bessie and Lucien. They ate in silence, relishing the luxury too much to disturb the pleasure of it with conversation.

They started back again and were soon in the narrow alleys. It was dim, as if it were always dusk on these midwinter days. There was no reality of Christmas here, perhaps not even any belief in its meaning.

They delivered the pies and ale, which were received with gratitude, expressed with few words and ravenous pleasure. They decided that Bessie would stay with Lucien to look after him while he healed. Henry, Crow, and Squeaky would continue to search for proof of who had been killed, and whether Lucien was involved or not, and if so, in what way.

It was decided that Crow would go back to Mr. Ash and see if he could persuade him to tell whatever else he knew.

"There has to be more," Henry said. "He is involved in it somehow, because he feels too intensely to simply be an observer."

Crow agreed. "What about you?" he asked.

Henry bit his lip. "I shall endeavor to learn something of this Niccolo—who he is, and above all if anyone has seen him in the last two days." He looked at Squeaky. "You are the best suited among us to learn more about Sadie, particularly if she is still alive, and if not, who else, apart from Lucien, would have wanted to kill her."

Squeaky considered that a very dubious compliment, but this was not the time to argue with what was clearly the truth. Henry himself would be totally useless at such a task.

They agreed to meet back at daybreak the following morning, at the latest.

The others were already waiting when Squeaky returned, carrying a jug of hot chocolate he had purchased with some money he had "liberated" from a less-deserving owner. He shared it, measuring carefully, then sat down on the floor to enjoy his portion.

Henry turned to Crow, his eyebrows raised questioningly.

Crow warmed his hands on his mug.

Henry had bought some pies. Squeaky refrained from asking what was in them; he preferred to imagine. He also did not ask what they had cost. Both were things he very much preferred not knowing.

The candles were getting low. One had already guttered and gone out. Lucien and Bessie were probably asleep. They had already checked on them, Crow with some concern.

"How ill is Ash?" Henry asked. "Could he have killed them?" His face was in shadow, so Squeaky could not read his expression, but he heard the strain in his voice. Rathbone must have seen things here that his quiet life on Primrose Hill had not prepared him even to imagine. And of course there was always the smell. Few middle-class people had experienced the smells of the gutter, the sewage, the decaying bodies of rats, the rot of old wood.

It brought back memories to Squeaky that he had worked very hard to forget.

Before the security of Portpool Lane there had been other places, ones that smelled like this, of stale wine, vomit, unwashed bodies, blood, and sweat. Above all he could remember the fear. It might be the sudden eruption of temper into a blow against the head, or the knife in the stomach of deliberate revenge. He never looked at his own body because he did not want to see the scars. Some had been from women, and that was better forgotten too. Perhaps he had deserved those, or at least some of them.

Hate was behind him now. Some people even trusted him, and that was like a delicate, precious flame in the darkness. He would kill to keep that, and the moment he did, of course, it would be gone, probably forever. Damn caring what people thought. It was against all the laws of survival. And yet it still beguiled him and drew him in.

It seemed that Crow was going to answer Henry's question about Ash. He was sitting with his back against the wall, his enormously long legs straight out in front of him. There was a hole in the sole of his left boot. His face was more deeply lined than Squeaky had ever seen it before. He looked more like forty-five than thirty-five. Squeaky recognized it as not just weariness but a kind of pain that darkened the energy of spirit and the hope that lit him. If that went out, it would be a darkness Squeaky would never find his way out of.

Henry was watching him, waiting.

"He isn't going to live much longer," Crow said quietly. "His body's rotting. He stands so still because he can't feel his hands or feet. If he moves he's likely to lose his balance. He pretends to carry the stick for an affectation, but actually he'd fall without it. I don't think he killed Niccolo or Sadie, but he knows who did. In fact, I think he was there. He knows something else, but I can't get him to tell me."

"At a price," Squeaky told him. "Don't give all your help away. I know you're a doctor, an' all that, but doctors charge."

An indescribable expression crossed Crow's face. For a moment Squeaky was afraid he would not be able to pretend that he had not seen it. He realized with a jolt that in spite of the years he had seen him coming and going, watched him patch up the injuries of all manner of people, he really knew Crow very little: not the man underneath the black coat, the flashing smile, and the bizarre humor. Now he had trespassed, to a place Crow did not want to let him into.

"I have nothing to give him," Crow said, without looking at either Squeaky or Henry. "His pain is beyond anyone's reach. He is closed in with it until it kills him."

Squeaky shuddered. Perhaps in a way that was true of all of them, a final aloneness. He disgusted himself by feeling sorry for the man in his absurd costume.

Henry leaned forward. "Is it who killed them that he will not tell you?" he asked Crow. "Or something else?"

Crow thought for a moment. "I think it is something else," he said finally.

"The reason they were killed?" Henry suggested.

Squeaky stared at Crow, then at Henry, then back at Crow again.

"It's something about Sadie," Crow answered. "Something secret, that he nurses inside him, because he knows and we don't. We are making a profound mistake about her. Something we be-

317

lieve is totally wrong. I'm trying to work out what it could be, and I can't."

"Do you think Lucien killed her?" Henry asked. Squeaky knew from the tightness in his voice that if Crow said "yes," he would accept it.

Crow looked at Henry as if Squeaky were not even there.

"No," he answered. "Because he had no reason to. She gave him the physical pleasure that he craves, and she was very skilled, by all accounts, at making men feel admired, important—even that she loved them, in her own way. I can't see how he would have deliberately sacrificed that."

"That's more or less what I learned too," Henry agreed. "Pleasure, admiration, a kind of emotional power are his weaknesses, but not violence. It seems the same was true of Niccolo, from what I could find out."

"Jealousy?" Squeaky put in. "Most men get violent if the women they think of as theirs pay too much attention to someone else. I've seen it over and over. You don't have to be in love. It's to do with possession, with being top. If someone can take your woman away from you, it's a sign that you're weak. You could love anybody at all, so your love is meaningless." He forced memories away

from him, things he had done in the past to make
sure no one imagined him vulnerable, the fear he
had instilled to keep himself safe. He could still
too easily see their pale faces in his mind.

Henry and Crow were both looking at him.

Squeaky felt as if the ugliness in his mind were
visible in his face, and they could read it. They
would be revolted. He was revolted himself. He
felt naked in the most painful and degraded way.
His skin must be burning.

"They said she was beautiful," he began defensively. "Beauty can have funny effects on men.
Lucien said it himself. Long black hair like silk,
and sea-blue eyes. Sort of mouth you never forget.
Comes into your dreams, whether you want it to
or not."

"If that is the sort of woman she was, she may
have had other enemies," Henry pointed out. "I
know you are playing devil's advocate, Squeaky,
which we need, but you must grant that that is
also true."

"I know the devil too well to make jokes about
him," Squeaky said grimly. "Or to plead anything
for him either."

"I mean that you are making the opposite ar-
gument, so that we see our case in the full light,

from all sides," Henry explained. "I was asking about Niccolo, but I learned a lot more about Sadie from the answers. She was very beautiful, and funny at times—although people who are drunk, or in love, are more easily amused than the rest of us."

He shook his head. "Even so, she seems to have been extraordinarily vivid in her personality, never a bore, which to some is the ultimate sin. But she was dependent on the cocaine, and without it she was very frightened." He stopped, his face in the shadow. "I think she may have had an illness, perhaps something like tuberculosis. What do you think, Crow?"

"I think you're probably right," Crow said softly. "Some of her vitality, some of her wild gulping at life was fear. I've seen it before. Do everything now, in case there's no tomorrow." He stopped abruptly.

Henry looked at him, then touched him very gently on the arm for just a moment before letting his hand fall.

Crow took a deep breath and let it out in a sigh.

"Is that right?" Squeaky asked. "Would she have died anyway? And you reckon she knew that?"

"I don't know whether she knew it," Crow replied.

"You're a doctor—you know!" Squeaky accused.

"I'm not a doctor." Crow looked at the ground.

Squeaky drew in his breath to ask him why not, then knew it would be intrusive, even cruel. You did not ask people questions like that. Crow was his friend, and friends do not trespass into pain, still less into failure.

"But it sounds like it," Crow went on. "The fever, bright eyes, pale skin with a flush on the cheeks, the frantic energy and the tiredness, the . . . the knowledge inside her that she has not long—the need to do everything now."

"You sound very sure," Henry said gently.

"I've seen lots of it," Crow replied, his voice cracking. He took a breath as if about to say something further, then let it out again without speaking.

Squeaky looked at Henry.

"No one can help that." Henry turned to Crow.

Crow smiled, his eyes filled with pain. "I used to think I could, when I was young, and stupid. My mother had it. That's why I wanted to be a doctor. I used to think I could cure her. But she died anyway."

"We all fail at something," Henry told him very quickly. "One way or another. Things that don't work out as we had hoped, people we love who don't love us, dreams that crumble. Time catches up with us, and we realize what we haven't done, what chances for kindness, for courage we have wasted, and too many of them won't come again. We see glimpses of what we could have been, and weren't."

Squeaky was stunned. What was this life Henry was talking about? It was surely not the life he had had himself, inventing and making things, having a son who was the best lawyer in London, a nice house, people who trusted and admired him. What failure had he ever known?

Henry's attention was on Crow. "But you have helped many," he said with growing conviction in his voice. "More important, you have helped some whom possibly no one else would help. Don't let yourself be crippled because it wasn't everyone. Nobody succeeds all the time." He smiled bleakly. "Think how insufferably arrogant we would become if we did. There would be no need for God."

Squeaky smiled. "Is He going to pick up the bits we drop, then?"

"I don't know," Henry replied. "But I don't mean to drop Lucien if I can help it. There's always a chance."

"You're a dreamer," Squeaky told him. "This isn't your world."

"Hell is everybody's world, at one time or another, Squeaky," Henry answered.

Squeaky blasphemed softly under his breath. "You've been here for days and you still don't have the least idea! Lucien's here because he wants to be!" He forced the words out between his teeth. He did not want to hurt this gentle man. He liked him, dammit! But somebody had to save him from himself.

Crow was staring at Squeaky.

"And you don't need to look like that either!" Squeaky snapped at him. "He came here for pleasure, no matter what it cost, or who paid it. He wanted to live in a world where everybody flattered him and told him how handsome and clever he was. He wanted to believe the lies—so he did. He didn't give a damn about anyone else, and now nobody gives a damn about him." He looked at Henry. "He's here because he chose it. And you can't change that."

"Of course I can't," Henry admitted. "But if he chooses to leave, perhaps I can help him believe that he can do it."

"It's too late," Squeaky said brutally, not because he wished to hurt, but because he couldn't bear the hope and despair that would follow. It had to end now.

"It's never too late," Henry said stubbornly. "Well, maybe it is sometimes, but not yet. There's still something to fight for. You are free to go, of course, but I would rather you stayed with us, because we need your help, and your experience."

Squeaky wanted to swear, but no words in all his wide vocabulary were adequate to suit his feelings.

"Well, I've got to stay, haven't I!" he said roughly. "You haven't got enough sense to find your way out of a wet paper bag!"

"Thank you," Henry said gravely.

"I've been thinking." Crow measured his words. "I've heard a lot about Sadie, because I asked about her. At least some of it has to be lies, but I can't tell which is which. Sorting out the truth might be our next course of action." He looked hopefully at Henry, then at Squeaky.

"So what did you hear?" Squeaky asked. "She's

a damn good whore, with T.B., and any other disease she might have picked up along the way. She
had long, black hair and blue eyes."

"She was tall and slender, with extraordinary
grace," Crow added. "And very disturbing eyes,
actually, according to those who were not in love
with her. One was green and one hazel."

Squeaky shrugged. "What does it matter?"

"Unless it was two different women?" Henry
pointed out. "Maybe it wasn't even Sadie at all?
Then Lucien would have had no reason to kill
Niccolo." A sudden hope lit his face.

"Lucien is vain, stupid, completely selfish, and
up to his eyeballs on opium, drink, and anything
else he can get hold of!" Squeaky said. "He doesn't
need a reason to lose his temper and kill someone!"

"But there was another woman Niccolo used,"
Crow argued. "Perhaps she was the one with the
hazel-green eyes?"

"Can we find her?" Henry asked eagerly. "Do
you know her name? Anything about her?"

"Rosa," Crow said, yawning. "Apparently he hit
her quite a bit. I asked if we could find her, but no
one's seen her recently."

"What does she look like?" Henry asked. "She

must be somewhere. Perhaps she's hiding because she knows what happened. Maybe she has a pimp who protects her . . . and he killed Niccolo, and Sadie just got in the way." He looked at Squeaky. "Or maybe it has nothing to do with Sadie. What do you think?"

Squeaky saw the hope in his eyes and hated to crush it. "Maybe," he said reluctantly. "I suppose. But if nobody's seen this woman, I don't know how we're going to find her."

"Look for her protector?" Henry suggested.

"Pimp, that's what you mean. The man who owns her."

Henry winced. "If you prefer."

"What if her pimp is Shadwell himself?" Squeaky asked, shifting his position because his legs were cramped. Hell, it was cold down here! He longed for the warmth of the Portpool Lane Clinic. "Do we want to go after him?" he added.

"He's the one with the opium, and probably the cocaine," Henry pointed out.

Then Squeaky had a sudden, wild idea, one that would really give them something to follow, if it were true. He leaned forward eagerly. "At first we didn't know if it was Lucien or Niccolo who was murdered," he said urgently. "We got different descriptions of Sadie, so maybe we don't know if it was Sadie who was killed, or this Rosa! Maybe nobody's seen her for a few days because she's dead!"

Crow stared at him, his eyes wide. "Nobody's seen Sadie either!" he argued, but he was leaning forward, wide awake now.

"We don't know that, 'cause we haven't been looking for Sadie," Squeaky pointed out.

"But why would anyone kill Rosa?" Henry asked, clearly puzzled.

"Well, maybe we should ask Lucien that." Squeaky replied. "Maybe there's a whole lot we should ask him, like exactly what he's done for Shadwell lately. Who else has he brought down here? Maybe there's someone in this we don't even know about." Squeaky drew in his breath and began again. "And let's ask Lucien what he knows about this Shadwell, an' make damn sure we get a straight answer this time. If Shadwell is Rosa's pimp, is he Sadie's too? And if he is, what does Lucien pay for her, and what else does he do to earn it?"

"You are right." Henry spoke before anyone else could. "We shall speak with Lucien again. However, I would be grateful if you would allow me to lead the questions." He pulled himself to his feet, a little stiffly. He had been sitting on the hard floor for some time like the others. He was cold, and his muscles locked when he tried to pull his coat more closely around him. It flapped open now as he walked across to where Lucien was huddled, half asleep.

Bessie looked up from where she sat with him, her face streaked with dirt, her eyes hollow. "I think 'e's a bit better," she said hopefully.

Henry knelt down. "Good. Thank you. I'm afraid we must disturb him because we have questions."

She nodded.

"Lucien," Henry said firmly. "Sit up and pay attention. I need to talk to you, as do Crow and Squeaky. There are many questions that cannot wait any longer."

Lucien stirred and opened his eyes. His face was almost colorless and shadowed with bruises. His cheeks were gaunt, but even so he did not seem quite as deeply shocked as he had a day earlier.

Henry moved to assist him in sitting up, and Bessie quickly helped him from the other side. He moved awkwardly and was queasy with pain, for a moment gagging as the wound in his side was stretched and the dried blood tore at his skin. At last he was propped against the wall.

"I don't know who killed him—or her," he said, biting his lips with pain.

"I assumed not." Henry said, moving to sit more comfortably. Crow and Squeaky were close, just a little behind him. "There are other things that matter, and may lead us to knowing who did."

"Nothing matters, Mr. Rathbone," Lucien contradicted him. "And it really won't make any difference. Either Sadie or Niccolo is dead, and everyone will believe I killed them, whoever really did."

"Shut up and answer what you're asked!" Squeaky told him curtly. "Mr. Rathbone decides what matters, not you."

Lucien gave a faint smile, looking at Henry. "Who's your charming friend?"

"Squeaky Robinson," Henry replied. "And for the moment he's right. There are several things we don't know, and it's necessary that we learn."

Lucien looked away.

Squeaky wondered if he was crafting some sort of lie that might excuse him. Or perhaps the man was simply afraid. For an instant Squeaky felt a surge of pity. It startled him. He knew better than that. Spoiled, arrogant young men like Lucien Wentworth had had everything given to them, all the privileges Squeaky himself had never even dreamed of! A safe home that was warm even in winter, enough food, even good food, clean and well-cooked, not anyone else's leftovers. They had beautiful clothes, always clean. People cared about what happened to them. They were taught to read, write, count, and speak like gentlemen. They didn't have to worry and be afraid of tomorrow.

So why was Squeaky sorry for him? Was it just because Hester would have been? Or was this all because of Henry Rathbone?

"Lucien," Henry said firmly. "I can't protect you, and I wouldn't even if I could. The only way out of this is to face it. And believe me, there is no escape. The pain is going to come, and the darkness, whether you run away or not."

Squeaky winced. He had wanted to interrupt; now he changed his mind. Henry's quiet voice was worse than anger or open emotion.

Lucien looked back at Henry. "I don't know who was killed, or who did it," he said again. "If Shadwell comes to take me himself, I still won't know. There's no use in you threatening; I can't help."

"I believe that is what you think," Henry replied. "Tell me more about Shadwell. Is he Rosa's pimp? And Sadie's?"

"He's Sadie's," Lucien answered. "At least . . . he owns her."

"And Rosa's pimp?" Henry asked.

"No." Lucien sounded doubtful, but he did not add anything more.

"Why Sadie's?" Henry persisted.

"Because he feeds her the cocaine she needs," Lucien replied quietly.

"And Rosa?"

"She didn't use it."

"Why does he feed Sadie cocaine?" Henry persisted.

Lucien did not reply but Squeaky could see him chewing his lip, biting. It must have hurt, but clearly less than the pain that burned inside him.

"She lures the kind of men few other women can," he replied reluctantly. "And she keeps them. They come again and again." A wry self-mockery lit his eyes and then went out.

Henry put his hand on Lucien's wrist, gripping him gently, but without allowing escape. "And why does he want you? What do you do for him that she can't?"

Crow turned to look from Henry to Lucien. For an instant Squeaky thought he was going to interrupt. The wretchedness in Lucien's face was now so consuming that he half-thought of intervening himself.

Then Crow leaned back again, saying nothing.

"I bring a different sort of people," Lucien said at last. "People with other tastes: torture, voyeurism, bondage. I didn't bring them enough though. Some things sicken even me. Perhaps if I had brought them, Shadwell wouldn't have killed whoever it was."

"Who was it, Lucien? Niccolo? Rosa? Or Sadie?" Henry asked him.

"I don't know."

"Who is Niccolo?" Squeaky put in. "Did you bring him here?"

"Yes," Lucien said quietly. "Months ago."

"Who is he?" Squeaky insisted.

"A young man with social pretensions," Lucien said with slight contempt. "His father made a lot of money in trade of some sort."

"So why's he here in this gutter, then, not in Society?" Henry said. He glanced to left and right. "This is hardly pretentious."

"You've got to be born into the sort of Society

he's aiming at. You can't buy your way in. I don't know his history, and I don't care." Lucien half-turned away.

Squeaky grabbed Lucien's shoulder and dug his fingers into his flesh.

Lucien winced and cried out.

"Don't you get superior with us, you useless little toad!" Squeaky hissed at him. "Who else've you brought to Shadwell?

"Only those who were more than willing."

This time Lucien was angry.

"Did Niccolo come for drugs, torture, or just women? Sadie in particular?"

"Women," Lucien said. "Sadie wasn't for him."

"Rosa?"

"Yes. He liked Rosa. She was pretty as well, very pretty. But there was a kind of innocence about her, where Sadie could make you believe she knew everything there was to know about pleasure, from the beginning of man and woman—from Eden." For a moment Lucien's memory seemed to drift back into another time.

"Were they on cocaine as well?" Crow asked.

With an effort Lucien forced his attention back to the present. "Who, Rosa? Not so far as I know."

"And Niccolo?"

"Brandy and cocaine."

"From Shadwell?"

"Probably."

"What else did he want from you? What do you do for him that makes you worth his time and his best woman? Sadie was the best woman, wasn't she?" Henry persisted.

"Yes."

"Lucien!"

"He wanted me to bring in better, richer people, friends from my own social class, young men with money who are bored with the tame pleasures of Society." He shrugged very slightly, to avoid causing pain to his wound. "Men who want to escape the predictable, the safe marriage to some nice, tedious young woman and the endless round of the same dinner parties, the same food, and the same conversation for the rest of their lives. They want wild dreams, passion, discovery of new places of the mind, fevers of the imagination and the senses."

"They want the poppy, or cocaine." Henry summed it up. "To give them the dreams they can't create for themselves. Then what are they going to do when they wake up, and all that is left is ashes?"

334

"Take some more," Lucien said huskily. "I know that. I didn't do what he wanted, which may be why Niccolo might be dead. To teach me the cost of disobedience."

"So Niccolo was dispensable?" Henry asked with a touch of bitterness.

Lucien looked angry, and his expression was answer enough.

Squeaky stood up, his knees creaking. He was cold and sore and so tired he could have slept almost anywhere, except this filthy sty.

"Right. Then we've got to find Niccolo, or Rosa, whichever of them is still alive," he said to all of them. He pointed at Lucien. "You're staying here. You're too sick to be any use, even if we trusted you—which we don't. And someone's got to look after you, which had better be Bessie. You do whatever she says."

He lowered his voice to a grim whisper. "And if you hurt her, or let anyone else hurt her, believe me, you'd rather fall into Shadow Man's hands than mine. He has some use for you, so he probably won't kill you. You're nothing to me, so I'll kill you in a heartbeat—except I won't. I'll do it slow. Got that?"

Lucien smiled, a little crookedly, but there was

warmth to it, no self-pity. "I believe you," he answered. "If Shadwell gets you, which I expect he will, I suppose you expect me to get her back to some kind of world above this one?"

Squeaky was startled. It was the last answer he had looked for. "Yes," he agreed. "That's just what we expect."

Lucien's very quiet laugh ended in a cough. "Poor Bessie. God help her."

Bessie stiffened.

"Never mind God!" Squeaky snapped. "You're all we've got—so you'll do it!"

They bought a good supply of food: mostly bread, cheese, and a little sausage. Henry found enough firewood to keep the stove going, barely, for a couple of days. Crow rebandaged Lucien's wound, then Henry, Squeaky, and Crow left the room quietly and set out on the quest to find Shadwell.

They descended farther into the world of pleasures.

"It's pointless," Squeaky warned. "Even if we find this Shadwell, he can't help Lucien, and he isn't going to try."

He was walking beside Henry as they came to the bottom of a flight of steps and turned left along a passageway with little alleys off to either side. The sound of laughter drifted from the left, along with the smells of wine, smoke, and human sweat, and something else indefinably sickly.

They both stopped.

"This Shadwell isn't keeping Lucien here against his will, you know," Squeaky said to Henry. "Finding him isn't going to do any good."

Henry ignored him, walking again with his hands in his pockets, shoulders hunched. It was bitterly cold down here and they were eager to reach a place crowded with people.

In one of the cellars it was definitely warmer, but the air was so thick with opium fumes it made Henry gag. Even Crow put his scarf around his mouth. In the dim light they saw more than twenty figures sprawled in a mockery of repose. Some seemed conscious, though not fully aware. Their eyes were glazed; they saw nothing of their surroundings, only the hectic world within their own minds.

Henry tried speaking to one or two of them but received no answers of which he could make any sense.

"Don't bother," Squeaky told him. "They wouldn't know their own mothers. Come to think of it, they probably never did. We aren't going to find Shadow Man here. The poppy's his servant, not his master. We'll do better going after the whorehouses. At least the customers will still be conscious."

Crow peered into the faces of some of the smokers. They were mostly men but included a few women. "He's right," he conceded. "This lot can't tell us anything."

They turned to leave, but found their way blocked by a bald-headed man with tattoos on his neck and the parts of his hands that they could see. His right thumb was missing.

"And what would you be doing in 'ere?" he said with a pronounced lisp, as if his tongue were malformed. "Yer lookin' ter come 'ere without payin', then? That ain't the way it works, gents. Yer come in, yer pays."

"We smoke, we pay," Squeaky told him tersely.

"Yer come 'in, yer pays," the man repeated. He jerked his hand sideways sharply and another figure loomed out of the haze to join him.

Henry put his hand into his inside pocket to find money.

"Yer wanna watch 'im!" Squeaky warned, seizing Henry's arm and holding it hard to prevent him from moving. He felt him wince. He would apologize later. Right now he must stop him from revealing that he had any money, or they would all be robbed blind, and lucky to get out uninjured. His instinct was to fight, and they couldn't win. These men would be armed with knives and razors, and possibly garottes as well. Opium was expensive, and therefore worth protecting. Henry had no idea what he was dealing with. With an ounce of a brain Squeaky could have stopped this idiocy before it got this far. He was getting slow, and that was his own fault. He was out of practice. Out of brains, more like.

"'E works for Shadow Man," he said to the others, but nodding his head at Henry. "'E looks like 'e's a gent, and 'e was, once. And them that started as gents, when they hit the gutter, they're worse than them as was born in it. 'E used to be a surgeon. What 'e can do with a knife," he held his finger and thumb a couple of inches apart, "just a little, very, very sharp knife," he said, shuddering, "you wouldn't want to know about."

Henry froze, his jaw dropped in amazement.

Crow smiled, showing all his teeth. "We call him the Bleeder." He caught the spirit of the act. "Looks like butter wouldn't melt, don't he?" He regarded Henry admiringly. "Looks like that until he gets right up close to you. Then it's too late." He raised his right hand so quickly the bald man did not even see it until it was almost at his throat, and then gone again before he could thrust it away.

Crow's smile widened.

"Oh, really!" Henry protested.

Squeaky looked at Henry sternly. "No, Bleeder! Not this time. 'E's only trying it on. 'E don't mean it." He turned to the bald man. "Do you, sir? Say you don't, an' I'll get 'im out of 'ere, no trouble, no blood. Blood's no good for business. People come 'ere for a little peace, a little escape. Blood puts 'em right off."

"Don't you come back, or I'll get you next time!" The bald man said it grimly, but there was no conviction in his voice. He stepped back, leaving them plenty of room.

As one, Crow and Squeaky took Henry by both arms and swung him around. Then they marched him back up the stairs into the alley, right to the far end and out into the narrow square before letting him go.

The fog was growing thicker, and the cobbles were slick with ice. The lamps in the street ahead were almost invisible, little more than smudges against the darkness.

"That was preposterous!" Henry exclaimed, but even in this dim light it was clear to see that he was smiling. "What on earth would you have done if he'd not believed you?"

"Put me fingers in his eyes," Squeaky said without hesitation. "But that could have ended real nasty."

"We'd better keep moving," Crow advised. "We can't afford to have one of that lot catch up with us."

"We want either Rosa or Sadie, whichever of them is alive," Squeaky said. "I'm thinking they aren't bought by just anyone with enough money. I'll wager anything you like that they do the choosing, not the clients, although they might think they do. Shadwell doesn't find their customers for them, they find them for him."

"You're right," Crow agreed. "So how do we get to where they'll find us?"

Squeaky gave him a disparaging look, which was largely wasted because the light was too dim for Crow to see it.

"Yeah? An' which one of us is a woman like

Sadie going to go for, then?" Squeaky asked sar-castically.

"Definitely Crow," Henry replied without hesi-tation. "You and I are too old, and don't look the part anyway."

Crow's jaw fell. He struggled for words but none came to him. For once even his smile failed him.

Henry patted him on the shoulder. "Your turn," he said cheerfully. "I think we had better fortify ourselves with as good a meal as we can find first. It's going to be a long night."

*A*s it turned out it was two long nights and many wasted attempts before they found the right place—a small, very discreet club where an excel-lent champagne flowed and both men and women made their availability startlingly plain. There seemed to be endless doors to side rooms, cur-tains, laughter, farther doors beyond with locks. People wore all kinds of costumes. Some were colorful, even picturesque, borrowed from history or imagination. Others were merely obscene. In some cases it was easy to be deceived as to whether the wearer was male or female. Some appeared to have bosoms and yet also wore large and very suggestive codpieces.

Almost every distortion of appetite was catered to. Two or even three men together was illegal, but commonplace enough here. A near-naked hermaphrodite, clearly possessing rudimentary organs of both sexes, turned even Squeaky's stomach.

A slim, pale boy offered himself for sexual asphyxiation, and Henry averted his eyes, his face white. Squeaky wondered how long it would be before someone lost control and the boy ended up dead.

"Would you fancy something to eat, gentlemen?" another young man asked. "What's your pleasure, sirs? Oysters to spark the appetite a little? Champagne? Chocolate, perhaps? Soft, dark chocolate to lick off a woman's body?" He giggled. "Or a man's if you prefer? Got a nice young boy that nature was generous to . . ."

For once Henry was lost for a reply.

Crow shook his head.

"We'll find our own!" Squeaky snapped, surprised to hear how hoarse his voice was. "Don't worry—we'll pay."

The man swiveled on his heel and went off in a pettish temper.

Squeaky looked at Henry's too-evident distress.

"Take that look off your face!" he hissed, digging his elbow sharply into Henry's ribs. "Yer look like you just bit into a rotten egg."

"I feel like it," Henry said, gasping and coughing. "What in God's name has happened to these people?"

"How the hell do I know? Look, I never dealt in this kind of thing!" He was indignant now. Did Henry really think this was commonplace to him? "What kind of a . . ."

Henry shook his head. "The question was rhetorical."

"What?" Squeaky was hurt.

"A question that does not expect an answer," Henry explained. "I don't really imagine that you know, any more than I do, what creates this out of people who must once have been . . . normal."

"Oh." Squeaky was relieved. A heavy, stifling weight had been lifted from him.

He was straightening his jacket and beginning to look around him when he saw her. She was standing almost ten feet away from them, leaning slightly backward against one of the pillars that held up the ceiling. It was not her laughter that had caught his attention, or any movement of the man facing her, it was the extraordinary grace of her body. Her face was lifted to look at the man, her profile delicate, her long white throat smoothly curved. Her hair was jet-black and her lips artificially red. She was the only person in the noisy, hysterical room who was absolutely motionless. And yet her very stillness was more alive than any action of the rest of them. It was Sadie. It had to be. Which meant Rosa was dead—or Niccolo.

"Crow!" he hissed urgently. "Crow!"

Henry looked at him, then turned to Crow, touching him on the arm.

Crow swung around, then froze. His eyes widened.

"Go on," Henry urged. "Now."

"But she's . . ." Crow protested.

"We've got no time to waste," Henry told him. "Do it now, or I'll have to."

Crow hesitated.

Squeaky moved behind him and gave him a hard shove in the middle of his back.

Crow shot forward with a yelp and stopped a yard short of Sadie.

She looked at him, smiling with amusement. "That's original—even inventive." She looked him up and down, quite openly appraising him.

The young man she had been speaking to snatched Crow's arm hot-temperedly and said something almost unintelligible to Squeaky, who was watching.

Henry was clearly anxious. He started to intervene.

"No!" Squeaky said sharply. "Leave him!"

Crow gave the young man a dazzling smile, all white teeth and wide-open eyes. Then he kicked him very hard in one shin. The young man howled with anger and surprise. Crow seized Sadie and marched her away to a moderately empty space hard up against the wall.

Henry and Squeaky followed almost on her heels.

"They're my friends," Crow explained simply. "We need to talk to you," he added.

"You're Sadie?"

She nodded.

Sadie was amused. Crow was unusual-looking—not unattractive, just eccentric. Perhaps that appealed to Sadie more than the typical spoiled and demanding sort of young man who frequented such places. Also, he was sober and did not have the faded, rather pasty look of so many of the other inhabitants of the night world of the West End.

Sadie raised her elegant eyebrows. "Really? About what?"

"About Lucien Wentworth," Henry replied.

Sadie's smile froze.

Squeaky moved around to stand closer to her to block her retreat. At this particular moment the dim lighting of the room was an advantage; even the crowding helped. They could hear from the distance cries and moans of all sorts, raw farmyard emotions under the gaudy paint of sophistication.

"He's . . . dead," she said, her voice faltering.

"No, he isn't, any more than you are," Squeaky snapped. "It was Niccolo or Rosa who was murdered, and you know that. Maybe both. Lot of blood on the ground. Who was it, Sadie, and why?"

She kept her face toward Henry, as if he were the one most likely to believe her lies. "I don't know. I didn't kill anyone."

"You may not have held the knife," Henry agreed. "But you sharpened it, and gave it to someone. Who? And why?"

She swallowed. The pallor of her skin was almost ghostly in the subterranean light. Her eyes were brilliant, very wide, with black lashes. There was a feline grace to the way she held her body.

Her beauty was strangely disturbing, but there was something ephemeral about it.

"I don't know what you're talking about!" she said angrily. "If somebody's dead, it's nothing to do with me."

"That's a clumsy lie," Henry told her. "You don't survive here not knowing who's been murdered, and why. If it was Niccolo, then you've lost a lover. If it was Rosa, then it could be you next."

She stared at him with venom naked in her eyes. "You bastard!" she said between clenched teeth. "You touch me and I'll make you pay for it in ways you can't even imagine. You'll wish someone would put a knife to your throat—quickly!"

"Is that what it was?" Henry asked, his expression barely changing. "Revenge? Discipline for taking something that belonged to you, perhaps?"

She looked harder at his face, and saw in it something she did not recognize. Perhaps it stirred in her a memory of some better time.

"I didn't kill anyone," she said, still between her teeth, but more slowly, as if she was now afraid.

"But you know who did, because you led them to it, didn't you?"

She shook her head and made short, jerky movements of denial with her hands.

"I couldn't help it! I have to do what he tells me, or . . . or he won't give me any more cocaine, and I'll die." Something in her hectic eyes brought back to Squeaky's memory the first brothel he had ever been in. He had been almost six, taken there by his mother, told to start work on cleaning up behind the customers, sweeping, washing, always being polite to people. "They put the bread on your plate," she had told him. "Don't you ever forget that, boy."

There had been a young girl there then, for her first time. He could recall the smell of sweat and blood and fear, no matter how hard he tried to forget it. And he had tried. He had filled his mind with a thousand other things: his own pleasures in women, some of whom he had even liked, victories won over men he hated, good food, good wine, warmth, the touch of silk. But he could still smell that fear sometimes, alone in the middle of the night.

"Then you'll lead us to him now," Henry said to Sadie, his voice breaking the spell in Squeaky's head and forcing him back to the present.

"He won't help you. Leave him alone."

Crow moved slightly. Squeaky saw the distress in his face, which was composed of embarrassment, revulsion, and an anger within himself that he could do nothing to control.

"I don't believe it's got anything to do with Shadwell," Crow said deliberately. "You killed Rosa and Niccolo. I don't know how. Maybe you killed Niccolo first. You could have held him in your arms, and put a knife in his back, then cut his throat. You lured Rosa there, and when she was stunned at what she saw, you used the knife again. Perhaps she bent over Niccolo's body, maybe weeping. It wouldn't be hard for you to come at her from behind. One single slice from one ear—"

"I didn't!" Sadie cried, lunging forward as if to scratch at his face, everything in her changing from the pleading to the attack.

Squeaky grabbed her, pinning her arms to her sides. She struggled, and she had the strength of desperation. He kicked her hard and her legs collapsed under her, pitching her forward.

Henry was startled and profoundly disconcerted. He bent forward to help her up. "I think you had better take me to Shadwell," he said clearly. "See what he has to say about it."

She surrendered with startling suddenness, as if all her strength had bled away.

Squeaky knew better than to trust her this time. He stood well back, watching, ready to move quickly if she changed her mind.

"I'll take you," she said, and turned and led them out of the hall, then along one passage after another, and down several flights of steps. It was damp and bitingly cold. The air smelled stale, and there was something on the walls that could have been mold.

Then Sadie seemed to change her mind. Almost doubling back on herself, she climbed a long, narrow flight of stairs upward.

"Where the devil are we going?" Squeaky demanded as they came outside into the night and followed her across a lantern-lit, freezing yard. The wind groaned in the eaves of the high buildings crowding around the small space. There were icicles hanging from broken gutters, and a rat scrabbled its way, burrowing among the discarded refuse for food.

Sadie avoided a wide door that looked as if it might have led to a tavern, and instead went to a narrow, poky opening between one stone wall and another. She turned sideways to get through the opening, and for a moment Squeaky was afraid she had escaped them.

He pushed his way through ahead of Henry and Crow. He felt in his pocket for his knife in case he should need it as soon as he emerged.

But there was only Sadie waiting for him. As soon as she saw him she started to walk away, knowing he would follow her. He looked at the pale gleam of her skin above her dress and wondered how she didn't perish with the cold. Then an uglier thought occurred to him: Perhaps, in all senses that mattered, she was in a way dead already. He had seen a despair in her eyes that made that easy to believe.

Were they fools to follow her into this deeper hell than the wild self-indulgence they had already seen? How could he persuade Henry Rathbone not to go with her, when they seemed so close to finding Shadwell, and perhaps enough of the truth to convince Lucien to come back into the warm, breathing world and pay whatever it would cost him to go home again?

Squeaky was disgusted with himself that he liked Henry so much. What use was liking someone? It only ever got you into trouble. And if he imagined that they would like him in return, then he was stupider than the most idiotic drunkard in the halls and taverns they had just left. When this was over, Henry Rathbone would go back to his safe, clean house on Primrose Hill, and Squeaky would go back to keeping the books for Hester in the clinic on Portpool Lane. It would be surprising if they ever met again. Squeaky would have sacrificed his own internal comfort for nothing at all.

At the far end of the alley Sadie led them into another open patch where there was a narrow, scarred door. She pulled a key from around her neck and opened the lock, closing it behind them again when they were inside.

Here a wider stair led down into a labyrinth. They heard laughter, the drip and gurgle of water, and voices that echoed along the tunnels through which she walked as surely as if the way were marked before her.

Squeaky tried at first to keep track of where they were going—left or right, up or down—but after a quarter of an hour he knew he was lost. He was not even sure how far below the surface they were. He began to feel steadily worse about the whole thing. What had happened to the sense that usually warned him of danger? Except that he knew perfectly well what had happened to it: He had let it slip away from him because he was a fool, wanting to be liked.

He caught up with Sadie and grasped her arm. She stopped abruptly.

"Where are we?" he demanded. "You've taken us round in circles! Where's Shadwell, then?" He held her hard, deliberately pinching the flesh of her arm.

She did not pull away, as if she barely felt it. "Not far," she answered. "I'll show you where he is, then I'll . . ."

There was the noise of a door slamming not far from them, and then soft laughter.

Squeaky froze. He swore vehemently under his breath, then looked across at Crow a yard away from him. Even in the half-light he could see the fear in his face. Beyond him, Henry was little more than a shadow.

Sadie turned to Crow. "He knows we're here," she whispered. "I thought I would trick him coming this way, but he still knows. We've got to get out. Come back another time."

"What does he do down here?" Squeaky demanded.

"We're not that far down," Sadie replied. She was shivering. "Tell me where you want to go and I'll take you there. You can come back for Shadwell any time." She took the key off the chain around her neck and passed it to him. Her sea-blue eyes were almost luminous in the gleam. "Where do you want to get out?"

Crow named an alley. It was quarter of a mile from the room where they had left Lucien and Bessie, but a tortuous and half-hidden route.

Sadie nodded. "Follow me." There was urgency in her voice now, and an edge of fear that had not been there before. "It isn't very far."

They obeyed. Squeaky glanced at Crow and knew that he would be trying to remember it as well.

She had not lied to them. It was perhaps twenty minutes later when they stood outside in the alley. The wind had dropped, and the fog was thick, so that it lay in a blanket over the roofs and trailed long, white fingers of blindness in the streets.

They parted from Sadie, and she was lost to their sight within moments. Crow crept forward, leading the way. He knew it well enough, even in this sightless condition.

Lucien and Bessie were waiting for them. Lucien was sitting up now and had a little color in his face.

"D'yer find 'im?" Bessie asked eagerly. She sat on the floor close to Lucien. There were several pieces of bread on an old newspaper, and the stove was still just alight. She gave them each a portion of bread, taking the smallest for herself. There was cheese also, but she gave all of it to Lucien. Squeaky wondered how many women she had seen do that for those they cared for, saying nothing of it, pretending they had already eaten their share.

"We know where he is," Henry told her.

Squeaky was less sure, but he chose not to argue.

Henry recounted to Lucien their finding of Sadie, and her story that she had had no part in killing either Rosa or Niccolo.

Squeaky watched Lucien's face, judging whether he knew all this: if it were lies, or the truth.

"Oh, just tell my father you couldn't find me," Lucien said to Henry. "For the person he wants you to find, that's true enough. You won't be lying."

"Yes 'e would," Bessie spoke suddenly. "'Cause you're lyin'." She looked at Henry. "Did 'is Pa say as 'e 'ad ter be a certain kind o' person, or did 'e just say 'is son?"

"He just said his son," Henry replied. He looked again at Lucien. "I did not imagine it would be easy for you. You do not simply walk away from people such as these. And before you leave, you have to prove that you did not kill Niccolo, or Rosa. You have to prove it to the people who cared for them, and you have to prove it to us. If you don't, it is going to haunt you for the rest of your life, quite possibly in the very unpleasant form of someone coming after you. Surely you are not foolish enough to imagine that going back to your home would put you beyond their reach?"

"No," Lucien agreed. "There is no such place of safety. There is always somebody who can be bought, whether for simple money, or from hunger of one sort or another—or out of fear."

Bessie was looking at him, chewing her lower lip, waiting to see what he would do.

"They don't know where you are," Squeaky put in. "We'll go and find him tomorrow."

Lucien hitched himself up on his elbow.

"Not you," Squeaky told him sharply. "You're not well enough. You'll just get in the way."

"But . . ."

"You'll stay here with Bessie. We haven't got time to be looking out for you. Do as you're told, unless you want me to set that wound of yours back a few days?"

Lucien met his eyes steadily for several seconds, then lowered his gaze and lay back again.

Bessie kept looking at Squeaky, trying to work
out in her mind what he meant, and if he would
really have hurt Lucien again. Squeaky turned
away. He did not want to know what answer she
reached.

A few hours later Henry, Crow, and Squeaky
set out again, this time to find Shadwell without
Sadie's help—or presence to warn him. Bessie
and Lucien were both asleep, and they did not
disturb them. There was really no need.

It was a short journey back through the streets
to where Sadie had left them, counted in paces
through the all-enveloping fog. They returned the
way they had come, and used the key to the door
that led downward toward where she had said
Shadow Man would be.

"What are you going to say to him, if he's
there?" Crow asked.

Squeaky looked at Henry expectantly.

"A devil's deal," Henry answered quietly. "But

one that will prove to Ash, and his friends, that Lucien did not kill Rosa."

"Or Niccolo?" Crow asked. "Doesn't it matter about him?"

"No, not much," Henry said, moving forward carefully on the slick stones. "I think we might find that Niccolo is still alive."

"There was a lot of blood for one person," Crow said unhappily. "If the second body wasn't Niccolo, who was it?"

"If I'm right, I'll explain. For now we haven't time for a lot of talking." Henry led the way down the steps and along the stone corridor.

Squeaky looked at Crow and saw the anxiety in his face. They both hesitated.

Squeaky swore. "Come on! If we don't go with him, the damn fool will go alone. Anything could happen to him. Why do I always meet up with such idiots?" He hurried and nearly missed his step on the uneven surface. Crow strode behind him. There was no sound but the scraping of their boots on the stone and the steady dripping of water.

The words "a devil's deal" kept going around in Squeaky's head. What had Henry Rathbone meant? He wanted to ask now, but it took all his concentration to keep up with Henry and Crow in these miserable winding passages.

Then suddenly he recognized a stairway up to their left, and in front of them a door with a brass handle.

"We're in the wrong place!" he said simply, catching Henry by the arm. "This is the room of that fearful little creature in the velvet coat."

"I know," Henry answered. "The man who knows exactly what happened to Rosa, I believe."

"He killed her? Why? What did she . . ."

"No. He didn't kill her, but I think he knows who did."

"Why didn't he tell us?" With every new turn of events Squeaky was beginning to feel worse and worse about this whole idea of coming back.

"Because he wants to take revenge himself on the man who did," Henry answered quietly.

"Why?" Squeaky asked. "What's Rosa to him?"

"Doctor Crow?" Henry prompted.

"I think she's his daughter," Crow answered gently.

"What? How d'you know that?" Squeaky was aghast.

"Do you remember Lucien saying that Rosa had unusual eyes?" Crow asked. "One hazel and one green?"

"Yes. What about it?"

"I asked someone else and they said the same thing . . ."

"So what does that matter?" Squeaky was growing impatient. "Are you saying that it wasn't Rosa who was dead, then? So who was it?"

"Yes, I think it was Rosa," Crow replied.

"The color of your eyes is something that doesn't change with age, except perhaps to fade a bit," Henry interrupted. "If you think back, you'll remember that Ash had odd eyes too. What do you think the chances are that they are closely related to each other?"

Squeaky let out his breath in a long sigh. "Yeah. I never saw that. So what's your devil's deal?"

Henry took a long, slow breath. "A Christian burial for Rosa, if Ash will admit that the second body was Niccolo, and that he killed him in revenge for his murdering Rosa."

"Are you sure he did?" Squeaky asked.

"No, I just think so. It makes sense. Who else would?" Henry asked. "Perhaps he didn't mean to, just lost his temper. Apparently he was violent. Maybe he was wild on withdrawal from cocaine. No one had seen him since her death."

"You mean you believe Lucien that he didn't do it," Squeaky concluded, not sure if he was pleased, frightened, disgusted, or maybe all three. He had not felt so confused in years, maybe not ever. He could not afford all this . . . feeling.

"Do you know of some reason I should not?" Henry said.

Squeaky swore vehemently and from the heart. "'Cause it's bloody stupid! It's dangerous," he hissed. He wanted to shout at Henry, but he could not afford to make such a noise right outside Ash's rooms. "You can't go around just believing anything anyone wants to tell you! You could get taken—"

"I said 'reason,'" Henry corrected him gently. "Not fear."

"Fear's a reason!" Squeaky was exasperated. "It's one of the best reasons I know. It's kept me alive, with my skin whole, for fifty bleedin' years!"

"And has it made you happy, Squeaky?"

"Yes!" He waved his hand in a gesture of denial. "No! Well—I'm alive, and you don't get very happy dead! What a question to ask!"

"You don't have to come and see Ash if you'd rather not," Henry told him.

That was the final insult. "You trying to say you don't want me?" Squeaky demanded. This hurt, badly.

"Not at all." Henry smiled and took Squeaky's arm. He turned to Crow. "Come, Dr. Crow, let us see if the poor man will accept our deal."

Our deal? Ours? Squeaky was about to protest, then realized he really wanted to be included. He banged on the door and then threw it open.

The room inside was empty. Squeaky was crushed with disappointment.

"We'll wait," Henry decided. "At least for a while." He sat down on the filthy floor.

They had not long to sit. When Ash returned he was still wearing the absurd lavender coat. His face seemed even more gaunt, the white painted skin stretched over the bones of his skull. He used the stick to prod the ground, as if he were not certain that it was firm enough to hold his weight.

"Well!" he said with interest. "And what do you want this time? You found Lucien. And Sadie." He said her name slowly, as if it hurt him.

"Indeed," Henry replied. "But we did not find Rosa or Niccolo. I think you could help us with that."

Squeaky looked at the terrible face, which was like a chalk mask. Crow was right; one of his eyes was hazel, the other quite definitely green. Perhaps Henry was right too that Rosa was this man's daughter. It made a sort of tragic sense.

Ash stood motionless as a garish figurine.

"In order to give them a Christian burial," Henry went on. "Or Rosa, at least. Perhaps Niccolo doesn't deserve one. They don't do that for men they hang."

Ash smiled. It was sad and horrible. "He wasn't hanged. Not strong enough to lift him, you see." He raised his hands, but stiffly, as if they would not go higher than his shoulders.

"How did you kill him?" Henry inquired as if it were no more than a matter of courteous interest.

Ash tapped his stick with his other hand. "Dagger in here," he replied. "Very useful. Had a proper sword once. Haven't the balance to hold it anymore now. Dagger will do. He didn't even see me. Just killed my beautiful Rosa. I put the blade through his heart. I was surprised how much he bled."

"He probably took a little while to die," Crow observed. "People don't bleed much after they're dead."

"Really?" Ash looked only mildly interested. "A Christian burial? Why?"

"Because I want something from you," Henry replied. "Of course."

"What?"

"That you tell people the truth, so Lucien is not blamed for either death."

"And you'll bury Rosa, decently, like a Christian?"

"I will."

"Where is she?" Henry said wearily.

Without speaking again Ash turned, leaning awkwardly on his stick, and led them out of the room. In the passage he started in the opposite direction from the one they had taken before. After a hundred feet or so they went into a small side room, cold and dry, where two bodies lay side by side on a table. One was a young woman, her long dark hair loose around her face, her hands folded as if totally at peace. Her eyes were closed. Even so, her features were a finer, almost beautiful echo of what Ash's might have been in his youth, before disease spoiled them.

Her dress was matted with blood where someone had stabbed her over and over.

The man, by contrast, bore only one wound, to the heart. His arms were by his sides.

They stood in a few moments' respectful silence. It was Crow who broke it.

"I'll carry her," he said quietly. "Do you have a cloth of any kind to wrap around her?"

*W*hen they were far beyond the hall and heading toward the way up, they came face-to-face with Sadie, and behind her Lucien and Bessie.

Henry stopped instantly, Squeaky, Crow, and Ash close on his heels. One glance at Henry's face was enough to show that he did not understand, but Squeaky did. It was all now horribly clear. Sadie had been so eager to help because she needed to see where they were keeping Lucien. Now she had gone back to collect him—for Shadwell! Always his servant, bought and paid for with the cocaine she could or would not live without.

Bessie had come as well, either with them or close after. Her ridiculous sense of loyalty would make her do that. Now they were all trapped. He didn't even need to turn around to know that the way would be closed behind them.

Shadwell was there in the half-light, as Squeaky had known he would be. He did not even notice if he was tall or short, except that he wore a frock coat, like an undertaker. It was his face that dominated everything else, every thought and emotion. The lantern on the wall threw his left side into high relief, illuminating the bony nose and sunken cheekbones, the wide, cruel lips. The darker side was only half visible, the eye socket lost, the bones merely suggested, the mouth a shapeless slash on the skin.

There was an instant's utter silence, then Henry spoke.

"Mr. Shadwell, I presume?" he said quietly. His voice was absurdly polite, and shaking only a very little.

Shadwell remained motionless where he was. "And you, sir, must be Henry Rathbone." His reply was almost gentle. As Sadie had said, it was a voice that crept inside the head and remained there.

"I am," Henry agreed. "We would be obliged if you would allow us to pass. We are taking the body of Rosa in order to give her burial."

"Ah, yes, Rosa." The man let her name roll on his tongue. "What an unfortunate waste. She was hardly Sadie, but she was still worth something. By all means bury her. Put a Christian cross above her empty soul, if it gives you some sense of your own worthiness. It will fool neither God nor Satan."

Squeaky gulped. He wished Ash had not had to hear that.

"All obsequies for the dead are to preserve our own humanity," Henry answered him. "Reminders of who we are, and that we loved them. The present is woven out of the threads of the past."

Shadwell inclined his head a little, allowing the light to shine on his face, making it look worse. "A silken rope to bind you," he agreed. "I will let the good doctor go, taking Rosa. The rest of you stay. I dare say in time I shall find a use for you."

"And Lucien," Henry added.

"And Bessie!" Squeaky insisted. How could Henry forget her?

"You make a hard bargain," Shadwell responded. "What do you think, Sadie? Could you teach this bony child to be a good whore?"

Squeaky looked at Sadie. Her face should have been beautiful, but now there was an ugliness inside her that soured it.

It was Lucien who moved. He stepped toward Shadwell, his head high, his arms held a little forward, still protecting his wound.

"I'll stay. I'll do whatever you need, even bring in men from my own society who want to come, if you let all these go, including Bessie. I'm of far more use to you than she'll ever be. She doesn't know or care how to please men. She has no art at all." He stood a little straighter, his eyes never leaving Shadwell's. His face was yellowish gray in the sullen light.

Shadwell's eyes widened, like sunken pits in his skull. "You trust my word?" he asked incredulously.

Lucien tried to smile, and failed. He was shaking. "Of course not. I shall bring to you every greedy and twisted man who can pay you, for as long as I know they are safe, including Bessie."

"Indeed. Or you'll do what? Are you threatening me?"

"Or I will kill myself," Lucien said simply. "I am no use to you dead, but alive and willing, I can bring men—and more women as lush as Sadie."

A look of anger and surprise filled Shadwell's terrible face.

Lucien had won the bargain, at least for the

moment. He knew it. His skin was ashen. He was entering a real hell: one that he understood intimately, could taste on his tongue and in his throat, and one that would never leave him.

Henry Rathbone was smiling, and tears welled up in his eyes. He watched and said nothing. That was when Squeaky knew that, for him, Lucien had redeemed himself.

Henry took Squeaky by the arm very firmly, so that his fingers dug into Squeaky's flesh, and pulled him away.

Bessie was on Squeaky's heels. Crow followed, still carrying Rosa's body. Ash was nowhere to be seen.

They walked as quickly as they could along the tunnels and passages, and up the flight of steps, slippery underfoot, lit only by a couple of rush torches soaked in pitch.

Bessie pulled so hard on the tails of Squeaky's jacket she very nearly tore the fabric. He stopped and whirled around on her, then did not know what to say.

Behind him Crow stopped as well, leaning against the wall, breathing hard. He carefully allowed the weight of Rosa's body to rest on the ground.

"We in't goin' ter leave 'im, are we?" Bessie said, her voice trembling.

"No," Henry answered her. "But we must think very carefully what we are going to do, and how. I think we are far enough away to take a rest. And we must keep our promise to Ash, wherever he has got to."

"'Im?" she said in disbelief. "'E's a—"

"It is our promise, not his," Henry reminded her. "But quite apart from that, he did keep his bargain."

"So where is 'e then?" she demanded.

"Probably watching us, to see if we keep our part," Crow said wryly. "He doesn't know you as well as we do."

Henry gave him a quick smile. Squeaky thought of all the sane, sensible people above them in the daylight, preparing for Christmas, buying gifts, getting geese ready to roast, mixing pastries and puddings and cakes. He could almost smell the sweetness of it. There would be wreaths of holly on doors, music in the air. Sometime soon there would even be bells. These people knew what Christmas was supposed to be.

"But we're going back for Lucien?" Bessie insisted.

"Of course we are," Henry assured her. "But we must do it with a plan. We have no weapons, so we have to think very carefully. Crow, you had better take Rosa's body somewhere safe, where it can come to no possible harm, and where we can be sure it will be given a Christian burial, should we find ourselves in a position where we cannot attend to that ourselves."

"You mean if we're dead!" Squeaky snapped.

"I would prefer not to have put it so crudely, but yes," Henry agreed. Then he turned back to Crow. "Do you know of such a place? Perhaps friends who owe you a favor? I am willing to pay; that is not an issue. I will write an I.O.U. that my son will honor, should that become necessary. Surely in your professional capacity you are acquainted with undertakers?"

Crow smiled, almost a baring of his teeth. "A few. It will take me at least half an hour to see to it."

"Then you had better begin," Henry urged. "In the meantime we will consider what weapon we can create that will be of use to us in battle against Shadow Man."

Crow picked up Rosa's body again. He staggered a little under her weight, although she was slight.

Squeaky realized how far he had carried her already, without a word of complaint or the request that someone else take a turn.

"We need a good weapon," he said unhappily, although a fearful idea was beginning to take shape in his mind. He did not want to look at it, not even for an instant, but it was there, undeniable.

"Crow!" he shouted.

Crow stopped. He was almost at the next bend in the passage. "What?"

"Bring some matches," Squeaky called. "Lots of them."

Henry stared at him. "Fire?" he said hoarsely. "For God's sake, Squeaky, we don't know anything about the airflow down here, or which tunnels lead to which others. We could end up killing everyone." His voice cracked. "We could end up setting fire to half of London!"

"I'll bet that little bastard Ash knows," Squeaky said darkly. "You shouldn't have let Crow take the girl's body. You gave away the one thing we could have bargained with." How could Henry be so clever and so stupid? Squeaky would never understand some people.

"We already used it," Henry pointed out.

"Well, we could've used it again, if you hadn't let Crow take her!" Squeaky protested.

"No, I couldn't. Quite apart from the morality of it, it isn't very wise." Henry smiled. "How can a man trust me if I've already cheated him once?"

Squeaky was obliged to concede that there was a certain logic in that. "Do you wish me to go and look for the little swine?" he offered.

"There is no point. You won't find him if he doesn't want you to."

Squeaky swore. He really needed more words if he was going to continue in Henry Rathbone's acquaintance. Everything he knew was insufficient to express the pent-up emotions inside him, the rage, the pity, the sheer, blind frustration of it all. Not to mention the fear!

There was a tiny sound behind him and he swung around. Ash was standing no more than a couple of yards away.

"Don't creep up on people!" Squeaky shouted at him. "You could get yourself killed like that."

Ash looked at him in disdain. "Not until after you've killed Shadwell," he replied. "You need me until then."

Henry looked at him. "We don't intend to kill

Shadwell, just to rescue Lucien, and Sadie if she wishes it."

Ash leaned on his cane. Henry offered him a hand to steady himself and he took it, reluctantly. "Same thing," he said. "He won't give up, and he knows these tunnels and passages far better than you do."

"Then you are quite right when you say that we need your help," Henry agreed. "We need to have some form of plan by the time Dr. Crow returns. He has gone to take Rosa's body to where it will be safe, and buried properly, if we find that we cannot do it ourselves."

"I know."

Henry opened his mouth to say something, then changed his mind. "Do you know these passages well enough to help us?" he said instead.

"Of course I do," the man replied. "What is your plan?"

Henry smiled ruefully. "We have very little yet. We wish to rescue Lucien and Sadie, and prevent Shadwell from following us out. The only weapon we have is fire."

Ash pulled his grotesque face into an even more bizarre grimace. "Then we must get Lucien out.

We can set fires that will trap Shadwell so that he cannot follow you. Sadie will not come. Lucien may. You must be prepared for any answer, and willing to leave them, or you will be burned as well."

"We know," Henry agreed.

Henry dug around in his pockets and found a piece of paper on which Ash could draw a plan of the tunnels, steps, and passages through buildings where Shadwell would likely be, along with the direction of drafts, and so the way fire would travel.

"We'll have to wall him in," Ash explained. "Here." He pointed to the end of a network of pathways.

"Doesn't he have an escape door, a back way out?" Squeaky asked. "I would."

Ash smiled. "That way." He put his fingers carefully on the paper. "Into the sewers."

"As long as we get Lucien," Henry said quietly, his face pale. "We may have to forgo getting Shadwell too."

Ash touched the paper again. "If we set fires here, and here, and maybe here, too, then we've got him. You'll need to collect as much rubbish as you can, stuff that'll burn easy." He smiled. There was something ghastly about it, and Squeaky found himself turning away from the sight. "I know where they keep the oil for the lamps," Ash went on. "And the tar for the torches along the tunnels where they can use a flame. We'll have a fire to make hell proud."

By the time Crow returned they had collected oil, tar, several piles of tallow candles, and as much old wood and rags as they could find without robbing people whose attention they could not afford to attract.

They crept forward together. Ash led the way, tapping his stick on the ground to make certain of it so his nerve-dead feet did not trip him. He was followed by Henry, Crow, Bessie, and Squeaky, all carrying or dragging behind them roughly made sacks of candles, pieces of wood, tins, bottles, and jugs of oil, and buckets of tar. When they reached the places the man showed them, they very carefully laid their fires, sometimes with a fuse made of torn and knitted rags soaked in oil, aided by a little tar. There was no time for error or for waiting and watching.

With shaking hands Squeaky lit a match, held it as still as his trembling hands would allow, then touched it to the rags. It ignited immediately. The flame raced along it and caught hold. He jerked back, watched it for another moment to make sure it was not going to die, then ran as fast as he could to the second site to set it burning too.

He knew Crow was doing the same with the other fires.

Henry, Bessie, and Ash made their way to the heart of Shadwell's territory, expecting to meet him around every corner or through every door or archway.

When they finally did, it was deeper than they had been before. They crossed a last threshold into a clean, stark cellar with doorways to both the right and left, and one to the back. The last must lead to the sewer, the other to the tunnel where the fire was already approaching. Shadwell was sitting in an armchair with Lucien in a chair opposite him. Sadie stood casually by a table with a cabinet next to it, filled with tiny carved wooden drawers.

"What now?" Shadwell asked, rising to his feet. "Have you changed your mind? Come to give me the girl and take Lucien in exchange? I'm afraid you cannot do that. You see, Lucien is right. He is of far more use to me than she could ever be. You made your bargain and it stands."

"I came back to ask Lucien if he wishes to leave," Henry replied. "You too, for that matter. Although I have no idea where you might go. I doubt there is a place for you above the ground."

For several seconds Shadwell did not reply.

"You are right." His voice was still very quiet, insistent, and the strange sibilance was even more pronounced. "My place is here, in all the stairways and passages that thread under the blind, busy world. This is my world. But you chose to come into it. Everyone who is here chose to be, but I choose who stays and who leaves. I let you leave once, but not this time."

Crow came up behind Henry. Squeaky appeared at his other side, but facing backward, keeping guard over the tunnel.

"Go, while you can!" Lucien said urgently. "He's right. I made my decision and I'll abide by it."

Henry could smell smoke drifting toward them from the passage beyond Squeaky: a sharp, acrid stinging in his nose. In another moment they would all be aware of it. And the flames could not be far behind if the man in lavender was right about the flow of air in the tunnels.

"Lucien!" Henry said urgently.

Lucien shook his head. "Let me pay my debts," he answered gravely. "Please tell my father that I did that. Go, while you can. You don't owe me anything. You never did."

The smoke was getting stronger. Suddenly Shadwell caught the odor of it. His eyes widened and his head jerked higher. The only way of escape was either past Henry, Crow, and Squeaky, or past Lucien through the door behind them, into the sewers.

The crackle of fire was audible now.

It was Bessie who broke the silence. She walked forward to Lucien, past the line of the door to the left. "Lucien, yer gotta cóme wi' us. Squeaky and me come back for yer. Yer can't stay 'ere . . ."

The door to the left crashed in and the fire spread across the room, cutting them off with a wall of heat.

"Bessie!" Squeaky cried out desperately. "Yer stupid little cow! What . . . Oh, God!" He tore off his jacket and put it half across his head, then bent and charged through the flames to where he could still just see her. The heat was terrible, but he was through the wall and out the other side to find Bessie gripping Lucien's arm.

She swung around.

Squeaky seized her, picking her up. She weighed almost nothing. He could feel her bones through the thin cloth of her dress. He turned, but the fire was taking hold. It was hotter, spreading already. He hesitated. How could he get her back through it to the way out? What if her clothes caught fire? Her hair?

There was no time to even think. He put his head down and charged. He felt the flames all around him for a terrifying moment. The pain was enough to make him cry out, but he bit it back, afraid to draw in a scorching breath.

Then he was out the other side, Bessie still in his arms. Crow clutched hold of him, throwing his coat over Bessie and holding it, smothering the flames that licked at her dress.

No one had noticed Henry going the other way through the flames toward Lucien, Sadie, and Shadwell.

Lucien stared at him, horrified. "You can't come with us!" he said urgently, his eyes flickering just once toward the doorway to the sewers.

"I don't intend to," Henry replied. "But if you hurry, you can come with me. There's still time to get back through the fire, if we go now."

But it was Shadwell who answered. "You want him, you must pay." He was standing close to Sadie, between her and Henry. He put out his hand and his strong, heavy fingers closed like a vise on arm. "If he goes with you, I will kill her."

Henry hesitated.

"Slowly," Shadwell elaborated. "Painfully."

"You are doing that already," Henry told him. "My leaving Lucien behind will not change that. As you have pointed out before, those who are with you are there by choice. I don't know what choices Sadie has left. Each decision we take can narrow them. But if she will not fight to save herself, no one else can do it. There comes a point when we all stand alone."

Lucien took a step toward them.

"Go, while you can," Henry ordered him. "I'm coming with you." He turned, and in that instant Shadwell let go of Sadie and put his other hand on Henry. His grip was like iron. For a moment, as he saw Lucien step into the flames, Henry was paralyzed. The pain in his arm took his breath away.

Lucien was gone. Sadie was still standing by the wall, stunned.

Henry swung around to face Shadwell. He had never physically fought anyone in his life. There was only instinct to prompt him.

Shadwell's face was close to his. For the first time in the red light of the flames, Henry saw his eyes, empty keyholes into hell in his uneven face. He could not bear to look at them. He bent forward a little and charged, knocking them both off balance and toppling onto the floor, kicking at each other. It was ridiculous and desperate. The heat was filling the room and sucking the air out of it. Henry was gasping already.

Shadwell was on top of him, holding his throat. He couldn't breathe at all. The room swam into darkness.

Then suddenly he was slapped, hard, and gasped for air.

"Get up!" a voice hissed at him. "Get up, you fool! Take my arm!"

Henry opened his eyes, expecting to see Crow and Squeaky, but it was Ash hitting him with the little strength he had. "Get out of here, down the sewer and turn left. Stay left at every turn. Go!"

Henry struggled to his knees. The fire all but filled the room now. Shadwell was on the floor, kneeling, rising, his back to the flames. Sadie was screaming, her clothes alight. Henry tried to lunge toward her but Ash kicked him in the ribs. Henry doubled up with the pain of it and found himself staggering forward. A hard shove from behind and he was through the open doorway. It slammed shut behind him. In seconds the room would be an inferno. Yet he was safe and utterly alone, unable to go back, unable to help.

The sour smell of the sewers was cold and damp, a balm to his seared skin. He was glad to step into the icy water and wade to the left. Feeling his way in Stygian darkness, he was too relieved to be afraid.

The water grew deeper, the current of it stronger as he went a little uphill. As Ash had told him to, he bore always to the left.

His feet were numb beyond his ankles by the time he saw light ahead, but he had not had to travel as long as he had feared. With a shudder of relief he made his way onto a ledge and upward to an iron ladder. He grasped it and climbed to the passage above.

There were sounds ahead, footsteps. Henry

froze. Then he saw the pool of light on the dripping wall. Suddenly the slime of it was gold. A whole lantern appeared, and the hand holding it, then the sleeve of Squeaky's scorched and ruined jacket.

"Squeaky!" Henry shouted with joy. "Here! Over here!"

Squeaky came forward at a run, the lantern swinging around wildly, as his feet slid on the wet surface. "Where the hell have you been?" he demanded, his face contorted with both fury and relief. "You had us scared half to death! You ever do that again, an' I'll . . ."

Crow was coming behind him with Lucien and Bessie. They were all filthy, skin scratched and burned. Their clothes were torn and in some places blackened by fire, but they were alive.

Bessie threw her arms around Henry, hugging him with more strength than he would have thought she could possess. Slowly he closed his arms around her and held her just as powerfully.

"You need to get those burns tended," Crow interrupted. "We should get out and find clean water, bandages."

"Yes," Henry agreed. "Yes, of course." Now that he thought of it, parts of him hurt appallingly.

Even in the semi-darkness here, he felt as if he was still on fire. He let Bessie go at last and tried to collect his wits.

Crow took him by the arm, but holding only the cloth of his sleeve, not touching his skin. "Come on. Lucien knows the way."

It seemed like a long time, but perhaps it was no more than half an hour before they were standing in the street. The lamps were lit and gleaming in the dark, shedding pools of gold on the snow. Icicles sparkled from roofs and gutters. There were a few carriages and hansoms around, and they could hear harnesses jingling, hooves muffled in the snowdrifts that were still fresh and untrampeled.

In the distance people were singing.

Crow, the least disreputable-looking among them, hailed a cab. They all piled in, although with difficulty. Henry needed a little assistance.

"Where to?" Crow asked.

Henry gave him James Wentworth's address.

Lucien began to protest.

"According to the driver, it's Christmas Eve," Henry told him sharply. "You're going home. Where you go after that you can choose, but tonight you owe us this."

Lucien sat stiff and afraid, but he did not argue.

It was not a long ride to Kensington, where James Wentworth lived, but to Henry, who was exhausted and very sore, it seemed to take ages; Only now, on the brink of impossible success, did he actually wonder if Wentworth really wanted his son back to forgive him. Perhaps it would instead involve some harsher discipline, some price for his disobedience and the family's shame.

When they stopped they had to fish between them for enough coins to pay the fare and offer the cabbie a bonus fit for Christmas Eve. They climbed out stiffly, helping each other, until they stood on the freezing pavement. The hansom jingled and rattled off into the distance.

The street was lit as far as they could see in both directions. There were wreaths and garlands on the doors. Somewhere far away church bells were ringing out across the rooftops.

Henry walked up the short distance to Wentworth's door, lifted the brass knocker, and then let it fall.

The door was opened almost immediately and the liveried butler stared in undisguised disbelief.

Lucien stepped forward. "Happy Christmas, Dorwood. Is my father at home?"

The butler gasped and his eyes filled with tears. "Yes, Mr. Lucien," he said gravely. "If you care to come in, sir, I shall tell him you are here." He did not even bother to ask who his companions were.

Inside, the magnificent hall was decked for Christmas, as if they had been expected. The Yule log was burning in the open hearth. There were garlands of holly, ivy, and mistletoe, with colored ribbons. Red wax candles glowed. There was mulled wine in a large bowl on the sideboard, and cakes and pies and candied fruit in dishes.

A door flew open. James Wentworth came out, his eyes wide, his face shining with joy. He went straight to Lucien and threw his arms around him, too filled with emotion to speak.

Then he let him go and turned to Henry, the tears wet on his cheeks.

"Nothing I can say is thanks enough." He all but choked on the words. "My son was lost, and you have found him for me—you and your friends. My home and all that is in it are yours." He looked questioningly at each of them.

"My friends," Henry introduced them. "Dr. Crow, Mr. Robinson, and Bessie."

Bessie curtsied, with a slight wobble. Crow stood beaming the widest smile of his life, and Squeaky bowed, really rather gracefully.

"How do you do," Wentworth replied. "Happy, happy Christmas."

ANNE PERRY is the bestselling author of two acclaimed series set in Victorian England: the Charlotte and Thomas Pitt novels, most recently *Buckingham Palace Gardens* and *Treason at Lisson Grove*, and the William Monk novels, most recently *Execution Dock* and *Acceptable Loss*. She is also the author of the World War I novels *No Graves As Yet, Shoulder the Sky, Angels in the Gloom, At Some Disputed Barricade*, and *We Shall Not Sleep*, as well as nine Christmas novels, most recently *A Christmas Homecoming*. Her stand-alone novel *The Sheen on the Silk*, set in the Byzantine Empire, was a *New York Times* bestseller. Anne Perry lives in Scotland.

www.anneperry.com